# Perfectly
# GOOD
# White Boy

Perfectly GOOD White Boy

CARRIE
MESROBIAN

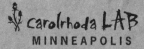
Carolrhoda LAB
MINNEAPOLIS

Carolrhoda Lab™
An imprint of Carolrhoda Books
A division of Lerner Publishing Group, Inc.
241 First Avenue North
Minneapolis, MN 55401 USA

For updated reading levels and more information, look up this title
at www.lernerbooks.com.

The images in this book are used with the permission of: © Danielle Carnito/
Todd Strand/Independent Picture Service.
Front Cover: © Danielle Carnito/Todd Strand/Independent Picture Service.

Main body text set in Janson Text LT Std 10/14.
Typeface provided by Linotype AG.


Library of Congress Cataloging-in-Publication Data

Mesrobian, Carrie.
        Perfectly good white boy / by Carrie Mesrobian.
            pages   cm
        Summary: After losing his virginity to an older girl who dumps him at
    the end of summer, Sean decides to join the Marines, but first he must get
    through his senior year of high school.
        ISBN 978-1-4677-3480-6 (trade hard cover : alk. paper)
        ISBN 978-1-4677-4628-1 (eBook)
        [1. Interpersonal relations—Fiction. 2. Sex—Fiction. 3. United States.
    Marine Corps—Fiction.] I. Title.
    PZ7.M5493War 2014
    [Fic]—dc23                                                        2013036749

Manufactured in the United States of America
1 – SB – 7/15/14

FOR **Adrian**:
ALL OF THIS, EVERY LAST BIT,
BECAUSE OF YOU

# HERE YOU ARE ALL EQUALLY

# AND MY ORDERS WEED OUT ALL WHO DO NOT PACK THE GEAR TO SERVE IN MY

# DO YOU MAGGOTS UNDERSTAND

# WORTHLESS!

## ARE TO
## NON-HACKERS

## BELOVED CORPS!

## THAT?

—Full Metal Jacket

# Chapter One

I stood in the back of the barn, in front of a pile of boxes marked "Tools," watching the party go on. The senior girls' spring party was usually down by the old railroad trestle bridge off Highway 10, but this time it was out on someone's farm, so they'd decided to make it a goddamn hoedown or something. The barn looked like a normal barn—red, kinda faded—but it didn't have a tractor or any animals, no haystacks or anything, just the boxes and a sound system and sawdust on the dirt floor, not to mention packs of screaming girls dressed like slutty cowgirls, in cowboy boots and bandanas and super-short shorts and long braids flying everywhere. It was loud as hell, and the circle around the keg was ass-deep in douche hockey player dudes. Eddie had ditched me for that Libby sophomore chick he was into, and I was regretting leaving the house for this shit. Eddie wouldn't have found the place without me; it was only by luck that I'd known where it was, since I'd gone hunting on the property last November.

I pushed my way through the douche hockey dudes to get another beer. I'd paid seven bucks for this stupid cup, and Eddie had brought his tent and shit; I might as well get loaded. But I'd barely finished the cup when the senior girls started dancing and screaming to this terrible country song, "The Devil Went Down to Georgia," and so I had to get out of there.

It was dark, and the moon wasn't out. I could see just a little of the farmhouse in the distance, past the rows of parked cars. Everything felt still and silent and good in the cool air. Like maybe this would be fun, maybe I could handle this whole thing after all, after my weeks of being a social hermit, sitting at home, avoiding unpacking boxes in our new place with my mom. Eddie hadn't expected me to say yes to coming to this party, even. He was used to me disappointing him in that way lately.

I walked toward the cornfield, which was nothing but dirt the same color as the night, trying to find the tree where Grandpa Chuck and I had nailed up the deer stand last November. Wondered if the handholds were still there. Grandpa Chuck didn't believe in those ready-made stands; you built it yourself, was his opinion. You brought some wood and made do. Enough crap to haul out there as it was, he said.

But I wasn't out in the fresh air five seconds when a goddamn Frisbee smacked me in the face so hard I dropped my beer. My nose gushed blood. People were laughing and yelling, but I couldn't see who it was. But it didn't matter, because it hurt so bad I wouldn't have been able to throw down anyway. Since the whole thing with Eddie back in February, I'd made a deal with myself I'd never hit anyone again.

Which was good, because it was this cute senior girl who'd thrown the Frisbee. She had a big ponytail, short denim skirt, really, really tight American flag shirt. Cowboy boots. It took me a second to recognize her through everything hurting and all the blood, but I knew her from school. Hallie Martin. She went out with this douche hockey player guy who always walked around with his mouth half open. Dan. He looked like a Dan too.

But now she was all over me, saying stuff like, "Oh, Sean, I'm so sorry... Your nose is bleeding! Oh my god, I'm soooo sorry..." Over and over she said sorry. While I said nothing back not just because it hurt but also because I was kind of in shock. Because Hallie Martin was a year older. And how did she know my goddamn name? I only knew hers because she lifeguarded with Eddie at the YMCA. That, and you just knew the names of hot girls, generally. It was the kind of information that just downloaded naturally, along with stuff like who was playing Monday Night Football that week or when duck hunting season started or whatever.

I let her drag me away from everyone, her holding one of my hands like I was five years old, my other hand pressed over my bleeding nose, until we got to her little tiny red girl-car. A Kia, for fuck's sake. She dug around in the console, which gave me a minute to catch my breath. Also to check out her ass. Which was shitty of me, but whatever.

She handed me a bunch of Dairy Queen napkins, and I mopped my face with them, trying to calm the fuck down. I wasn't really down for girls hovering around me like this, even if they were a foot shorter than me, like Hallie Martin; it made me feel like a total chump. Plus I was getting blood all over my shirt. I didn't want to drip it on her and her cowgirl outfit too.

"I'm so sorry!" she said about a million times. I nodded at her, turning away and pinching the bridge of my nose, making blood rain down the back of my throat. I didn't want to spit blood while talking and look like more of a freak.

"I'm Hallie," she said, turning around with me.

Like I didn't know!

She moved like she wanted to shake my hand. But I was holding bloody napkins in one hand and my nose in the other, so it was a little hard.

"Sean," I said.

"I know who you are," she said. "You're kind of hard to miss."

Which wasn't good to hear.

"You're a year behind me in school, right? You're friends with that kid Eddie, right?"

Well, that was a little better than being Violent and Crazy, the labels everyone probably gave me, along with the side-eye, since the thing in the library went down in February. Though it made me feel like Eddie's butt boy.

"I totally love that kid," she said. "I lifeguard with him at the Y. He's so funny."

I nodded. I was out of things to say. The bleeding was pretty much done too. Just a trickle. She handed me another napkin from her car; I looked at her ass again. God. Then we both stood there, like, duh, how did this even happen?

I stared at the blob of bloody napkins in my fist.

"There's a trash behind the house," Hallie said, grabbing at my elbow. I could feel her fingernails. Long and sharp, making me shiver. Christ.

"Come on," she said.

We started walking then. Like we were together. I was feeling a little less dumb, though I still worried there were boogers and blood all over my face. But Hallie kept talking.

"Carenna doesn't have keys to the house, because it's her uncle's farm, but we set up a bunch of recycling and stuff for later."

Carenna was another hot senior girl. She was homecoming royalty, but not the queen. One of the runners-up. Hallie was cuter that Carenna Whatever-Her-Last-Name-Was, but she hadn't been in the homecoming court. Clearly there was no justice in this world.

"You guys really planned this out, huh?" I asked.

"Well, it's our last year together, you know? I leave for Madison this August, so we had to start early. And a spring party is kind of an Oak Prairie tradition, you know? Carenna thought it wouldn't be so big, though. This place is hard to find. Or so we thought."

"Wasn't that hard to find. I went hunting out here in November," I said. "My grandpa and I built a deer stand up in that tree over in that cornfield." I pointed and she looked, not that there was much to see in the darkness. "Eddie and me found the place no problem."

"Lucky for you, huh?" she said. Smiled at me. She was pretty damn cute.

And she was right: I was pretty damn lucky. And goddamn, it felt good. Things were moving in a positive direction at crazy speeds, light years away from the funk I'd been in, sitting around our shitty rental, not wanting to unpack boxes or settle in. I sneaked a look at her, down at the top of her head, as we walked. Her hair was shiny and golden and her pony-tailed bobbed as we walked past the dark fields.

"People shoot at deer in cornfields?" Hallie asked. Like she thought I was some kind of crazy lunatic.

"Well, I was up in the deer stand when I shot mine, but yeah."

"You shot it from a tree?"

"Well . . . yeah, but . . ."

"I owe you a beer, Sean," she said. "Come on."

●

So, then I just kind of fell into this hole. The Hallie Martin Hole. It was a decent place to be. She smelled really good. And she looked even better. Hallie's hair, when she pulled it out of her pony-tail, was dark reddish blond. She was a lot shorter than me, but most everyone is. I couldn't stop looking at her.

I had no idea why she was hanging out with me.

But I went along with it. Me and Hallie drinking more beer. Me and Hallie drinking shots of tequila. Me and Hallie playing bad Frisbee. Me and Hallie and her friends, getting introduced. Me and Hallie, suddenly, this *thing*.

Of course, Eddie was not around to witness this. Which was too bad. He would lose his mind when he found out. Still, we were kind of on a need-to-know basis these days, Eddie and me. We'd been friends since we were ten years old. So I didn't say shit to him about him always dogging younger girls and his swoopy gelled-up hair, and he never said shit about why I broke his nose right before Valentine's Day and he had to go to the St. Albans Dance looking like hell. I could have told him why, of course. But when I tried to explain, he said he knew, and then we just waited in silence in the principal's office, him holding the ice pack the nurse gave him, until our parents showed up.

My phone beeped. As if Eddie'd realized I was on to something. He'd sent his typical text. Too lazy for words, he'd only send photos, and they were usually gross. Porn shots or whatever. This time it was a shot of two horses fucking. I wondered what it meant, but couldn't text back or laugh, because me and Hallie were sitting around the bonfire and she was surrounded with her friends and they were whispering and laughing and the girl Hallie'd been playing Frisbee with said, "He'll be perfect," and another one added, "Way better than fucking *Dan*," and then Hallie looked at me and smiled and I was so embarrassed that I got up and went to take a piss in the bushes.

I mean, this was fun and everything, but she was going to college, and I had another year of dumbass high school.

Fuck.

I finished pissing. I turned around. And there was Hallie.

"Hey," I said. Hoping to god she hadn't been watching me piss.

"I thought you were leaving," she said.

"No, me and Eddie are camping out all night."

"Did you set up your tent yet?"

"No. Maybe he did. I don't know." I thought of the horses fucking photo. Wondered if that meant the tent was now occupied?

Then, though I'd barely had done up my belt, with no plan or asking or anything, I just moved forward, closer, kind of towered over her, in a way that made her seem smaller than before, in a way that made me want to scoop her up and put her in my pocket, like she might run away. Before something else about this weird, good situation would break. I just reached out to her waist and hooked her toward me, my hand gripping the edge of her skirt, looking for anything to grab onto. And I kissed her. I was sorta wasted and not thinking much beyond *GRAB SMASH GIRL*.

But she was into it. Which was amazing in itself. Because it couldn't have been that smooth. She was on her tiptoes, wobbling in those damn cowboy boots. But somehow, it worked.

So we made out. Nothing really involved. I maybe touched her boob over her shirt a little by accident, but it was mostly kissing. This all went down with us both up against a tree in the dark, away from the rest of the party. She smelled like bonfire and tasted like beer, but her mouth was super soft and warm.

After a little while, she pushed back from me, folded her fingers beneath my belt, looked down. Right at The Horn I was rocking there. Jesus.

"Carenna and I set up our tent already," she said. "She might already be in it. But do you want to go and see? It might be more private . . ."

"Okay," I said.

"Do you want to get another beer?"

"No. Do you?"

"No."

We walked quickly toward where all the tents were, between the house and cornfield. Nobody saw us. And we didn't say a word to each other. She checked that her tent was empty and then she told me to take off my shoes, so I did, and stood there while she took off her cowboy boots. Then we went inside.

Once she zipped the flap shut, bam! We were back at it.

Except now she was under me on top of a bunch of sleeping bags and blankets. I didn't check my watch, but it couldn't have been that long until we were both stripped down to our underwear. But maybe it was longer, because of the way it happened. My shirt for her shirt. Then her bra, but only after I spent a lot of time feeling over it. Then my jeans. Then her skirt. There was a strict kind of order for the whole thing, unlike the other drunk hookups I'd had. But I followed everything she did. I was so turned on I would have done anything she said, anyway. Except she didn't say anything. It was mostly signals: her hands going here or pushing mine there.

Finally, she did talk, though. Just as her hand went down my boxers and started rubbing my dick, she said, "We can't have sex, okay, Sean? I can't yet. Okay?"

What? "Okay," I said.

"You're not mad?"

Was she kidding? We were almost *naked*. My hands were on her *tits*. She was giving me a *handjob*. Why would I be *mad*?

"Why would I be mad?"

"I don't know. We just can't do it tonight. But I've thought about it, and I've got this plan, okay? I'm not just being a prude."

JESUS. I was about to come all over her, pretty much, and she was talking about being a *prude*?

"Obviously you're not," I said. "Not that you're . . . you know . . ." I sort of nudged her hand off my dick so I could actually talk like a normal person.

"A slut?"

"I didn't say that. I just . . . what's your plan?"

"It's not really a plan," she breathed into my ear. "More of a *rationale*."

"Okay . . ."

"If we do it tonight, then what would we do next weekend?" She laughed in my ear and all my hair stood on end. Christ.

"Next weekend . . . ?"

"Well, that's when we'll go out on a real date. Next Friday's my birthday and I turn eighteen. So we could do something fun for that. Okay?"

I felt like a baby again. I wouldn't turn eighteen for months.

But I just said okay, and we kissed again, but her hand didn't go back into my boxers. Which was fine. Everything else was so great. Her body, her whispering into my ear, all of it weird, but still great.

Then a girl voice shout-whispered right outside the tent.

"Hallie? The cops are here!"

●

We got dressed faster than hell. It was a total disaster. My watch snagged on the sleeping bag. She couldn't find her shirt. The tent flap zipper jammed. She wanted to run toward the house, and I knew they'd check there and all the other outbuildings, so I had to convince her to go toward the cornfield. It was like she'd never been caught at anything and didn't know how to be sneaky, almost.

When we'd gotten to the tree with the deer stand, she looked at me like I was crazy.

"You want me to climb a tree?"

"The deer stand's up there. It's like a little platform. We can sit on it. You'll see it soon enough. Grab the little wooden handholds. It's not that high up."

"How do I know those handholds are safe?"

"They're fine! I nailed them up myself! Just go!" I kind of just pushed her into it, put out my hands so I could boost her up, and then she laughed so loud I had to shush her. Seriously, she seemed like she'd never been busted before for anything. The climb wasn't a big thing, given that Grandpa Chuck wasn't the most fit old guy in the world, but Hallie hadn't struck me as the tree-climbing type. Still she launched up that fucker in no time and I followed her, surprised at her speed. The Horn didn't mind seeing flashes of her panties, either.

But once up in the deer stand, I sat on the outer half of the platform while she clutched the tree trunk like she was scared now. We were quiet. Watching and listening. Flashlights scanning around the barn and outbuildings. Cops hollering. The red swooping glow of the cop-car lights making everything all swimmy and sickening. Reminding me of the day in February, my dad in the bathroom. Which was nothing I wanted to think about up here with Hallie.

"Do you think they'll see us?" she whispered.

"Not if we're quiet," I said.

"Are you sure? Wouldn't they check up here?"

"How would they know there's a deer stand?"

"I don't know."

"People don't tend to look up, generally," I said. "Plus, just look at that fat fuck." I pointed toward the one cop who stood in the headlights of his cop car, talking into his radio. "You think *he's* going to climb up and get us?"

"But it's like a treehouse, kind of?" She ran her hand over the little two-by-fours we'd nailed up there. "A little treehouse that someone started and didn't finish. Won't they see the little ladder things? Don't you think . . ."

"Shhh . . ." I said. "They'll only check if they hear something."

Honestly, I was more concerned about the sex mood being totally killed, and since I had no idea how it had started to begin with, there was pretty much no way I could get it going again without seeming completely dickish or awkward. And Hallie was pretty freaked out. So I let her talk, all her worries, how her parents thought she was at Carenna's house for the night and that she'd just been given her car as a present from her parents and everyone would be so pissed if she got busted, because they thought she was so good and perfect with her awesome grades and everything. It sounded like she might cry, and I didn't know what to do. Like hold her or tell her it'd be okay? But I couldn't say that, because what did I know?

"They'll never find us," I said. "We're being quiet. It's too dark out here; they'll never come out into the mud. Look at how dirty your boots are." I pointed, and she knocked one boot on the tree trunk, raining clumps of mud down below.

"Don't!" I said, putting my hand on her knee. Then snatching it back, which freaked her out even more. Like the cops would be there any second now, seeing a little hunk of dirt from a tree that far away. So I tried to distract her again.

"Hey, Hallie," I said. It was the first time I'd said her name. I'd just known it and had never said it. "I'm gonna make a guess here, but I'm betting there's no way those are your cowboy boots. Because you don't seem like the kind of person who *owns* cowboy boots . . ."

"I don't?"

"No."

She smiled at me and I was all The Horn. Again.

"What makes you think that, Sean?" she asked.

"I bet you came into the Thrift Bin—where I work," I said. "With all your friends you planned the party with. And you all laughed at all the junky shit and weird-smelling old clothes. But you guys found everything there, anyway. Tried it all on, laughing your asses off. All those bandanas and hats and shit."

She leaned closer to me. "How'd you guess?"

"Shh . . ." I said. One of the cops was talking into his radio, and I was trying to listen. Wondering if he'd call for more backup. There were only two cars here and that meant they were only just busting the party. They'd need more cops if they wanted to round people up and give them underage consumption tickets.

She whispered into my ear. "No, really, how'd you guess?"

Her voice in my ear tickled. Damn. Having The Horn up in a tree in a deer stand was one experience I'd never banked on.

"I've seen it a million times," I whispered back. Then her arm slinked around me and pulled me closer and it was nice, but I was nervous so I just kept talking. Told her some more about the Thrift Bin. About how nursing homes donated all this crap from dead old people. About how people left half-eaten Happy Meals and dirty diapers in the customer bathroom. About how homeless people came in and changed into new outfits in the dressing room and then walked out, leaving their nasty reeking hobo clothes on the dressing room floor.

She listened to all of it, which was good, because it stopped her from freaking out. And she clutched me closer so I could tell her more. Her favorite part was when I told her about the little shelf of strange shit we kept in the break room. Which was the idea of this girl in my grade named Neecie Albertson, who just started working in the back room sorting donations. Neecie was this sort of quiet nerdy chick; she had bad hearing, I guess, because back in junior high, she used to have to carry around this little bag with, like, equipment in it, including a microphone the teachers clipped to their shirts so she could hear them during lectures. Though she stopped doing that in ninth grade for some reason. Anyway, Neecie liked collecting all the weird, broken, shitty trash that got donated. And it got so huge that one day Kerry, my boss, said he'd build a shelf for it and nailed one up quick on the break room wall with old boards he'd scrounged from pallets behind the Dumpster. People would give Neecie stuff they found while sorting, and then she'd decide what she liked best from that day and put it up on the pallet-shelf thing with a little caption about it. Which was pretty entertaining. Wendy, the store manager, loved it. Thought it was perfect for the staff to do when it was sucky and hot with no air-conditioning in the back donation room. Everyone took turns trying to find stuff that Neecie would put up there. Usually it wasn't anything we could sell. A used douche kit. A girl's diary. A greasy pack of playing cards with naked-lady pictures on them. A full bottle of booze with another language all over the label.

"That sounds so cool," Hallie said.

"Not as cool as being a lifeguard. Wish someone would pay me to sit in the sun all day."

"It gets so hot and sweaty. And the kids are totally annoying. Their moms too. It's mostly just really boring. But it looks good on college applications, so I did it."

"Lifeguarding gets you into college?"

"Well, no," she said. "But my parents thought it was a good idea. I did a million other things to get into college. You know. You'd have done them all last year. Junior year's the big year for that. ACT and stuff."

I shrugged. "I didn't really do shit," I said.

"What are you going to do after you graduate, then?"

Great. Now Hallie Martin had something in common with my mother. And my brother Brad. And Grandpa Chuck. Everyone asked me that question, had been asking me that since forever. I was so fucking sick of that goddamn question.

"I don't know. Maybe I'll work at McDonald's. I hear that's a good career path."

She pushed me a little. "Come on! Be serious."

I gripped her waist harder; suddenly, I felt like we might tip out of the goddamn deer stand and splatter on the ground.

"I don't know. Might join the Marines or something."

"Really?" She sounded, again, fascinated, in the same way she had about the Thrift Bin stories. Like I was somewhat crazy and she couldn't wait to tell her friends about it. Though I didn't really get it. Oak Prairie was still a pretty small town in a lot of ways, even though now it was becoming a fancier expanded outer-ring suburb of Minneapolis. But even so, plenty of people here still chose the military after high school. Not the people who were popular or worth a damn socially, obviously. But people like me? I didn't exactly come from a family of high-rollers or geniuses. My brother ran a tree-trimming service. My dad, when he had a job, worked for a farm equipment place. My mom was the only one with college. She was a school psychologist, though; that didn't make much money either.

"I don't know." I suddenly felt a little dumb. I mean, I hadn't thought about it that much. Not much beyond that the Marines seemed like the coolest of the military branches to join, at least. I didn't have a thing for airplanes or ships, plus Grandpa Chuck had been in the Navy and talked shit about it all the time. And Brad had once considered the Army, but my mom had freaked out a little, being that she's all about nonviolence and whatever because of all the fucked-up abused kids she deals with, but then Brad met his fiancée, Krista, who drove that whole Army idea out of his mind.

"Joining the Marines," Hallie said like she was testing it out. "I mean, wouldn't that be like just saying, 'Come kill me in a war?'" she asked.

"They do give you a gun, you know."

She laughed, and I shushed her. She held me tighter around the neck, and I could feel her boobs against me again. God.

"You must be really brave," she said, pulling away again.

"Not really."

"You're way braver than me," she said. "Way tougher."

This made me think that she knew all about the thing with Eddie. There was a lot of shit that had happened this year, until my dad finally left, but the day I broke Eddie's nose and got suspended for a week was what everyone knew about. But I wouldn't have called any of that "tough." Or *brave*. I hated that word: *brave*. I knew that when it counted, I was not brave at all. Even if this girl, this beautiful awesome girl, thought I was.

Cars began pulling out, and we leaned forward to see what might be happening. I was listening to the cop radio, or at least trying to. Hallie had rested her head against the tree trunk. Like she was tired of me. I wanted to keep telling her stuff so she'd laugh. But I was running out of things to say. And I was getting pretty fidgety, because her being deathly quiet just lit up my ass with worry that she would tell me this was a mistake, all of it, the kissing and getting in the tent and everything else. Like, any girl who was worth anything good might get to a point after so many hours in a deer stand that she decided what was wrong with this situation wasn't the cops but *you*.

It was five in the morning when we came down. Though the cops had been gone a while before that, Hallie made us wait because she worried they might come back. Which I thought was unlikely, but I just went along with it. I climbed down first and waited for her to climb down, too, trying not to be super gross about looking up her skirt, but then not caring, given that I'd done it on the way up the tree, too. But once we were back on the ground, the touching thing seemed over. Because it was near dawn and the party was busted and now Hallie had to go back to normal. Stop getting naked with random younger guys and turn back into a pumpkin or whatever.

The sun was just coming up over the cornfield. The dirt was black and sticky as fuck, all plowed up in thick rows for spring planting. It was amazing we'd been able to run as fast as we had through it. I supposed Hallie's cowboy boots were actually useful in that. My shoes were completely caked, and I dragged them on the gravel and stretched my legs out.

Hallie found a ticket on her car, for illegal parking or some stupid shit. We went looking for Eddie's car and the tent we'd set up, but no luck.

"Can I get a ride?" I asked Hallie as she dug through her bag for her phone and stuff. I felt a little shy about asking, but I didn't have any choice, really.

"Sure," she said. In this sort of yeah, whatever kind of voice that just killed me, really. That's the problem with getting what you want. Then you have to worry about it being gone.

"Thanks," I said, and then gulped, because she slipped off her T-shirt and changed into a clean tank top. Swapped out her cowboy boots for flip-flops. All like it was no big deal. Like I just got an all-access pass to her body from here on out. Or maybe it was friend-zoning, like Eddie always warned against? Still, I had The Horn for her again. How could I not?

But then she lent me her toothbrush, didn't even think that was gross, me using it or spitting toothpaste all over the ground. She actually laughed, watching me do it. And once our teeth were brushed and she had washed her face with the hose from the back of the house and she put on fresh lip gloss and stuff, she kissed me. And made fun of my sticking-up hair. And said she thought I was cute.

Then, the sun in my eyes making me wish I had the sunglasses I'd left in Eddie's car, she drove us back to town. Everything so easy. Like we planned it. Maybe she *had* planned it? But it felt like both our ideas. Like it was all meant to happen.

I'd think about that morning so many times. How I was dead tired and probably still half drunk and my balls ached but how it all was so good. How she stopped at a gas station to wash the mud off her windshield. How I bought her a giant orange juice and myself an Amp and a box of donuts and how she freaked out and said, "What do I need a dozen donuts for, Sean?" How I said she could have one or two, but the rest were for me. And how that made her laugh, and how that was good, very good, but that I was only half kidding and ate most of the box. And how she drove me home, then, but I wouldn't let her come up the drive, saying it was so my mom wouldn't notice.

I should have felt stupid then, but I didn't. Even a mile from this crappy house I hated, kissing her good-bye in her tiny red perfect girl-car—which was all smooth and glossy like a make-up case—was pretty much the best I'd felt in a while.

Her mouth full of sugar flakes and cherry filling. Her little laughs in my ear. My hands climbing up her shirt and The Horn hard as hell in my jeans. How fucked up and good life was. One minute you're drinking beer in a barn, the next life sends a Frisbee bashing into your face and a girl so beautiful and perfect you can't decide if it's some giant joke or just you getting what you deserve, finally, finally, after so many years of not.

## Chapter Two

I came into the kitchen to see my brother Brad laying on the kitchen floor, pulling the guts out of our broke-dick dishwasher. Brad hadn't lived with us for years; he had an apartment with his fiancée Krista, but since we'd moved to the rental, he was over all the time. Helping my mom with stuff. Seeing if he could get salvage titles for the motorcycles the previous renters had left in the backyard. Loading up other junk in the yard, a busted microwave and an old hot water heater, and taking it all to the dump. Fixing all the broken stuff the last renters had wrecked, everything from towel bars to closet door hinges to busted windowpanes and screens. So much shit needed fixing. Which I guess was good. I couldn't fix shit.

That morning, I said my usual Brad-greeting: "What's up, idiot."

Brad gave me my usual Sean-greeting: "What's up,

douche." Then went back to his grunting on the floor with all his tools. I started making peanut butter toast and gulping a ton of orange juice out of the jug, not saying anything. Lately, talking to Brad meant him launching into a list of jobs I needed to do around the house for Mom.

When I turned to put away the orange juice, my dog Otis jumped up on the counter and ate one of the pieces of peanut butter toast, and I yelled at him and Brad laughed. Brad was like that: the kind of brother who thought it was super amusing when shitty things happened to other people. Or at least to me. Two weeks before, on the Fourth of July weekend, he'd made us demo one of the crappy old sheds in the backyard because the rambler's landlord knocked money off the rent in exchange for the labor. I'd ended up getting stabbed with a rusty nail and had to go get a tetanus shot, and Brad laughed at that, too. But when I tried to blame our dad for any of this, for me having to sweat my balls off on my one day off from work, or for anything else, either, Brad told me to shut the fuck up.

"I'm busting my ass to help you and Mom out," Brad had said as we walked into the quick clinic to get my shot. He looked at me with his lips all thin. "Quit acting like a dick."

I wanted to say it wasn't him, it was our dad, but Brad stomped off ahead of me, and that was that. No discussion. No more laughing, either.

It was one main reason I didn't get along with Brad. Maybe some brothers like each other, or at least have a good time together. But we never did. All Brad did was save the goddamn day and then laugh at me when shit went south. He'd never say one bad thing about our dad. Never once. And no one else could, either. Brad wouldn't have it. It drove me crazy.

I left Brad to be the dishwasher hero, happy to have a job. Happy to be able to get away from the rental and go to work, where there was always something to do and none of it made me feel guilty. It was a normal shift like any other at the Thrift Bin: Wendy was wearing a weird outfit; Neecie Albertson was tagging clothing; Kerry was saying sleazy things; a cashier called us to help carry out a loveseat to the car of this four-hundred-pound man who was driving around on one of those Medicare motor scooters. His wife smelled like baby powder and diapers and bossed us ridiculously about loading the damn thing into their crap-filled minivan. Your basic Thrift Bin regulars, hoarder customers. That day must have been a sale day; the regulars/ hoarders crowd always came in on those days to swoop down on whatever they'd been waiting to get marked down.

After the loveseat thing, Kerry bought us Taco Bell for lunch, and then we baled tons of unsaleable clothing into the rag baler, which Kerry was training me on because soon as I turned eighteen, I could legally use it, and then he would cele-brate because he hated baling. I remember thinking that would be cool, to be the one doing the baling for a change, so Kerry could handle the donation door (and all the customers and their annoying tax receipts) instead of me.

It was a heat wave, a mid-July kind of thing. The Thrift Bin was pretty horrible in the back, with no A/C.

"Sweating like a whore in church," Kerry kept saying. He always said it around Neecie Albertson too, like he wanted to make her react. She never reacted. I was proud of her, in that way, but also waiting for her to finally crack. Kerry was relent-less in his grossness to girls like that.

Despite the heat, Wendy was in a good mood. She even

changed the radio to the country station when Neecie asked her to, though everyone else hated country, especially Kerry: it made him extra bitchy. But then a bunch of weird injuries happened: one of the cashiers punctured her thumb with a tagging gun, I got a big scrape across my forearm shoving a busted baby buggy down the compactor, Kerry dropped a box of books on his foot. Wendy told everyone to relax—the accidents and injuries freaked her out. She busted out a box of popsicles and made everyone take a break while she filled out injury reports and we all shot the shit, looking at all the crazy things on the break room shelf, laughing at this book called *The Christian Guide to Sex*, which of course didn't have any pictures in it and Kerry was surprised the whole book wasn't just a bunch of blank pages.

I didn't find out what Neecie picked for the break room altar because my shift ended before hers, but it was a choice between a million-year-old condom that came from some old guy who died at the nursing home, some nasty Polaroids of this chick in a bikini sitting on an ugly couch smoking a cigarette, and a crucifix made out of wire hangers. Wendy had found the condom; Kerry had found the Polaroids. I'd found the crucifix.

Wendy even let me go a little early when things slowed down, which was awesome, because there was a party out at Prairie Lake where Hallie's cousin's cabin was. Everyone was going waterskiing, and I wanted to get out there fast because it was supposed to thunderstorm later, and I loved waterskiing.

●

Hallie had been drinking all day. Everyone had been; it was kind of a sloppy all-day-swimming thing. Which was good; I had met all of Hallie's friends, but I still felt a little weird being around them, since they all had known each other forever and had a million inside jokes and talked about people I didn't know. And her cousin was in college and so *everyone* was talking about college, like they were already there or something. I was glad they were all drunk by the time I got there.

We went out on her cousin's boat. Hallie wore a white bikini, and she looked tanned and sunburned, both at once. She was drinking this crap that her girlfriends always drank: these super sweet malt liquor bottled drinks that made their mouths a bloody red color, and she was being kind of crazy. Like, loud. Telling her cousin driving the boat to go faster and swearing a ton more than normal and touching me more than usual in front of everyone. And screaming laughing when she got up on skis. Just being really drunk, I guess.

Around seven we came back to her cousin's cabin because everyone wanted to get some pizza in town. The girls changed out of their swimsuits; the guys finished their beers; everyone scooped up keys and purses and hashed out who was sober enough to drive.

"Do you want to go?" Hallie asked as she stood on the deck in her bikini, wrapping a towel around her waist.

"Whatever. You decide."

"I just feel so . . . I don't know. I'm not hungry. You're probably hungry, though, right?"

I was really hungry. And pizza sounded good. But I was always hungry, I guess. I could eat an entire pizza first thing in the morning. But I looked at her and saw everyone leaving, and I didn't care where they were going.

"Okay, let's just stay," she said. "Okay?"

"Cool. Yeah. Fine."

From the deck, we watched the guys wrap up the ponykeg in a trash bag and load it into someone's trunk, taking the party with them, or maybe just getting Hallie's cousin to return it for another.

Hallie went inside and brought me back a Coke, and we sat watching the sun get low over the lake. Though I was exhausted, I felt pretty good. It was hard to get alone with her sometimes. If we weren't at a party with a bunch of people, then I'd be at her house, late long nights where we'd sit on the couch and watch TV, and I'd wish her parents would just go to bed already so she'd calm down and let me touch her.

"... plus he's totally got a girlfriend at back at college," Hallie was saying. She was talking about her cousin.

"So?"

"So he's hooking up with all these other girls while he's home," she said. "It's so shitty of him."

I shrugged. Her cousin was sort of a douchebag, in my opinion, but that wasn't anything I'd ever bring up, since he let us hang out in his parents' cabin and had bought us alcohol a lot this summer.

I stretched out my legs so the sun could dry off my wet board shorts, gulped the rest of my Coke.

"I've met his girlfriend," she said. "She's really nice. She's really pretty, too."

I didn't get why she was saying any of this. Hallie was always talking about girls she thought were pretty. I didn't think about girls' prettiness all that much since the end result was The Horn. Looking at Hallie now, her legs all tan and firm and strong—and man! I wanted to just ... *bite her*. Right in the thighs. Not like I was some kind of vampire or any kinky weirdness. Just that, all the time, I was ready to practically, you know. Eat her up.

"Maybe he doesn't like her anymore," I said.

"Well, then he should tell her!" she yelled. "Not cheat with someone else. I feel like I owe it to his girlfriend to tell her. I feel like I'm lying."

"Is that why you didn't want to go back to town with him and everyone else?"

She looked at me then, and she smiled and I felt like I'd won something.

"Kinda," she said. "Yeah." She looked happy that I had figured this out, but also still kind of sad.

"Come here for a minute," I said. And she did.

That was also weird, because I never really told her what to do, ever. I was always waiting for her, really, to do everything. Go out, make plans, let me touch her. Always waiting.

She wrapped herself in my lap, and the chair I was on almost fell over, and I laughed and she freaked out, but I wouldn't let go of her and we kissed for a while, and then she started talking again. She did that a lot, the whole make-out-then-stop-and-talk thing, which was fine, I guess, though The Horn wasn't a fan. I mean, The Horn did what it did, no matter what I wanted. It sort of ruled my life in a way that got embarrassing sometimes.

Still, I liked her on my lap, even though my thighs were starting to get numb, and I liked how her hair smelled, even though it tickled me as the sun sunk and the breeze blew up from the lake. I liked how her left boob smashed against my shoulder. Since school had ended, I'd been with her almost every

26

single day but it never got old, being with Hallie. Especially when we could be alone together, touching like this. I'd barely seen Eddie all summer.

"It's going to storm," she said, slapping a mosquito on my arm. "Let's go in."

We went inside the cabin and poured bowls of cereal, which we ate standing up in the kitchen. Then she said she wanted to go lie down in bed for a while. The sun was setting, orange everywhere across the lake, but the clouds started covering it, making it feel like it was later than it was.

"Do you mind?" she asked. "I just feel so icky."

Did I mind? "Fuck no, I don't mind," I said. Sometimes I wondered if she was crazy. Even though we always ended up doing whatever she wanted to do, she always asked me what I thought about this or that: *Is this okay? Do you mind? What do you think?*

Like I was going to complain about getting in bed with her. Like I wouldn't do whatever she said.

Upstairs, we moved all the clothes and stuff the other girls had dumped on the bed and got under the covers. It was hot, though, so she had me get up and open the window. The storm wind started rushing up from the lake and it felt good on us.

Then I just did my normal waiting thing. Let her curl herself around me. Listened to the bugs buzzing around the screen of the window. The sky rumbling. Waited to see what she wanted. From that first night, Hallie wasn't weird about sex stuff, not uptight about getting naked at all. But she had these standards.

Like: No calling each other pet names. No dirty talking. No popping her boobs out of her bra without unhooking it first.

No using words she thought were gross, like "tits" or "pussy" or whatever. (Not that I would. Not to her face, at least.)

It reminded me of those signs they have up at the swimming pool. But instead of No Running, No Spitting, No Horseplay, it was all her things she didn't like. I sometimes imagined it written up like that when she talked with her friends about other guys (Dan, her hockey player ex, was often mentioned) who had broken all these rules.

No feeling her up before kissing her.

No touching under the bra before taking off her shirt.

No sticking my hand down her pants before I touched her boobs.

*No no no no.*

It wasn't like she'd smack me over the head with her purse about it or anything. But she'd say "No," or "Wait," or just move my hand. So I learned quick. It sort of embarrassed me, anyway, to be the one who wanted more than she wanted.

She started kissing me, then. Nice, but basic kissing. Being that we were both kind of sandy and sweaty in our swimsuits, I thought it wouldn't go far; Hallie had a thing about that, too. Her definition of what it meant to be "clean" or "ready to go out" was a thousand miles different from mine. Plus she'd already said she felt icky; that could have meant anything.

But that night, just when I got her bikini top off, she stuck her hand down my board shorts. Right on The Horn. Which, though out of order, was more than cool with me.

Then, next, she tugged my shorts down and pulled them all the way off. Okay, *that* wasn't normal. She didn't ever strip me like that. Ever. Just pushed my boxers or whatever down a little if she was going in that area. It was like she couldn't have me be all the way naked or something. She was the same way about her own self, too. Let me touch under her panties, but never pushed them down. It was like she was thinking it didn't really count if she was still wearing her stuff or something. I had to try to get her off like that, with her panties still on, and while I think she liked some of it, I was pretty sure I'd never managed to get her off for real. Which bugged me, because she got me off all the time.

So after getting me all naked like that, all unexpected, when she touched my dick again like it would just be the usual hand-job or blowjob of the past few weeks, I was kind of bummed out, honestly. I mean, it sounds stupid, but changing the rules got my hopes up so quick, made me thinking she'd finally want to have real sex. Handjobs were nice, but I was getting a little sick of them. I'd been jerking off since I was thirteen. I was a professional. And then there was the awkward "time to mop up the jizz" moment that I never could get used to doing in front of another human being.

Blowjobs I had less to complain about. I mean, I wasn't completely stupid. But it was like she didn't get the point of sex stuff. The reason she did her hair and makeup, the reason I put on a collar shirt and picked her up on time and took her out for dinner and went to the mall with her while she looked for crap for her dorm at college and every other goddamn thing. People did all that because there was getting off at the end of it. Because you liked it and you liked each other and all of that felt good. That was why we were both here, right?

Hallie sat up, swung herself over me. As if she could tell I was being a bastard about her handjobs and blowjobs in my head.

"Hallie, what . . ."

"It's okay," she said. She put my hands on her hips. Her bikini bottoms were slightly damp, and she moved like I should push them down, so I did. Her body felt sunburned, warm, but her bare ass was cold, which would have been funny to me, except for right now things were serious. She was looking at me. Watching me. Not smiling or talking. Even when I put my hand between her legs, she kept watching me. She was wet as hell. Which was good. Great. Girls can't fake being wet, Eddie told me once. But the rest of her was very tense and still. Like I was taking out her stitches or something.

*Why is she still looking at me?*

I kissed her so she would stop looking at me. Thought about the condoms that lived in my sock drawer. Condoms that were almost an hour's drive away. I wanted to punch a hole in the wall for not planning ahead. But then, maybe I'd read things wrong again.

A couple minutes later, she pulled back off me.

"I have condoms," she said. "And I've been on the pill since March. It takes three cycles to work. Three months. But it's been longer than that, just in case. So it's all set now. Sean? Do you want to? Because we can. It's okay with me. I've never done it before. But we can. Okay?"

This was a lot of information at once, so I guess I couldn't help it, then. Because *March?* The barn party was in April. Was she still with Dan the hockey player in March? According to Hallie, they'd gone out for a million years. She even had a framed picture of him and her together on her nightstand, which she got rid of the first time I went over to her house. Because Hallie and Dan had been a *couple*. They went to *dances*.

They *ate lunch* together. They posed for pictures that were then *framed*.

But now she was saying she hadn't fucked him. And now she was saying she wanted to fuck me. Except Hallie would never say "fuck" like that.

"All right." My voice was a whisper. "Where are they?"

She reached around, her boobs swinging in the air, and grabbed her bag, handed me a condom.

The little packet crinkled in my hand. How do I know she's really on the pill? What if she's lying? Does she know I've never done it either? What if she did it with Dan? And other guys too?

What if I come the second I put the condom on me?

Finally, she was looking at me funny and so I just ripped open the packaging. The second I did that, she laid back, her wrist over her eyes, like she couldn't bear to watch what came next or she was getting herself all mentally prepared or something dramatic. This hiding her eyes from me and my dirty condom business might have made me feel bad, but instead I was relieved to go through the whole thing on my own. Chucking the wrapper on the floor. Slipping the little circle-blob from the packet. Unrolling it, all slippery, with its weird Band-Aid smell, down my dick. I mean, it was pretty gross, if you really thought about it for a minute. I was glad she wasn't watching.

"Did you get it on okay?" she asked from behind her wrist.

"Yeah," I said, laying myself over her. Though I actually didn't know. It wasn't like she handed me the little instruction booklet that came in the box. Or that I would have read it. Had *she* read it?

"You ready and everything?" I asked. Which came out

sounding so weak-ass! But she nodded. Put her hands on my shoulders. She still wasn't really looking at me, but at least her wrist wasn't over her eyes.

So I kind of nudged her legs apart with my knee. She was a little resistant, like she couldn't really believe that was required. Like it was my shitty idea. My fault for biology, for being a guy, that I had to press her open all gross like that.

Since just sort of pushing around my dick right there seemed very, well, *icky*, I reached down again to figure out what was where, kissing her at the same time so she wouldn't notice I was being all clinical about finding the exact spot. But I guess she had the same idea, because then her hand knocked against mine and for a minute both our hands were down there, pushing and moving around, getting everything set up in the right place. Once it was clear things were all set up, my dick nudged her right in the exact spot and her entire body went still again. Like I was a Tyrannosaurus with bad eyesight and she was the prey trying to hide.

"Hallie?"

"Yes?" she asked. Her voice was high and soft.

"Hey," I said. Then she was looking at me. Weirdly. Like this was the part where I did the sex version of pulling a rabbit out of a hat. Like suddenly my dick should do something really brilliant, like produce a laser light show full of fireworks or something. Which, strangely, it didn't feel like doing. I was basically completely panicked.

Stalling, I asked if she was ready again. And again, she nodded.

There was nowhere else to go. Nothing else for it. So I just pushed in. Slow.

And then, not slow.

Holy shit.

"Holy shit," I said.

That day, like most days, I wasn't any better at not blurting stuff out.

"It's okay?" she asked. Now she sounded panicked.

"Yeah," I said, closing my eyes. Completely unpanicked. It was like I'd transferred my panic to her because this felt better than okay. "Okay" was not the word. *It felt better than I could believe.* For a minute it felt so good that I was pretty sure it would now have to be over. That that initial good feeling would be all I'd deserve to get and she'd change her mind or something.

But then I moved in her, back and forth. And there was more.

More more more. Jesus. *Fuck.*

It took a little while to get in sync, but it happened eventually. My hands in push-up mode, hers around my lower back. Her head tipped back, her boobs bouncing.

So. Fucking. Awesome.

Then Hallie's nails dug in my back and she made a sound like, "Ow!"

"Are you okay?"

"Yes, yes," she said. "It only hurt at first. Keep going."

*It hurt at first?* She seemed fine to me. At least from my side of things. But what the fuck did I know about hurting? God.

"You've really never done it before?" I asked.

"No," she said. And looked a little peeved.

"Okay," I said, really quick. The last thing I needed to do was piss her off! But goddammit. Both of us damn virgins! Though she didn't know that about me. She'd never asked! I mean, maybe she guessed it, but right now it felt like it was my job to know everything. She'd done the birth control part; now I had to step up and do my side. I kissed her, just for reassurance—hers or mine, I didn't know.

Then I just kept, well, *doing it.*

She was all breathless, too, which was funny to me, since I was the one doing most of the work. Not that I cared. I didn't. It was great.

*It was so fucking great.*

But I was getting increasingly brainless. I hadn't counted on the old "think about baseball scores" myth actually being useful, but I didn't want it to end. I mean, I wanted it to end, sure. But I also wanted it to go on feeling this way forever.

what is not sexy what is not sexy think about what is not sexy . . .

And the first dumb thing that came to mind? My Grandpa Chuck's new shotgun. The one I'd killed the buck with in the deer stand I'd sat in with Hallie at the barn party. So, then I just closed my eyes and ran through the list of all the other guns that I had ever used.

The 12-gauge. Oily as fuck the first time I touched it.

The .50-cal flintlock. The one my grandpa didn't like me to use.

The .410. Had to use that when I was a kid. Brad gave me so much shit.

Then I opened my eyes and looked down at her and we kissed a whole bunch but I just couldn't do it any longer, even though it hadn't probably been more than thirty seconds. I couldn't think. About guns or anything besides everything "good" and "wet" and "awesome" and "fuck."

I choked out, "Hallie?" Like I was asking permission.

She said in my ear, "Just do it, Sean." Four magic words like a switch, and so I just did it, I came, everything came, and for a minute everything was black but so excellent and I collapsed on her, feeling her arms around me and like I might sleep for ten years.

I lifted my head up. A minute later. A thousand minutes later. I looked down at her, her hair everywhere on the sheet. There were no pillows—what had happened to them? Did she move them? I barely knew where I was.

"Hallie?" I said. Looking down at her. She had sweat between her boobs. I thought I should pull out of her, but it felt so good, still, to be in there. I never wanted to be anywhere else on earth.

"Yes?" she said. Looking straight up at me.

It kind of hit me, then. Crazy. Like something that would happen to someone else, not me. Like Brad asking Krista to marry him on the beach in Florida on their vacation, under a full moon and bonfire on the sand and everything all beautiful, at least the way Krista always told it. Or a TV-show thing, where the music kicks in and the hero looks at the girl and everything becomes so meaningful. Totally cheesy. But that's exactly how it was. Except all in my head.

"You all right?" I asked. My throat was instantly scratchy. Like I'd drank sand.

"Yeah," she said. Lifted up to kiss me, and everything lurched down there in a way that seemed dangerously impregnating but she didn't let me move. We kissed a little more, and the whole time that same dramatic television feeling was in me. The urge to say it. I'd never said it to her, never meant to say

35

it to her. Had never said it to anyone else, besides my mom. Though I hadn't said it to her, even, since I was probably ten years old.

*I think I love her. Hallie. I think I love her. I do.*

"I think I love you," I said.

She stared at me. Quiet.

I looked away. It was raining now, lightning and heavy clouds over the lake. The water all chop and whitecaps.

Several more centuries of silence. She cleared her throat and I could feel it all rumble down there again, so I got up, turning so she didn't see everything hanging off me, and went to the bathroom.

I chucked the condom in the toilet. Then I pissed on it, trying to push it under the water, like all this was its fault.

*She's leaving in a month. Stop being such a pussy. Go in there and deal. At least get your clothes back on.*

In the bed, Hallie was sitting up, wrapped in a sheet—again, another TV-style detail. I didn't know what to do. I wanted to touch her again. I wanted to leave. I wanted to scream at her.

I scanned the floor for my clothes.

"Sean?"

"Yeah?"

"What are you standing there for? Get back in bed."

Christ. I didn't know if I was in trouble. Or if it was okay now.

I got in bed with her and she curled next to me, and the second I felt her all naked and she laid her head on my chest I was thinking it would be okay. Maybe.

Then she covered us both up with the sheet, like the cameras were rolling, and I could feel her foot next to my foot, her legs sliding beside mine, her breathing on my chest in that caved-in spot that seemed to defy any sort of fitness attempt to fix it, and everything snapped back to good. Or not exactly good. But better. Feeling like I could sleep a thousand years again, I shut my eyes.

*Maybe she didn't hear me.*

She stretched up. Put her mouth just beneath my ear. My eyes whipped open.

"I think I am, too," she said.

And I knew instantly what she meant. We stared at each other and then we kissed some more and then she laughed and I laughed and I rolled her on top of me. The words caught between us.

Words that I kept hearing for the rest of the night. Even after everyone came back to the cabin, drunker and smelling like pizza, and we rushed back into our clothes, we were still watching each other, across the deck and the fire pit, both of us knowing what had happened but acting normal, not saying anything, and the ride back into town, both of us holding hands across the long bench seat of my car, not talking, just listening to music and knowing the secret of everything.

# Chapter Three

Hallie pulled up her skirt but left her bra and shirt on the seat between us. My car was the kind that was big with senior citizens back in the eighties, all plush and padded, with that weird velvety fabric for seats, which made it hot as hell in the summer, even with the windows open. I was sweating so much my hair dripped.

She was leaving for college. Tomorrow.

Which was why we'd just done it, for the last time probably, at one of our favorite spots, down below the old railroad trestle by the dried-up riverbed six miles out of Oak Prairie, between the RV dealership and about twenty miles of cornfields. The railroad trestle hadn't supported a train since I'd been coming here, back in junior high. Now it was just a place for kids to act like shitheads because it was out of the way, through a bunch of dirt roads that had originally been a KOA campground, but now nobody who hadn't taken them before would be able to figure them out. The first time I'd come here was with Eddie and his older cousin, when we'd smoked pot for the first time. Back then, the river was deep and kids sometimes jumped off the trestle into the water. I'd jumped it a dozen times myself. When the river dried up, like it had this summer, it was just a stripe of mud and beer cans and trash. Lots of used condoms too. I pulled on my boxers and got out to add another one to the collection.

Getting back into the car, my foot caught on a plastic to-go cup on the floor mat. Hallie's soda cup. I hated trash in my car. I chucked it out the window.

"Litterer," Hallie said. "God, Sean." She sounded like a mom. I ignored her when she talked like that, generally.

"What time you guys . . . get on the road?" I couldn't say "leave." Or look at her.

"Five a.m.," she said. "My dad wants to leave earlier, though. He's saying four. My mom refused. Thank god." She kind of laughed.

"What's the rush?" I asked. "Don't you have all day to move in?"

Just talking about her moving in made me feel like shit. It took so much energy to act natural, I thought my heart might stop.

"There's this orientation for parents at noon," she said. She went on to explain the details of the day, but I could barely listen. None of them mattered; I wouldn't be there for any of them.

"Sean, we should talk about this," she said.

*No, we shouldn't.*

"I'm so glad everything happened that happened," she said, wrapping her arms around me. Her boobs jiggled against my ribs.

I couldn't speak. Or move.

"Sean?"

"What." My voice was all crackly, like my nuts hadn't dropped.

"We can't help it that this all turned out this way. But it'll be fine. It'll all work out."

"Hallie, you're going to college five hours away," I said.

"I don't mean that."

"Well, what the hell are you even talking about?"

"Us. Being together. For this summer. I'm glad we were able to do it."

*Were?*

I looked up. Though her hands were nowhere near my neck, I felt like she was strangling me.

Then she kissed me. She leaned against me more and our skin pressed together, all sticky. Like, you could even hear it being sticky, when it touched and pulled apart.

"I like you, Sean. I love you. I didn't think I would. But I do. Love you. And we had so much fun this summer, you know? It was more than I expected. But I'm glad it was."

*Was.*

She kept kissing me. Around my face, on the cheeks. My forehead.

I kind of wanted to shake her. Ask her what she was talking about. But really, I just wanted to leave. I pictured her, standing in the dry creekbed, in her underwear. And me driving away, driving fast, her standing there yelling after me. The image rushed so close to the surface, right under my skin. Right under where she was kissing. So I didn't move. Couldn't. She kissed my shoulder, and I thought, *now I have to hate you.*

Finally, she stopped kissing me and sat back. No matter how half-cocked she was sounding now, Hallie wasn't dumb.

"Did we . . . you just broke up with me," I said. "Right? Hallie?"

"I don't want to call it that, Sean." She picked up her bra and put it on.

I turned away from her.

"Well, what do you want to call it?"

"Can't you just appreciate it for what it was?" She ran her hands over my arms a bunch. I pictured her again, screaming after me, the Buick kicking up dust as I sped away.

"I don't really get what you're saying here," I said.

"Sean, come on. I will always feel good about it. Because it's, like, love, you know? It's good. Love is always good."

"Okay."

I wondered if she'd cry, if I really left her here. What she'd do. Would she walk the whole way home? Hitchhike? A girl couldn't hitchhike in her underwear. No. Maybe I'd toss her phone out the window at her?

 "Plus you never know where we'll end up. There's so much possibility in life, you know?"

Nope: no phone. Just her clothes, then. She could walk. She might not always act like it, but at the end of the day, she was strong. Physically at least. She might cry the whole way, but it wouldn't matter. I'd be gone, no matter how much she cried.

"Sean? Do you get what I mean?"

I got what she meant. I got that she had dumped me and

seemed to think it was something pretty great, from the smile on her face and the glowing sound of her voice and the way she was squeezing my shoulders now like a python and when you couldn't love someone anymore you had to hate them. So, I hated her now. I had to. I had to, because I was in love with her and she was doing this. Whatever this was. Why was she doing this?

"Okay," I said. It was a strain to keep this still, but I didn't trust myself. The image of her in my rearview mirror as I sped off was so clear—what the hell was wrong with me? But it wouldn't go away. Almost clinically, I kept walking through it. Like it was a math problem or something. Wondered how I'd get her out of the car. Would I trick her? Carry her out? Would she fight me? Would she be surprised? What would she say? She'd probably yell. And there'd be no tricking her. I'd have to remove her physically, which I could do, but not easily. She wasn't as tall as me, but I was skinnier. She was like a woman, Hallie. Built. While I was tall, a lot of me still looked like a boy. *Skinny little weasel*, my dad used to tease me, Brad laughing. Dad and Brad, being built and stocky and football-player-like. I started feeling around for my shirt.

"So, we're, what?" I asked. "Friends?"

"We're more than friends," she said. "We always will be. But we have to accept . . ."

Her voice got all choked-sounding. She wouldn't look at me. Then she wiped her eyes. We stared at each other, then, and I felt a little sorry. For imagining ditching her in the dirt. For the fact that we'd never again talk like this, have sex like this. For hating her, too.

"We have to accept that our lives are changing," she said,

clearing her throat. Her voice sounded so bad that it made me feel like crying, too. And I didn't even really understand what she was saying. But she kept talking, looking at the hollow spot in my chest. It made me straighten up, square my shoulders so it wasn't as noticeable.

"And we'll be able to see each other, again. When I come back home to visit. But we have to be thankful. And we have to let each other be free, because . . ."

"Hallie?"

"Yeah?"

"Look at me, okay?"

She looked up. And stopped talking. Finally. She'd been sounding like some shitty paper I'd write for English, where you just go on and on for the sake of the word count but not really saying anything.

"So, we're done, then," I said. "This is it."

"For now," she said. "It's just geography. I want you to have your freedom. It's your senior year, you know? But who can say where this might go, so . . ."

*Fuck geography. I'm leaving. Never coming back.*

"Okay, okay," I said. "I get it."

*I don't get it.*

"You could meet so many new people too, Sean. You have to believe that. We have so many opportunities right now, it's crazy if we didn't . . ."

"I know," I said. Then I kissed her. Like it would do any good, really. Like there was a point to it any more. But she kissed me back and that stopped the talking, which was weird but I wasn't complaining and then the leaving her in the dust and driving off idea dissolved and things got to the point that

43

we might do it again. Hallie was like that, sometimes, with sex. She just wanted it when she wanted it, the fact of which kept me in a constant state of semi-hardness since we'd first done it.

And I swear, even having just done it, and having just broken up, even in the weird way Hallie was explaining it out to be, we would have fucked again. Except a bunch of cars showed up, kids coming to get wasted, and Hallie always freaked out about that, about anyone seeing her like that. So I drove her home and we didn't say good-bye, but talk to you soon, something casual like that, like it was nothing.

•

I drove around for a while before I went home. It was late, but I wasn't tired. For some reason I decided to drive over to our old neighborhood. Our old house.

It wasn't a big house, but it was much bigger than the rental. We had a two-car garage, attached, and above it had been Brad's room, where he could climb out his window to the backside of the garage and sneak out. He'd never let me do that when he still lived with us, but I did once he moved out, of course.

The For Sale sign was still up; at least the notice from the sheriff wasn't on the door anymore. The grass looked long and shaggy; there were those freebie rolled-up newspapers nobody ever read in a pile on the front step.

I didn't want to slow down, but I did anyway. Parked. Looked at the front living room, which had a curtain drawn shut across it. We always had that curtain shut, too. It looked like we could have still lived there, except the lawn wasn't mowed and I'd always done that job. Not just because toward the end, my dad was too wasted to be trusted around machinery, cars or even something basic like a mower. But because I liked it, mowing. Liked those stripes on the grass, how much it made everything seem better than it was. You could look back at the whole lawn and see something. Progress. Change.

Then I worried Eddie might see my car, me sitting here like some kind of stalker. I reversed and turned around so I wouldn't have to pass his house, which was only four houses down, and headed back to the rental.

No one was around when I walked in the door. Otis stood there, barking, his tail whacking against the wall. Dogs are idiots, sometimes, how they get so happy they hurt themselves. I petted Otis, gave him a treat from the little jar my mom finally unpacked for his dog treats, and he clunked down on the floor to gnaw on it.

Then I went into the kitchen and saw my mom had gotten some groceries. Cereal and more orange juice. But I couldn't find a clean cereal bowl, so I poured a bunch of Frosted Flakes into a giant mug my mom used for drinking tea and went to the table. Which was covered in stuff for Krista and Brad's wedding—ribbons and hot glue and paper—and a pile of mail that was all OPEN IMMEDIATELY and SECOND NOTICE. Basically, the shit we'd been flooded with the past couple of years with my dad not working. I put all the mail and wedding junk to the side so I wouldn't spill on it and started eating. Sometimes after sex I'd be hungrier than shit, and this time was no different. Hallie always thought I was weird for being that way, but she was sort of uptight about food and dieting and stuff like that.

In front of me was another unopened box, marked BASEMENT/OFFICE, in Brad's crappy handwriting. This didn't make sense; the office in this house wasn't in the basement. My room was in the basement, right next to the laundry and the furnace. And the office was just another little dinky bedroom across from my mom's upstairs. My mom hadn't really set it up as an office yet; there was nothing in there but books and a desk. And she didn't have an office at our old house. No wonder the box was still sitting there, unopened.

I finished my cereal, then drank the sweet milk, then some orange juice. Then I sat there and looked at the BASEMENT/OFFICE box. School started in two weeks, and Hallie was leaving in just a few hours. And it would all be fine because of geography and all our opportunities, who could say where it would all go. All of this freedom. All of our possibilities. All of it so good.

# Chapter Four

I was not going to be a dumbshit about Hallie. I was not. It was my senior year; I'd waited my whole goddamn life for it. Not the stupid glory parts, like sitting in the senior section at pep rallies or getting lockers on the first-floor hallway. Just, really, being the oldest in the school for once. Being the ones who knew the most. Who nobody could say didn't belong there. When you were the oldest in the school, you could finally relax.

I didn't even tell Eddie about Hallie until after the first week of school. And then it was only because he asked.

"She's at college now," I said.

"Oh," he said.

"Yeah."

Then he started saying crap about Libby, the girl he'd been circling around all summer while I'd been up Hallie's ass. And how Libby had a cute friend and that I should hang out with them all.

"She's a sophomore," I said.

"No, she's a junior now," Eddie corrected.

"Whatever. Still."

"Her name's Emma. She has nice tits."

"Well. Okay."

So after school one day, before I had to be at work, me and Eddie hung out with Libby and Emma. Emma did have nice tits. And she was cute enough. But kind of shy, and not saying much, and after a while I said I had to go.

"Let's do homecoming, you guys," Eddie said all of a sudden. I stared at him.

"Totally!" Libby said. "That would be super fun!"

Emma nodded. Smiled. She was cute. She seemed so little, though. So much younger.

"Yeah. Okay," I said.

So I went to homecoming with Emma and Libby and Eddie. Emma and me drank wine before the game, then went into the dance. Emma had this really low shirt on and it was hard to not look down it while we slow-danced. I'd kind of avoided dances most of high school, because I always felt dumb about asking girls to dance, but having someone automatically to dance with was kind of decent. Made me wish I'd had the chance for that with Hallie, actually.

Afterward we went to a party at Tristan Reichmeier's grandmother's house, a hockey player party, but they had beer, and Libby offered to drive us because she didn't want to drink during soccer season. So I got kinda lit with Emma, and the next thing I knew, we were sitting in this room with embroidered cushions on the sofa and making out. It all happened pretty quickly, and at first I wondered if that was because Emma thought she owed it to me or something. Not that she liked me, just because I was older. But it wasn't like I was forcing her or anything; she was all over me and seemed into it. It was kind of funny, in a good way, actually, because I'd never expected her to be like that; she'd always been kind of quiet. But just as I got to feel, in the real, her tits, she climbed off me, said she felt bad. Then she got up and walked into the kitchen and barfed into the sink while a bunch of people stood there like assholes, staring and laughing. I got her some paper towels and then texted Eddie to get Libby, who showed up right away and took Emma to the bathroom to clean herself up.

Emma was sitting in this lawn chair on the patio, her head in her hands, all miserable, while Eddie and Libby went to get the car. I just waited, feeling bad for her, standing by these two guys smoking cigarettes and watching my own breath go in and out like smoke too, and then Eddie texted me a picture of a girl sitting on top of this giant red dildo that couldn't possibly have been real and I was going to text him back when I got another beep.

Hallie.

how's it goin, sean

I didn't text back because Libby pulled up. She took me home first, because I lived the farthest out. Thankfully Emma was asleep when Libby pulled into the gravel drive of the rental, which was good, because I didn't want her to see where I lived. Though probably Libby would tell her, anyway. Plus I kind of felt like it was my fault, for it ending up crappy.

But that's not what kept me up after I got home. Lying in bed, I stared at Hallie's text on my phone in the dark. Wondering what it meant. Thinking I'd text back in the morning. Or maybe I wouldn't.

Wondering if this was good. Or bad. Or just being friends.

I kicked off the covers. Otis harrumphed at me, pissed that I'd disturbed his billionth nap of the day.

What did I even say back? Nothing sounded good. Not "fine" or "good" or even "hey"—I was starting to see Eddie's point in just sending photo-texts.

What if I sent her the red dildo girl? "Hey, Hallie. *That's* how I'm doing."

Otis sat up in the dark, yawned audibly. Like he was sick of my bullshit.

I got out of bed, then. Took a piss. Looked at myself in the bathroom mirror. All lanky. The chest hollow looking deeper. Sharper. Like I should eat more and ease up on the Amp for breakfast.

Then, while Otis watched me from my bed, I rolled onto the carpet and did a couple of push-ups.

Maybe I'd join the Marines, like I'd told Hallie that night in the deer stand. Maybe I would. Then someone else could tell her how it was going for me.

⬦

The thing about working at the Thrift Bin, though Kerry was a dick sometimes and the work was hard and sometimes gross and the customers were crazy and cheap and left chicken wing bones on the shelves as they dug through all the merchandise in the store, was that it was never, ever boring. There was always some weird thing happening. Two ladies fighting over a leather coat. Kids knocking over a display of breakable figurines. Someone donating a loaded handgun inside a box of embroidered pillowcases and sheets.

Tonight's example of this was Kerry's discovery of a pile of used thongs in the parking lot by the donation door (Wendy's policy was that we didn't sell any underwear or panties unless they still had the tags on them; bras were okay, though, for some reason.) We all went and stood outside in the parking lot, staring at the pile of blown-out elastic and talking about what the hell had happened.

"Maybe it's some kind of subliminal message," Wendy said. "*Sell more thongs.*"

"Maybe we should bag them up and sell them as special lady-of-the-evening accessories with all the Halloween costumes," Neecie said.

"Maybe next week we'll get the matching bras," I added.

"Maybe all of you are fucking cracked," Kerry said. "A whore empties out her car's ashtray and you're all standing here acting like it's the secret meaning of life. Jesus." He kicked the pile of thongs into a box with his boot and huffed back inside. Kerry did that sometimes. Just shit on everyone's good time. Like this was the millionth pile of used thongs he'd dealt with today and the rest of us were babies for even pausing about it.

The rest of the shift was pretty basic. The Be Like Jesus group showed up, a bunch of giggling little junior high kids with braces and skinny girls wearing more makeup than they had any right to and their dorky youth pastor in a Captain America T-shirt making them pray before they starting unpacking bags and boxes of donated junk, acting like it was this super holy, sacred activity instead of one step above Dumpster diving.

People's behavior in a thrift store is so predictable. The girls freaked about finding some dude's old brief underwear; the guys lost their minds at touching a bra; the dorky pastor kept telling all these unfunny jokes like he was super "wacky" and then got kind of high-horsey with Wendy, asking her why we thought it was okay to sell Bibles: "Shouldn't those be given away for free?"

What a total douche. How did he think a nonprofit place like the Thrift Bin made any money by giving shit away for free? The Thrift Bin made money for United Way or something like that, stuff that helped poor people or kids with diseases or disabilities or whatever. There was a point to it, the Thrift Bin. But there was always some customer wanting something for nothing. Like we were just a big garage sale and needed a FREE box at the end of the driveway.

The Jesus group's job was to unpack clothing on the table in flat piles so that Wendy could sort through it to see if any of it had stains or rips. Then I went around and emptied all the trash they created as they ripped open bags and boxes. People don't donate their cast-off junk with any sort of organization, obviously, so the kids would open a box and find an alarm clock and a bunch of broken dishes and a pile of socks. My job was to collect the obviously broken junk for the trash and take all the nonclothing and put it in another bin for later sorting. I mean, the Thrift Bin might have been a secondhand store, but Wendy really made it so that we didn't just put out any old shitty shit for sale.

Later that shift, while I was working through a bunch of

cardboard with a box cutter, Neecie came up and started talking to two of the Be Like Jesus girls. One of them looked like her, blond. The other was dark-haired, with a fairly significant rack. Sometimes you saw girls like that in junior high, who were all filled out in a way that they weren't thrilled about, and this girl was totally like that. All hunched over and uncomfortable. I watched Neecie talk to the girls. Neecie was actually smiling and putting her arms around their shoulders, and it was weird; I'd never seen her do that. She always seemed stiff and serious, whether she was ignoring Kerry's gross comments or evaluating stuff people gave her for the altar shelf thing.

"Do you know those girls?" I asked her as we both went back to the break room to get something to drink.

"My sisters. Melanie and Jessamyn."

"Oh." I didn't want to knock them, then, for being in a dorky Jesus group.

"My mom is making them do youth group," Neecie said, like she could tell what I thought. "It's family tradition. Of horribleness."

I laughed. Again, surprised. Neecie cracked open a giant cans of iced tea, watermelon flavor, and I drank my Amp, and we stared at the stuff she'd put up on her little thrift hall of fame.

"What's on tap tonight?" I asked.

"I don't know," she said. "One of the cashiers found a pencil sharpener that looks like a nipple. But I don't think that's on purpose. It's just bad design."

"Lame."

"I know. Why would you ever put anything *into* a nipple? It's not even anatomically correct."

I was wondering about that when Kerry came in, yelling.

"Hey! You ever gonna do your job or what? Shit's piling up, idiot." Wendy must have been piling up the reject clothing for Kerry to bale, which of course would make him all hacked-off. As if he had it so bad. As if he'd be any cheerier in my place, listening to the dork pastor's jokes. And as if it were my fault I wasn't legal to work the goddamn baler. But I felt like he was also trying to act all badass in front of Neecie, which just bugged me more. Neecie always ignored him anyway, since she started working here.

The rest of the shift, I kept my head down, did my shit, and tried to avoid Kerry. At the end of the night, when I took the goddamn cardboard recycling bin out, I came across another interesting thing: Neecie Albertson, standing back by the Dumpster, arguing with someone.

I stopped pushing the recycling bin when I heard her. I couldn't tell if she was alone or on her phone. Wendy was sort of strict about not using your phone at work. There were just too many places you could lose it or break it.

"I can't, okay," I heard her say. Walking closer, I could see she had a phone to her ear. I wondered how she could hear on it.

"Tristan, I have to drive my sisters home . . . I know. Normally I would . . ."

TRISTAN? TRISTAN REICHMEIER? What the fuck was she talking to *him* for?

Then Neecie again: "I couldn't text you in the middle of work! Fine. Whatever . . . If I can get out, I'll try. No . . . I couldn't get there in time between school and work. I don't know why you can't go and do it . . . it's your idea . . . but you always have hockey! I mean, when is that *not* going on . . . ?"

It *had* to be Tristan Reichmeier. Tristan played hockey. He was, like, the hero of hockey at our school. Really good at it, actually. Everyone kind of lost their mind about him about the hockey. But Tristan Reichmeier always had a girlfriend. Girlfriends. And none of them were nerdy weird deaf Neecie Albertson.

"Fine, I know," she said. "But you know what you want to get more than I do. Okay. *Okay!* But I can't promise anything."

He must have hung up, because I heard her swear to herself, and then I started rolling the recycling bin again and Neecie turned and looked a little surprised to see me but just rushed past without saying anything.

•

When I got home from work, another round of Brad and Krista's Wedding Planning was going on. This had been happening since forever, it seemed like, since Brad asked her to marry him when they were in Florida on vacation and now every minute there was some new project going on all over the kitchen table and if I wasn't careful I'd get sucked into it. To top it off, Steven-Not-Steve was there too. Steven-Not-Steve was this guy my mom had met in her Al-Anon group, and who she said wasn't her boyfriend, but he was hanging around a lot for someone who was not a boyfriend. Steven-Not-Steve stood at the kitchen counter, drinking a beer. Which was weird; my mom usually didn't stock beer. I wondered if she was losing her mind about the wedding planning, too. Or maybe Steven-Not-Steve was losing his mind? Either way, Steven-Not-Steve wasn't usually here on weeknights, though he'd been showing up more and more lately.

"Hello, Sean," Steven-Not-Steve said. He was always formal, careful around me. Just like his clothes: Steven-Not-Steve always wore stuff that was tucked in, always took his shoes off when he came into our house, too, which wasn't a rule or anything.

"Hey," I said, edging around Steven-Not-Steve to get to the refrigerator and the orange juice. I'm kind of a fan of orange juice. My mom buys gallons of the stuff, just for me. I normally drink it out of the jug, because I'm the only one who drinks it anymore, but since Steven-Not-Steve and his dumbass polo shirt were here, I used a glass.

"Pretty excited for your brother's wedding, I'd imagine," Steven-Not-Steve said. Which, what was I supposed to say to that? No? Yes? Neither answer was right. What a dumb question to ask.

I nodded, slipped away, hoping I could just nod at my mom and Krista too and not get roped into anything. But then my mom came up and said, "Oh, hi, honey," and Krista looked up and said, "Hi, Sean!"

Krista was pretty, but she had this squeaky voice. And her hair was this blondish color that couldn't be real. And she wore those fakey plastic nails and a lot of makeup. And she liked to fake-tan. And sometimes her thong stuck out of her jeans in a way that made me turned on and grossed out all in one shot. But the thing was, Krista was very very nice. She was always so happy to see you, and unlike the rest of her looks, that part wasn't fake. Like, there was a reason she was the manager of Applebee's; probably people were so taken in by her welcoming them to the dumb restaurant, they just wanted to eat everything and like it so they wouldn't disappoint her.

"Hi, Krista," I said, guzzling my juice.

"How are you, honey? Sean, your hair is so long! I can barely see your eyes! Can we get your opinion?" Krista said, and I wanted to die, because that meant no slithering down to my room to jerk it in the shower or stalk Hallie online or just be alone for five minutes to think my own thoughts.

But I went over to the table and looked at what my mom and Krista were doing, which was making "Save The Date!" postcards that were like some kind of weird pre-invitation to the wedding and featured a picture of Krista sitting on Brad's lap next to some palm trees, which meant this was taken during the Fateful Florida Vacation. There were four different versions of the thing, the same picture, but framed with different designs. The table was covered in little bits of colored paper. It looked like Otis had gotten into some paper recycling and shredded shit up, like he did when he was a puppy.

Which reminded me.

"Where's Otis?" I said, since he hadn't come to the door to greet me. That was always his habit. At least, it was at our old house. Here, Otis was as disoriented as me, except instead of eating cereal out of mixing bowls and drying his body with Pokémon beach towels because we couldn't find the normal towels in any of the boxes, Otis had taken to hiding behind the furnace things in the basement or under my mom's bed, and running away along the highway, eating garbage and making me freaked out that he was going to get hit by a car.

"He's somewhere," my mom said, distracted. "So which one do you like, then?" She pointed to the cards again.

I motioned toward one of them and then yelled, "Otis?"

"That was the same one Steven liked," Krista said, frowning, as if that had some meaning. Like it was a man conspiracy. I went into the living room, where Otis's dog bed lay empty by the fireplace. Of all things, the rental had a fireplace. Brad said it didn't work, though.

"Mom, did you let him out and forget to bring him in?"

"What? No, he's inside. Check my office," she said, not even looking up from the table. "He's been going in there lately."

I found Otis under the office desk, between stacks of my mom's psychology books. He looked happy, was thumping his tail. And he got up and followed me to my room like nothing after that. But it was weird. Otis was almost twelve years old; we'd had him since I was in kindergarten. He was part German shepherd, part something else the vet and my mom could never settle on. He was big and furry and kind of fat, but he was great. He jumped on my bed and lounged for a minute, licking himself in all his gross places, and then, while I was in the shower, something else must have caught his dog-attention, because he was gone when I came back to my room.

I put on clean boxers and opened the window above my bed. It was still hot, even though it was now technically fall. The rental didn't have air-conditioning. Our old one had it. Our old one had everything good, really. Everything good, except for my drunk father.

Even a shitty house out on the freeway, with trash tossed out of passing cars getting caught in the fence, and semi trucks roaring by all night long and the goddamned muddy yard and gravel drive making everything look like we were hillbillies cooking meth or something, even that was better than living with my dad when he was drinking. But it still wasn't great.

I considered, pretty intensely, for a period of three to four minutes, doing my homework. But then I just got into bed. Because at the moment, I felt like doing nothing. Which meant one thing, really.

Doing nothing, jerking off; they were kind of the same for me. Not because I felt really sexual, necessarily. Mostly I jerked off for no real reason. Because I had a hand and it could go easily down my boxer shorts. And because, why not just do that when all else failed? I lay in bed, listening for everyone to shuffle out—Brad honking the horn of his truck in the drive, Krista's girl shoes making pointy clacks on the linoleum, Steven-Not-Steve jingling his car keys. I waited until I heard my mom call down that she was going to bed, and I yelled back "Good night," and then, finally, I could do it. Finally.

I'd worked myself up decently when my phone buzzed from across the room, still in the back pocket of my jeans. The little sound it made when I got a text. My hand froze midstroke. I listened again. In case I'd just imagined it. I didn't think it would buzz again. Then it did.

Of course, even though my hand was all covered in lotion, I still got up to look. I couldn't resist. It could have been Hallie texting again. I'd never replied, but that didn't stop me from thinking she'd text again.

Buzz.

I got up, wiped my hand off on a T-shirt lying on the floor, picked up my phone.

But the texts were from an unknown number.

don't tell anyone about that okay? pls?

Next one:

this is neecie from work btw

Like I knew any other Neecies!
The third:

sorry to bug you. nobody can know. he'll get really mad. pls don't tell anyone Sean

I stared at the screen. I kind of hate texting, because my phone's an old piece of shit and my thumbs are giant. And worse still, my hand was all slippery. So I just hit the call button on her name and let it ring. Figuring she wouldn't pick up, because that's why you text, right? Because you don't want to actually talk to anyone?

But of course, Neecie picked up.

"Hello?"

"Hi. It's Sean."

"Hi.

"How did you even get my number?"

She sighed, very loud. "From the staff phone list that Wendy gives out."

"Oh." I always got that list; Wendy updated it whenever someone was hired or quit, but I never looked at it. I only had Wendy and Kerry's numbers in my phone. There was no one else who worked my job that I could call to sub in for me, anyway.

"Hey, sorry to bug you about this, but it's really important you don't say anything."

"About what?"

"You heard me on the phone behind the store, right?"

"Yeah."

"Okay, about who I was talking to."

Great. We'd have to go through this dumb little quiz game, circling around the situation.

"Right. Tristan. Tristan Reichmeier. Hockey guy."

"Shit."

"I won't say anything," I said, sitting down on my bed. Otis started scratching at the door, and I opened it up for him. He instantly jumped up next to me and started snuffling around my crotch.

"Goddammit," I said, pushing him away.

"What?"

"Nothing."

"I can't hear very well on the phone," Neecie said. "Sorry. That's why I texted you."

"Oh. Okay."

"Well, thanks, Sean," she said. "I know it's weird, but just . . . thanks."

"Is he like your boyfriend or something?"

"What?"

"Your boyfriend," I said, louder and clearer.

"No," she said. "It's not like that. It's kind of . . . I don't know. It's just like, you know. Hooking up. I guess."

"You have sex with him?" I said. Blurted, really. Whoops.

"Umm, well . . . ," Neecie said. "I guess. If you want to put it like that. Yeah. But it's just sex. Not a real thing or anything. Okay?"

"Okay."

Neither of us said anything for a minute. I was being silent, punishing myself for blurting. I worried for a minute that she'd hung up. Like she was one of those people who don't say goodbye and just hang up when they're done talking. Brad was like that.

Then she said, "I mean, it's just stupid drama. And it's, like, no big deal to me that you know. But it'd be worse if other people found out. Just Ivy knows, so far."

Ivy Heller was this girl Neecie was always hanging around with. She was one of those chicks who barely talked but always dyed her hair weird colors like purple or blue and then, if you looked at her for one second, being that you couldn't really help looking, since most people don't have purple or blue hair naturally, she'd give you a shitty evil glare like you were being discriminatory or something.

"Sean? You there?"

"Oh, sorry. Yeah. Don't worry, it's cool. I won't say anything. I mean, I don't really know the guy, anyway."

She didn't say anything. I wondered again if she'd hung up. I wondered if she'd even heard me.

"Hello?"

"Sorry," she said. "I'm here."

"What's your name short for?" I asked. Because I'd just thought of it. Blurting still happening, I guess. But it occurred to me, talking to her, imagining her on the other end, what she was looking like, and whether her family was around her, like her mom and dad or whatever, and wondering what made them name their baby daughter Neecie. Like, it had to be a nickname, obviously. Nobody named a baby "Neecie." It'd be like naming a baby "Bill" or "Vicky" or something like that.

"What?"

"Nothing, it's nothing," I said.

"Okay, well . . ."

More silence. I didn't know if I should bother repeating my dumb question. Now that I was super curious.

"I have homework, so I better go," she said. "Again, sorry to bug you."

"It's fine."

"Okay. Bye then." Then she clicked off so quickly I felt a little surprised. Weird. Neecie was weird. And not just her name.

Then, it was like I'd just drank a whole can of Amp. I just felt hyper. Like I could run around the goddamn block. Except we didn't live on a block anymore.

So I rolled on the floor and did some push-ups. Then some crunches. Just to knock off some of the hyper feeling. I hadn't talked on the phone to a girl in a million years. A girl not Hallie. With Hallie, we usually texted, not talked.

The floor was crumbly and gritty and gross, but I just laid there, breathing hard, Otis trying to lick my face, human sweat being like the sweet nectar of the gods for dogs, I guess.

*Just sex?* I couldn't fit it in my head: Neecie was too nerdy to have sex.

I laid on the floor for a long time. Imagining Neecie Albertson having sex. Jesus. It wasn't hard to picture, actually, me being me, and The Horn and all.

I got up, brushed the crap off myself from my nasty carpet and got into bed. But still, I couldn't wash out the whole Neecie Albertson sex thing.

Then I felt like jerking it again. Which was pretty gross of me.

But then the channel switched to Hallie again. The first time she'd given me head. We were at her house; I'd been lying on her bed, the one with the big purple blanket, in the same position I was now. And we'd had a dumb fight just before it happened too. But I couldn't remember what we'd fought about.

The only part I remembered was how it was basically the best feeling in the world. Total relaxing luxury. Not having to do anything at all but lie back and feel it. Feel *everything*.

And when it was over, it was just over. Nothing for me to clean up, no condom to ditch in the bathroom. And it was quiet, too. Hallie'd get up, without a word, and then come back, usually drinking a glass of water, and then she'd lay down beside me again and still not say anything. That first time she'd put her head on my stomach, her hair tickling me a little. She was always oddly quiet and peaceful after doing that, like she didn't need anything from me, like she was feeling as good as I was, though I doubted that was true. I didn't care, though. That first time, I remembered looking down at her and thinking, *I would do anything for you. Anything. Name it, and I will do it.*

But then I couldn't jerk it anymore. Because then my eyes were just leaking, dripping down over my temples, into my ears, all over the pillow, and it was like I was being crushed from the inside, like my organs were failing. I sat up, then, and dropped to the floor and did twenty more push-ups, so fast I thought I'd choke. Otis didn't even move, just slumped his head on his paws as if to say, *Enough of your up-and-down shit, man. I'm not moving anymore.* Finally, I got back in bed. Otis settled his hot head on my shin, and I listened to the water heater kick on and scream for a million years until I finally fell asleep.

# Chapter Five

We were in a stand of trees between two cornfields, me and
Eddie and my grandpa and Brad. Deer hunting. It was earlier than fuck, the sun not all the way up, and it was kind
of cold, but not as cold as Eddie was bitching it was, and
though I didn't like smelling like the doe piss that Grandpa
Chuck insisted we had to wipe all over us, and I was sick
of Brad telling everyone what to do every second, it was
good to be here. I loved deer hunting, especially with my
Grandpa Chuck.

Eddie was nervous. He wouldn't stop whispering questions
about what was going on, and I didn't exactly know the plan,
either, because this was Brad's deal. Brad had been out hunting
a couple of times this season but hadn't bagged one yet, so he
was extra bossy. I was just glad we weren't at the same farm
where I'd met Hallie last year.

"You two, up that stand over there," Brad said, pointing at me and Eddie, then at a tree down at the edge of a frost-covered cornfield.

"Why do we have to go up?" I asked. The wind was kicking up and it'd be worse in the tree.

"Don't be a bitch," Brad said. "You can't track for shit, and you know it."

"I'm a better shot than you," I said.

"You can't be still for one second, though," he said. Which was true. We just stared at each other. Eddie looked back and forth at us.

"Grandpa's on the south end," he said. "Once he crosses the road, you're cleared."

I nodded. Then I nudged Eddie and we headed toward the deer stand.

"We have to set up a deer stand?"

"No, there's one up there," I said. "The guy who owns this land? He leaves them up for people."

"Jesus," he said, struggling to catch up with me. "Your brother's all professional."

"He's a dickhead," I said. "He takes all the fun out of it."

"What's it mean, to be cleared?"

"You can't discharge a firearm across a road; that's illegal. Technically, that little road there?" I pointed. "Where probably just the farmer and his family go across once in a while? That counts as a road. But, still, it's kind of a big deal, and the guy whose farm this is? You have to respect their safety and whatnot. Which isn't, you know, hard to understand. So Brad means, once we see my grandpa, we know he's flushed anything ahead and we can come down."

"Oh. Do you always do this, in the middle of a farm?"

I stood at the bottom of the deer stand, motioned to Eddie to go first.

"Sometimes. It's a fuckload easier than tracking through woods," I said. "Plus, there's corn and crap for the deer to eat. Makes sense. And it's less noisy, too, for us. Less stuff to give us away. Plus you can see better from up high, too."

Eddie could barely make it up the deer stand. It was kind of hilarious, when I thought of of Hallie doing it in no time flat. Eddie and all his swimming and lifeguarding and caring about his clothes and how tan he was, losing his mind when he broke a pair of his expensive sunglasses. He'd wanted to go hunting with my grandpa and me forever.

Once we got up top, Eddie was still winded. And he looked freaked. Normally, deer hunting was no big thing; we went, tried to fill our tags—sometimes succeeding, sometimes not—and my grandpa did all the field dressing and then we'd haul it out and go have a big breakfast somewhere and then he made it all into venison and that was awesome. We'd eat venison all winter long. But I hadn't really ever given much thought to the details until Eddie asked me all these questions today. But now he wasn't talking. Just breathing his frosty-ass breath out, looking around the fields. Like it wasn't deer coming but some kind of enemy.

I ran my hand down the stock of the shotgun my grandfather had given me for today. It was a nice gun, a 12-gauge, better than the .410 he'd given Eddie. But I had the M16, the Marine-issue rifle, on the brain. I'd watched a show about the history of Marine snipers, and it was pretty cool, what they could do, the scout snipers. The M16 was a pretty sweet-looking gun, too.

I liked the scope especially. It was sort of a little-boy idea, but I wished I had it now, since shotguns, having no range, don't have scopes. At least I didn't have the goddamn .410. Eddie seemed unlikely to fire it, though. He held it too tight, for one thing. Like it made him nervous. At least the safety was on. I told him I'd tell him when to take it off. I really didn't want him shooting at shit up here, when I thought about it.

Guns didn't make me nervous, for some reason. I got how they worked. Pretty simple, really. Not a lot of time for dicking around when it came to guns. You cleaned them, you loaded them, they worked.

"I don't see your grandpa," Eddie said, looking through the binoculars.

"Give it a while," I said.

"What do we do? What if you see one?"

"You don't have to take any shots," I said. "It's fine. It'll be over pretty quick, anyway. If it happens at all."

"Oh." He breathed out a long, visible exhalation.

I'd figured Eddie wouldn't like hunting, but we hadn't done anything together, with no girls at least, in a long time. I just wanted to be normal with him again. Do stuff. Get past the whole broken-nose thing, the whole ignoring him all summer for Hallie thing. We'd picked him up in my grandpa's Suburban at three thirty in the morning, and Eddie's mom had been standing on the doorstep in her bathrobe, handing him a little tiny cooler and his backpack, as if he was going to kindergarten or something. She looked at us, all decked out in blaze orange, like we were nuts. Eddie's dad had been there, too, in his windpants and stocking cap, smiling and putting his earbuds in like he was about to go out for a run.

Eddie's dad was pretty fit, he ran marathons and stuff, but he was the kind of dude who got his hair cut every week and liked to golf for fun, not kill things in the woods. And Eddie had two sisters. It wasn't a big man cave, Eddie's house.

"Why do you want to kill a doe?"

"I don't," I said. "Brad's the one with the doe tag."

"But why would you want to do that in the first place? Don't you want the mothers to live and have more baby fawns and stuff?"

"There's too many of them, bucks and does, in the first place," I said. "That's the point of the hunting season. To reduce the population. Too many deer, and they'll starve. The cute little fawns won't have anything to eat."

"What if the doe is pregnant?"

"She won't be now," I said. "That's not till spring. Jesus Christ. How come you don't know all this shit? This is like Science 9 shit, Eddie."

"It's just weird, is all."

"Why would you want a doe, though? What's the big deal with a lady deer? Doesn't Brad want, like, a giant trophy head with antlers and stuff?"

"Shh," I said. Because I could hear something. That little picky sound deer made. Skittering over stuff. Deer were dumb. They didn't know how to keep their steps quiet.

We kept listening, and then soon enough, I could see something. I pointed.

"Where?" Eddie said, reaching for the binoculars.

"Shh," I hissed at him. I wondered if Neecie'd be able to hear this. Probably not. Neecie wouldn't be a hunter, if we were cavemen. Some giant creature would probably have eaten

70

Neecie, with her bad ears and all, if she'd been alive back in the Stone Age.

Which meant probably she wouldn't be a Marine. Couldn't pass the physical requirements. They'd talked about that in the sniper-scouts show. You had to pass a vision test, so for sure you couldn't be a Marine if you couldn't hear. For some reason, as I raised my shotgun and exhaled, the way Grandpa Chuck had taught me, I was bummed out for her.

Then the deer stepped into view, right in front of me: a buck, not a big one, but big enough, judging from the size of its rack. And then, in that weird slidey way deer have, instantly there was another beside it. Like a magic trick, like it had slipped out of the other deer's pocket. Then another. Three of them, pausing in a row. Like they thought it'd be sneakier if they were hiding behind each other or something.

"Right there," I said as quiet as possible. Pointing.

"Where?" Eddie looked panicked. Like they were going to attack us or something.

"Shh," I said again. And then, as if they'd heard him, they were running across the cornfield, kicking up frost and dirt, and Eddie was about to say something but I didn't hear it because that's when I unloaded the 12-gauge, all five shots.

"Jesus Christ!" Eddie said. He'd been knocked with the brass as they'd been spent. I wanted to laugh. The 12-gauge's trigger was slicker than normal; most guns, you squeeze the trigger, you don't pull it. But the 12-gauge was especially light; the barest squeeze made a pretty damn loud shot.

"What the hell, Sean!" Eddie said. He looked like he might have shit his pants. Which made me laugh. That, and I was happy. It looked like I'd got at least two of them. Maybe even all three of them. Two bucks and maybe a doe. Unless it was a first-year buck. We'd need to get closer to see for sure.

I put the safety on, nudged Eddie to start moving. But he just sat there, his breath coming out of his mouth, all dumb.

"Seany, you do all that shooting?" My Grandpa Chuck, calling up.

"Yeah," I said. "There were three of them. I got at least two. Maybe all of them."

"No shit," my grandpa said. "That's unbelievable."

"I know."

"What if they're not dead?" Eddie whispered. *Now* he was whispering. Like it still mattered.

"If they're not, they'll be soon enough," I said. "Doesn't take long for them bleed out."

"God," Eddie said, looking sick. Like he didn't want to come down from the tree.

Eddie had no idea how lucky this was. Not just one good shot, but two or three? If I'd got them all, then I'd filled almost all our tags. Something Brad couldn't say this year. Or last year, either. I mean, I wasn't happy to make things dead. But what did people do before, when there were no grocery stores and stuff? This was how you ate. This was how you lived. It wasn't like we were doing it to be mean. If you wanted meat, well, you had to deal with deadness.

"Where's Brad at?" I asked my grandpa once Eddie and me were both on the ground.

"Should be along soon, I'd guess."

My grandpa looked thrilled; his face was bright red and smiling. He was old, in his late sixties, I think, his face was all leathery and wrinkled, and he didn't have any hair anymore, even white hair, but he didn't seem so old when we were hunting. He had a full kit of good gear he wore; he wasn't all sloppy like you'd expect an older guy to be; he rocked the high-tech stuff: wrap-around anti-fog Oakleys, layers of Under Armour, waterproof Gore-Tex, that kind of thing. He made the rest of us look like kinda bad, actually, amateurs tossing blaze orange vests over our chests. Brad in his stupid duckhunter's camo, me in my old Carhartt coat and Eddie in his snowboarding jacket. But I liked how serious my grandpa took it, hunting; I liked that he was always trying new things every year, not just being crabby and traditional about things. He was always reading stuff about it. He'd been a veterinarian before he retired, so animals were kind of his thing. That was another part of this; it wasn't so much about killing things, hunting. It was doing stuff with my grandpa. He'd always taken us hunting. My dad never went with us; he had some hang-up about guns or hunting. Or maybe he was just being pissy about Grandpa Chuck; he and his dad didn't get along that good. But me and Brad had been going hunting with our grandpa since we were little. Grandpa Chuck had been the one to sign us up for gun safety classes, taught us how to shoot tin can targets out at his house in the country. I'd got my first doe when I was thirteen.

"Let's get to it, then," my grandpa said. He put his arm around Eddie's neck and started telling him about field dressing as we hiked out to see my kill. I was trying not to run toward it, be so obvious and proud, but goddammit, I couldn't wait to see my brother's damn face when he strolled up.

The sun was rising, hot and white, when we got to the kill

site. Sure enough, there were three of them. All three tags, in one go, still steaming in the morning chill. I couldn't believe it, all over again. Grandpa slapped me on the back.

"Think this time you'll want to field dress them?"

"Hell no, Grandpa."

"Chickenshit," he said. Laughing.

"Hey!" I said. I was smiling like crazy. "You expect me to do everything around here?"

I got closer to see where I'd hit the deer. Two in the chest, one in the neck. One was still alive, its hooves wavering in the air. That was the doe. The other two were bucks, their racks sticking into the mud. My grandpa knelt beside the doe, put his hand on her chest, and pulled out his field kit, laid it on the ground. Then he pulled a knife from it and slit the doe's throat. Her hooves stopped moving pretty quick then.

"Whoa," Eddie whispered to himself, stepping back, his eyes on the blood puddling in dark lines in the corn rows.

My grandpa put his gloves on, started on one of the bucks.

"Jesus," Eddie muttered, his hand over his nose, when my grandpa made the first cut, breastbone to balls. The guts started tumbling out of the white-fur belly, all vivid red and blue, and Eddie stepped back from the smell. I started breathing through my mouth, swallowing a lot to avoid the stench; my grandpa had taught me and Brad that.

"First time's the hardest," my grandpa said, glancing at Eddie, who looked like he wanted to barf all over his shoes. I tried not to laugh, for Eddie's sake. "This one's a second-year buck, Sean," Grandpa Chuck added.

"Sure that's a second-year buck?" Brad, adjusting his ball

cap, out of breath from running. "Looks like a first-year. You should have stayed up in the stand. Waited for more."

I didn't say anything. Saying anything would give him something to argue with. And right now, Brad couldn't argue with shit. I'd filled my tag, plus his damn doe tag, plus Eddie's. If he wanted to sit around and try to fill the last one, he could do it himself.

"More than enough work, dressing these three," my grandpa said. He glanced back at Brad. Brad put his hands on his hips in a kind of bitchy way.

"Are you . . . is that normal to do that? Cutting around the asshole?" Eddie asked my grandpa.

Grandpa Chuck didn't even look up. "You don't want to nick the intestines; you'll ruin the meat."

"Jesus Christ," Eddie said, his face squinching up like he was trying to hold in puke. But he didn't stop looking.

"There's a little creek down a ways," Brad said. "Saw some tracks over there from last night's snow. Might be another place to check out."

The buck's gut sack slid out then on the ground, the blood in the dirt thick as oil. Eddie stared at it like he was hypnotized.

"Be a waste not to try," Brad continued.

"Are you just going to leave all that . . . all that stuff, here?" Eddie pointed to the innards my grandpa had just removed from the first buck. "Just let it sit here? On the ground?"

"That's what ravens and buzzards are for," Grandpa Chuck said. "Think of it this way: everything living's just waiting for the dinner bell."

"I mean, I could go next weekend too," Brad said. "But Krista's got the weekend off so we can do this wedding thing . . ."

I wondered how long he was going to talk to himself. It made me feel even better, for him to sit there babbling to himself about his unfilled tag.

"Do you skin the fur off, too?" Eddie asked.

"Some people do," my grandpa said. "I like to take the hide off once I'm back home. It's a little easier at home, in my shed. I've got all the equipment. It's not as cold, either."

"It's twenty-nine degrees, are you kidding?" Brad asked.

"Wind's coming up," my grandpa said, moving on to the next deer. "Eddie, will you get that tarp out? We'll need to wrap that one before we tie it up."

Eddie squatted beside my grandpa and got to work.

"So, we gonna keep going or what?"

My grandpa sat back on his heels, looked up at Brad, put on his fancy mirrored Oakleys, the expensive-but-cheesy kind the hockey players at school always wore. For some reason, they didn't look douchey on my grandpa's face, though.

"I'd say we pack it in, son," Grandpa Chuck said. "Gonna be more than enough work getting these out of here. Seany blew his wad early, but we still have to haul everything out. Might as well do it and then go get some breakfast."

Brad nodded. He wasn't going to argue with my grandpa. He never did.

"Look at it this way," I said. Blurting. "We can drive back early. Krista'll be thrilled. More time to do wedding stuff, right?"

Eddie laughed, like he wasn't expecting it. I stepped back, myself; Brad would have hit me if my grandpa hadn't been there. But I didn't care. I set down my shotgun and knelt beside Grandpa Chuck, handing him whatever he asked for, my back to Brad, looking at what I'd done and letting myself smile as much as I wanted.

# Chapter Six

After I overheard her talking to Tristan Reichmeier, Neecie Albertson didn't talk to me at all in school. Which was weird, because while we'd never been chatty, before we at least acknowledged each other, since we worked together and sat by each other in dumb Global Studies. But now she wouldn't even look at me. Even when I was looking at her. Like if I said "hey" to her, it would pop her secret with Tristan into a big splattery mess.

I watched Tristan more now, though. Him at his locker with his stupid hair he couldn't stop shaking off his forehead constantly, and that stupid black cap he always wore, in that total douche way. Him at lunch acting like a shithead with his hockey friends. Him surrounded by girls, the hot ones, plus this chick Hannah, who I think was supposed to be his current girlfriend, or just maybe the girl he'd be public about, or whatever. He'd put his arm around that Hannah chick and she'd always be laughing at whatever he said. You'd never in a thousand years put Tristan with Neecie. Never ever. She'd achieved ninja status in this, in my mind. Because you can't do the simplest, littlest shit in high school without a dozen people noticing one second later. I wondered how long it'd been going on. How it'd ever started.

One Friday during lunch there was a college-career fair. They'd had them last year, too, but I'd skipped them all. Was planning on skipping this one, too, until Neecie came up to me while I was standing outside the gym, debating whether to go in. You could get free pizza if you went and got your thing stamped by a certain number of booths, and today the caf was serving nasty turkey tacos.

"What's up, Sean?" Neecie said. All normal. Wearing her usual T-shirt and hoodie and jeans, her hair the long straight sheet of yellow everywhere. Drinking her giant can of iced tea—peach-flavored today—and holding a piece of pizza and a bunch of handouts and brochures.

"Nothing."

"You going in?"

"No."

"I only went for the pizza," she said, laughing.

"I'm shocked you don't care more about your future."

"I already applied to the places I wanted to go. I don't need any more information. Here," she added, handing me the pile of handouts. "Go expand your horizons. I don't need any of this shit. You just have to talk to six places. It's no big deal. Go to the Marines' guy. He's giving out water bottles and nobody's at his table. He's all lonely, and there's no line. Plus he's really kind of cute."

I looked at her.

"Well, anyway," she said. "Just saying."

"How long have you been with Tristan?" Blurting.

She almost dropped the pile of papers she was dumping into my hands. She stopped, looked around. I grabbed the stuff, lowered my voice.

"I mean, has it been a while?"

"Since summer," she said. "Since July."

"Oh."

"You can't say anything," she said.

"Who would I say anything to?"

"I don't know," she said. "Here. I'm not hungry, anyway." She handed me the pizza and then she was gone, and I just watched her ass walk away like an idiot, until she turned down the senior hallway. I sat down, then, and looked at all the handouts from colleges I'd never get into, eating the pizza, which was a little cold and greasy, but still good.

The Marines brochure showed dudes climbing up ropes and standing in formation and sighting rifles with pretty sweet scopes and running in combat boots and doing pull-ups. I had been decent at pull-ups, back in tenth grade. I was skinny, so it wasn't as hard for me to heave my weight up, probably. But still.

I would have kept sitting there, eating and looking at the handouts, but then I saw Emma and Libby coming down toward me and I didn't want to deal with that. I mean, I didn't hate Emma or anything, but I hadn't really talked to her since our failed make-out. And I supposed I would have made out with her again, but I didn't really want to have a girlfriend anymore. Well, I guess I would have had sex with someone. So maybe that meant I wanted a girlfriend. But I didn't want to deal with any of it. Not since Hallie. I jumped up and tossed all the handouts into the recycling, and that was how I met Sergeant Kendall for the first time.

●

The next Friday, while driving to my follow-up appointment at the Marines recruiting center, I started to wonder if maybe Neecie was crazy. Like, actually mentally ill. Pathologically lying about this. Or delusional, hallucinating. Maybe playing some complicated joke on me.

The Marine recruiting center was in this little junky strip mall, which included a shitty grocery store that sold expired spaghetti sauce and 3.2 beer to anyone with a pulse, a place that did those fakey nails like Krista had, and this kind of porn store, which wasn't super porny. It sold "novelty" gifts like dick-shaped pasta and feather boas for bachelorette parties. There was some porn and sex toys and crap in the back, everyone said, but you had to be eighteen to go in so I didn't actually know for myself. Really, except for the hooker nails, it was kind of one-stop shopping for a kid who just turned eighteen and didn't have Internet, I suppose.

Sergeant Kendall remembered me. I was sort of surprised about that. We shook hands, he called me Sean Norwhalt, all formal, like he spent his evenings memorizing names of kids he'd met at career fairs. Which maybe he did. He looked like he was basically on top of everything. He wasn't wearing the same uniform like last time, just a basic button-up and matching pants, but it was a uniform—you could see that in every inch and ironed seam. I felt like a slob in comparison.

But just like the first time we'd met, I couldn't stop looking at him. Also, we were standing up. He was standing up, in front of his chair, and though I had a chair, too, I felt weird getting all comfortable when he was standing. And also wondered if maybe this was a test or something. Or some Marines ritual I needed to observe.

So, standing, he started going over some stuff with me, about Delayed Entry, and how I'd need to graduate on time in order to qualify, and I was nodding, but I was barely listening. Just staring at him. Studying him. Maybe it was because he was black. In Oak Prairie, there aren't that many black people, beyond that one African minister's family, but they were from somewhere in actual Africa where they spoke French for some reason and his church was the weird one where everyone got all nuts with the praise music and speaking in tongues. Not that I went there; just that was what people said. His daughter was this girl named Mahali or something and she always wore a fancy dress every day to school, which alone made her weird, even though she was pretty. Also, she was like Neecie, off-limits from sex stuff, even though she had a nice rack and all. Plus she was a couple grades below me, and so I didn't really keep track of her like you did other hot chicks, maybe also because of her minister father and French-accent weirdness too. Not that I'm racist—I'm not—but anyway, it was just unusual for me. Talking to a black dude.

Plus, everything about Sergeant Kendall was so polished and scrubbed. Like, my fingernails were all dirty and needed cutting, while his were trimmed and short. And his hair was short, like a dusting of black color on his scalp. While my hair had become kind of a mop lately. Which I liked, I liked having mop-hair, you didn't actually have to do anything with it, which was nice. Hallie had loved my hair.

He'd asked me about my job history and I told him about the Thrift Bin; then he moved down a list of stuff on a form.

"Are you involved in any sports, Sean?"

"No. No, I mean, I was. Not currently. I used to swim, though."

He nodded, like he was a little bummed out.

"There's a fitness requirement all recruits must pass. Pull-ups, crunches, and a timed run. There are also weight and BMI standards, which, just from looking, I think will be okay with you. How tall are you?"

"Six one or so." He looked at me more, nodded again.

As if that didn't make me feel gay, him giving me the whole up-and-down. But also kind of happy.

"The timed run's a mile, right?" I asked.

"A mile and half. And we ask that you finish in thirteen minutes, thirty seconds. So . . ."

"Okay, that's doable."

I thought it was, at least. I should have talked to Eddie about this. We used to run sometimes, back when we swam together and were all gung-ho about making varsity and keeping in shape in the off-season. Eddie still did that, as far as I knew. But I hadn't. And my running shoes were shit. I needed new ones; my old ones were covered in cement from me and Brad pouring a patio out at Grandpa Chuck's place.

Sergeant Kendall nodded and smiled at me. I smiled back. We were smiling at each other, like two people on a date, almost. And then he told me to have a seat. I tried not to look too relieved to finally sit down. In case that was also part of the invisible test or something.

Sergeant Kendall handed me a DVD, which he said showed proper technique for pull-ups and crunches, and told me to keep on with the running, and we made another appointment to meet after my birthday. There was a list of documents I needed to bring for that meeting, and I had to register for Selective Service, too, which I'd forgotten about but needed to do, and I stared at all the papers seriously for a minute before saying anything. I was kind of bad with paperwork. I didn't know where half that shit was before we'd moved; I didn't exactly want to ask my mom where it was now, either.

"I really want to do this," I said, like maybe he could see me getting all bummed out. "I do."

"I'm glad," Sergeant Kendall said.

I felt like it was clear on my face that I was all freaked about the paperwork part. But he just stood up, and so I stood up, quickly, ready to be dismissed. I shook his hand and took the papers and then I walked out.

But before I could even dig my keys out of my jacket pocket, I saw Neecie Albertson. She didn't see me, though. Because she was coming out of Private Delights. Which was the real name of the porny store. She had a brown paper sack with something in it. And she was digging in her bag for something and then she dropped her phone and the battery knocked out of it and then she was picking up all the little bits of stuff and when she stood up again, she saw me, standing there in front of the Marines place, staring at her.

She looked completely freaked.

Then a red truck pulled up to the curb and she practically leaped toward it and got in the passenger seat.

Tristan Reichmeier's red truck. It was nice. New. She buckled in, and he drove off, not even seeing me, or if he did, he didn't care. And I knew she'd text me, later. And I knew, then, that I'd call her again. I just knew.

●

"He didn't see you, so don't worry about it," Neecie said.

"I'm not worried about anything," I said.

"He gets kind of nuts about things. Like, he's paranoid, I swear."

"He's just being a douche," I said. Then tried to gulp it back when she looked across the table at me and stopped cutting her pancakes. "Sorry," I added.

She didn't say anything. We were at IHOP. It was Friday night, almost nine o'clock. Neecie had texted me ("please don't say anything," again) two hours after I saw her. So I just called her, and she said she was at work, and I said I'd come get her. I pulled up to the group of employees standing around waiting together for everyone to get picked up by their rides in the parking lot at the Thrift Bin—Wendy's rule, as the store wasn't in the greatest part of town—and when Neecie climbed in, Kerry stood there smoking and looking at me like, *Really? You and her, huh?*

But Neecie didn't notice Kerry. She said she was hungry and didn't want to go home. Which was why we were here. At IHOP. IHOP, of all places! But I didn't mind IHOP. I'd never gone to IHOP with Hallie. Hallie tended to avoid things like pancakes because of the sugar and carbs. She was a little crazy about her body and nutrition. I've never given one shit about nutrition; I ate like I was trying to fill out my chest hollow or something. I slopped up my Rooty Tooty Fresh 'N Fruity like it was my goddamn job.

"Thanks again for coming to pick me up. My car's getting fixed."

I shrugged, and then she went back to her pancakes. Which she ate all tidy. Cut in this perfect grid. And which was a short stack that was taking her ninety-nine years to finish. I'd eaten three times the amount of food in half the time it was taking her to deal with her little two pancakes.

"Why didn't you just have Kerry take you home?" I said, joking.

"Ugh, gross. I hate that guy."

"Well, he doesn't hate you, just so you know. He thinks you're cute."

She set her fork down. "You're kidding, right?"

I shrugged. I suddenly didn't want her to know about this. I just wanted her to beware without giving her the specific details.

"I would have walked home before I'd ask that asshole."

"He's not an asshole. Mostly."

She shook her head, like she didn't believe me. "He's the reason I tell Wendy to put on country music. It's my private passive-aggressive revenge. Jesus. He really thinks I'm cute?"

Now I laughed.

"I'm glad you were around, because Ivy's mad at me," she said. "Honestly. I just hope you're not weirded out by me or anything. But yeah, I would have had to call my mom, probably. Or begged Wendy for a ride. I just . . . normally I'm not like this."

"Like what?"

"I don't know. Bugged. Asking people I barely know to eat pancakes with me and pick me up."

"Going into the sex store with Tristan," I added.

Her face did that red thing again, completely red, from the neck up. It looked like a rash. Or a disease. Except I was watching it happen in real time.

"He didn't go with me," she said. "He's not eighteen yet."

"So he made you go in there *for* him?"

She looked down at her little squares of pancakes.

"It's so dumb. I can't even explain it. I mean, it's . . . Is my face all red?"

"Yeah."

"Fuck," she said. She pulled a little tube of cream out of her bag, started rubbing it all over her neck and face. It smelled like grass. Or plants. And girly stuff. I wondered if it was medicinal or something. I tried not to stare but kind of failed.

"I suppose I should probably tell you the whole long sad story of Tristan and me and how this happened."

"If you want."

"But you'll probably be like Ivy and get annoyed with me."

I admit, I was pretty much dying of curiosity to hear the whole story. Mostly because it was so weird, and thinking of her doing it with Tristan Reichmeier—much less *anyone*—was still pretty hard to for me to accept. But while I was wanting to know how the hell everything happened, I also wasn't super eager to hear about how they were secret star-crossed lovers and how it was all "different" with them or some other crap.

"I won't get annoyed."

"Yeah, right," she said.

"You can tell me whatever you want," I said, all casual, like I didn't care.

"Okay," she said. Then she was quiet, just ate the rest of her pancake squares, and when the waitress brought the check, I took it and paid it while Neecie went to the bathroom. And then we left, and it felt all weird and date-y because I'd paid and she was thanking me and we were walking out together and I even held the door for her, because my mom was sort of insistent about that kind of thing. My dad too. He was a prick about being a gentleman even when he was totally drunk out of his skull.

We got in my car, and Neecie sighed and smiled while she put on her seatbelt.

"I totally love this car," she said. "It's like sitting on a sofa. It's so soft. It's, like, a sofa on wheels or something."

I shook my head, started the car. "It used to be my grandmother's," I said.

"What?"

I looked at her.

"It's easier for me to hear if you look at my face when you talk," she said.

"Oh."

"I mean, I have hearing aids now, so it's not like junior high. You don't have to clip a microphone on your collar. Remember that?"

"Kind of." I sort of felt dumb that she brought this up. So bald, too, like it wasn't a big shameful deal.

I repeated what I said about the car, this time looking directly at her, and she nodded.

"It does smell kind of grandmotherish," she agreed. "It's

so clean too!"

"You don't have to tell me anything about Tristan, Neecie," I said. My hands were on the gearshift, but I felt like I couldn't talk while looking at her and drive safely at the same time. "It's totally not my business and I don't even . . ."

She interrupted me. "You're nice," she said. "I should totally tell you. Even if it's kind of a long dumb story. It'd be interesting to see what you think."

"I'm not exactly qualified to give boyfriend advice."

"Tristan's not my boyfriend, though," she said. "You can drive, Sean," she added, pointing to the gearshift.

I reversed and started driving.

"Ivy's got one opinion of the whole thing. Ivy's got a whole set of opinions, really."

"About Tristan?"

"About guys in general. Are you really joining the Marines, Sean?"

I was surprised. Again. I nodded, since she didn't have to hear nodding. And I didn't want to explain the whole thing, either.

"Wow. That's pretty crazy."

"Why?" I asked. A little pissy.

"I just never thought about doing something like that. Personally. It's a little strange, in general. Not that you doing it specifically is weird. You'll have to tell me more about it. If you want."

I nodded. I wasn't going to talk about it yet. Not because she was a jerk or anything. Just, because. I couldn't.

"Where do you want to go now?" I said. "Home?"

"No," she said. "Can we go to your house?"

Now I felt like the one all flamed-up and embarrassed. I didn't really want her to come to my shitty house. I had no idea what her house looked like. It was Friday, which meant my mom had a bunch of Al-Anon crap she went to with Steven-Not-Steve. But maybe not. Maybe she'd be home after all. Maybe Neecie would walk into a big wedding planning session with Krista and her thong sticking out of her tight jeans?

But I didn't feel like saying no. Back even when we lived in our old house, when my dad was living with us, I always said no to anyone coming over, even to Eddie. I didn't want anyone seeing my dad all shitty, even if he wasn't always shitty. You just never knew, really. But wedding planning was better than my fucked-up dad sprawled all over the living room. And maybe Neecie's house wasn't anything great? Maybe her parents were shitty too?

"All right," I said. "I don't know who's home, though. My mom might be there with her boyfriend."

"That's fine," she said. "Mine's probably home with hers, too. But my sisters are the main thing I'd like to avoid. I just can't handle them blabbering at me lately. Let's go to your house. I want to see how the real Sean lives."

90

# Chapter Seven

The rental was empty when we got there. Otis was nuts, though, jumping up on Neecie, and she petted him a lot, saying she didn't mind, but I didn't like him doing that and banished him to his bed in the living room. Neecie followed him into the living room and looked at all the books on the shelves that my mom had finally unpacked and asked about them and I was like, who the hell knows, I don't read that much, and then she gave me shit for not reading but in a nice way, and then I asked if she wanted anything to drink, because I wanted some orange juice right then, and she said no, but then she had to ask about Brad and Krista, because the kitchen table was covered in wedding shit, this time little mini flowerpots and packets of seeds.

"What is she trying to grow?"

"First it was poppies. Orange ones. She wanted the wedding to be pink and orange colored or something. Until my mom's boyfriend told her that poppies were, like, the symbol of war and death. Now it's something else. Something pink? I can't keep track of it all."

"Where's your room?" she asked.

"In the basement. Kinda. It's not really a basement. It's just downstairs."

"Is your room super clean?" she asked. "Because your car is always super clean. For a guy, that is. Or is it a shithole?"

"Well . . . yeah." I was sort of surprised she was that direct. The whole rental was a total shithole, as far as I was concerned.

"So now I want to see it."

"Why?" I said. But I led her downstairs, and she flopped on my bed, which was sort of made since I'd pulled most of the blankets off.

"Not as bad as I imagined," she said. "You should see Tristan's room."

I didn't know what to say to that. Because there was no world where I wanted to see Tristan's room, ever, so I just kind of stood there, looking at all the crap on the floor, which Otis helpfully sat down on and wagged, as if he were poolside at some swank hotel and not laying on a pile of dirty clothes. He looked up and panted at Neecie as if to say, *Isn't this the greatest? Sean's room's the best! He totally lets me hang out here all the time! It's pretty awesome! I'm so happy you're here! You should pet me!*

Neecie walked around, though it wasn't like my room was giant. I didn't really know what to do. I could have turned on the TV, I guess. Or some music. But I was just sort of stupid-feeling about the whole thing. Our house wasn't nice; my room wasn't cool. My Xbox was seven million years old; it'd been old when Brad gave it to me. I imagined Tristan's house. His parents were divorced, so he had two houses, plus a house on Prairie Lake. There'd been lots of parties at that lake house. It was the kind of lake house that looked like it belonged on the beach in Miami. There was even a gate and a security system.

I looked down at our security system, who was wagging and sniffling Neecie's ass while she looked at something on my desk. Great.

She held up a little photo of Hallie. Taken that day at her cousin's cabin.

"Is this your old girlfriend?"

"Hallie. Yeah."

"Is Hallie short for something else?"

"I don't think so. I think it's just Hallie. What's Neecie short for?"

"I am never telling you that. Never ever ever."

"That bad, huh?"

Neecie shrugged, ignored me, looked at the picture again. "She's pretty."

"Jesus!" I said, turning around. "Why does every girl say that?"

"What?" Neecie turned around. "I couldn't hear you."

I felt embarrassed, didn't want to repeat myself, but did, because it seemed unfair of me to not tell her when she had been so clear with me earlier about what she required in order to hear.

"I don't know," she said. "Maybe, jealousy? Maybe, just, we're describing stuff? Or trying to be nice?"

"Why be nice?" I asked. "Hallie—whatever her real name is on her birth certificate—dumped me. Plus, it's not like she's around to hear you say she's ugly."

"She's not ugly, though."

"Yeah, but that's not the point! Like, why do girls always talk about that shit?"

"What shit?"

"I mean, girls. Why do they think about that shit all the time? Who's cute, who's not. Who's fat, who's skinny. Who gives a damn?"

Neecie looked down at Otis, who was now seated at her knee, his tail wagging along the floor and scattering a pile of crunched-up Global Studies homework.

"Clearly your dog and I give a damn," she said, reaching down to pet Otis. "Don't we, Otis? We totally give a damn." She petted him around his ears and collar, just exactly where he liked to be petted, and he wagged even harder.

"Otis?" I said, kind of loud. "Otis doesn't give a shit about how anything looks. Otis'll eat his own crap if you let him."

"Gross, Sean!"

Then the door slammed and my mom called, "Hello? Sean? Are you here?"

"Fuck," I muttered. "My mom's home."

"I'm downstairs!" I yelled back.

"Will she get mad if I'm in here?" Neecie asked, suddenly all nervous. "Can you have girls in your room?"

"I don't know," I said, honestly. "It's never exactly come up before."

"Your girlfriend never came over to your room?"

"She didn't like to."

"Why?"

"She said I was a slob."

"Wow, that's kind of bitchy," Neecie said. "Sorry," she

added when I rolled my eyes. "Listen," she said, putting her hand on my wrist. "Just tell her I'm gay. That's what my mom thinks. That's how I keep her off my ass about guys and going to prom and whatever."

"You told your mom you're *gay*?"

"No, I just let her assume that."

"*Really*? How is that *better* than just not having anyone like you?"

Since that came out kind of harsh, I pretty much deserved the shitty look she gave me.

"It's *better* than her knowing about me doing it with Tristan at science camp last summer."

"You had sex at *science camp* with Tristan?"

She nodded. "He wasn't at science camp. He was just at the U for some hockey thing, but we were in the same dormitory for two weeks."

"I'm not telling my mom you're gay."

Then my mom was in the doorway.

"Sean? What's going on? Where's Otis?"

Neecie let go of my wrist. Otis rushed my mom so she could have the honor of petting him.

"Oh, hello," my mom said, pushing Otis away and looking at Neecie. Her face was sort of shocked and blank. "I didn't know you had . . . that anyone was with you."

"Hi, Mrs. Norwhalt," Neecie said. "I'm Neecie." She bounced up to my mother and held out her hand and they shook hands, like this was a business deal or something. Though Neecie was doing a nice, polite thing, I could tell my mom was standing there thinking, *What the hell, Sean?*

Still, my mom, being used to dealing with complete social

95

disasters for her job, was impressed by manners. She shook Neecie's hand and smiled. "Nice to meet you," she said.

"Likewise!" Neecie sang in this cheery voice. But her face was bright red. My mom was nodding like she was in psychologist mode, trying to be all warm and nonjudgmental and loving. Affirming everyone's *choices*. That kind of shit. The way she was about my dad, for some insane reason, when he'd been the biggest prick ever, pretty much.

Then Krista barged in the doorway, wearing her standard skintight shirt and jeans.

"This is Neecie," my mom said to Krista. All polite. As if it were normal, me having a girl over.

Krista shook her hand, too. It was so weird. I'd never noticed girls shaking hands like this. Hallie and her friends were always hugging and kissing each other's cheeks, though. Like they really loved each other, even though they talked shit about each other constantly behind their backs.

"We're doing the flowers now," Krista said. "We got grow lights and everything. I found this website where it's all laid out. It's so AWESOME! Your brother's even here tonight! Isn't that AWESOME? Come on up and help us!"

Krista thought everything was *AWESOME*. Not just Brad and her wedding plans—putting flowerpots on each of the guest tables for favors to take home—but margaritas, certain reality shows, cars with leather interiors, strapless bridesmaid gowns, Weight Watchers fudgesicles, giant sofas that looked like they were ready to explode from overstuffing—these were considered *AWESOME* too.

We trailed behind Krista and my mom; Neecie yanked my shirt back a little.

"Your mom seemed fine about everything."

"That's because she's used to dealing with fucked-up kids for her job," I said. "You act normal, and she's all impressed."

"Wow. I didn't have such a high bar to clear, then, huh?"

I laughed. "You don't have to plant the flowers."

"No, I'll totally stay," she said. "I've never heard of anyone using orange in their wedding colors."

"Krista thinks orange is *AWESOME*. And pink and orange? Even more *AWESOMER*. But she has to scale back to just pink."

Neecie laughed. "I suppose it might be okay. Sort of Dreamsicle-y. But I don't have any issues with pink, actually. It's summery. Nice."

I thought we'd have to redo the whole introductions thing with Brad and Neecie, but Krista rushed through it after Brad stuck his head in the door and said he was going to buy Otis some more dog food.

"What's going on, douche," Brad said after he'd said hello to Neecie.

"Not much," I said.

"Then why can't you pick up the goddamn dog food, idiot?" Brad asked. "I don't even live here anymore."

"Nobody told me to get Otis food!" I said.

"Proves my point," Brad said. Then he slipped back out the door. Obviously, someone didn't want to plant flowers for his own goddamn wedding.

Then Krista took over. She had a whole process. We had to wipe out the pots and add this stuff from a packet and something from a jar and then the dirt and all these steps and she basically was demonstrating it like she was on a cooking show except a lady on a cooking show wouldn't be wearing flowered gardening gloves to protect her plastic nails and a shirt so tight you could see her boobs pop out with every breath she took. Krista didn't seem to get that the rest of the world would notice her boobs or her thong whale-tail, as if being Brad's fiancée erased those things for everyone else. I didn't want to notice these things, but she was always so huggy and close with me. I felt like a total creeper about it.

Our kitchen table being circular, Neecie could see Krista's face and my mom's face, and all three of them babbled together without even including me, which was okay. Neecie seemed back in School Mode, like she was being called on to participate in class, something she did when she had to, though she never volunteered. It wasn't clear to me whether she enjoyed this kind of behavior or if it just came so natural she didn't even notice. Either way, the conversation went along fine. Until Krista asked Neecie about her post-graduation plans and Neecie told her about the schools she was applying to.

"That's wonderful that you're going to college," my mom said. And I was sure she'd use this as an opportunity to rail on me for not applying anywhere yet.

But Krista was the one who brought it up. It was like they took turns, rotating who would bug me about the future.

"Sean is so smart," Krista said. "He really needs to go to college."

"I don't know about that," I said.

"You're just thinking grades are the only thing that matters," my mom said.

"Well, they kind of are. When you're talking about *school*," I pointed out.

"Test scores are also important," Neecie said, but it was in this shy peep of a voice, like she knew I wasn't loving this discussion.

"Community college is a good place to get started," my mom said, trying to sound all casual as she patted seeds into the black soil.

"Totally," Krista agreed. "And the tuition costs way less."

"I guess it's up to Sean, though," Neecie said. "He's got to decide, right?"

Then nobody said anything, even Krista, and we just went back to miserably potting the goddamn flowers until Brad busted in carrying the dog food on his shoulder.

"I got that Senior Formula for weight loss," Brad said. "Since Otis is kind of a fatty."

"He's not that fat," I said.

"He's fat as fuck, are you nuts?" Brad said, unloading the kibble bag into the giant bin in the pantry with a big rushing clatter.

"Hon? Who's that friend of yours who went to DeVry? The one who makes all that money installing furnaces?" Krista asked Brad. Then they traded the guy's name back and forth and asked me if I knew him, and I shrugged.

"Don't you think Sean would do good in that kind of program?" Krista asked Brad, like Brad was my dad.

But Brad just shook his head, like he didn't even see the point of discussing me. He adjusted his cap on his head and said, "Babe, I'm starving. I didn't get any dinner yet. What did you eat?"

"There's stuff for sandwiches in the fridge," my mom said.

"I want a pizza," Brad said, and then, because he was the man, he called for pizza, and a little bit later, me and Neecie were sitting out on the back deck in the dark while Brad ate pizza in the living room and Krista and my mom set up the seedlings in the base- ment under the grow lights, which made it look like they were growing weed. They were probably the first people in the history of the world to buy grow lights for something actually legitimate.

Neecie was eating a piece of pizza, all careful with each bite. It was kind of cold, and she had zipped her hoodie up her neck, her long hair trapped underneath it, like she wanted the extra layer for warmth. It made her look a little weird, but also like she didn't give a shit, which was nice. Hallie was always worrying about her looks; flipping her hair, checking herself out in mirrors, all that.

"Your family's nice," she said.

"Uh-huh," I said.

"They are. They seem really nice."

"Brad's kind of douchey."

"Well, yeah," she said. "But he asked me what I liked on my pizza, didn't he?"

Neecie was such a bright-sider sometimes. Finally, she said she needed to get home and so I drove her back into town. She lived in an okay neighborhood, not one of the fancy develop- ments or anything, but not anything like the rental. Once I was in front of her house, she turned to me.

"Your mom doesn't know about the Marines thing?"

"No," I said. "And she'd freak if she did."

"Well, you have to tell her sometime."

"Not after I turn eighteen."

"I'm sure she'd notice, Sean, if you suddenly went off to boot camp."

"By then it'd be too late."

"I guess," Neecie said. "But I don't see why you can't just tell her. I mean, explain why you're doing it."

I didn't have anything to say to that. I thought she'd expect me to explain why I was doing it, the Marines. Though I wasn't really doing anything yet. But she didn't. She just kind of hung out with me in my car, talking.

I don't remember much more of the evening, though I know we sat in front of her house in my car for a long time. Eddie texted me a photo of a naked chick smoking from a bong shaped like a dick, which was his way of saying he needed me to get some weed from Kerry for him, but I just ignored it. Because I didn't care. It was nice, just sitting there, talking, her being just so regular and not hyper, her hair trapped under her hoodie, her hands on the knees of her jeans, not making me feel weird like she wanted to go on a date or anything. Like, people who said guys and girls couldn't be friends had to be wrong. Because that's what it felt like. Like there was no bullshit or games. Like we were just friends.

So that was the first night we hung out, even though there wasn't a big thing said about it. After that, we just kept hanging out like it was normal. Like it wasn't a secret that got us together. But, still, we weren't really *together*. I didn't want to fuck her, and she didn't want to go out with me, either. I didn't care if I picked her up after she'd been with Tristan. I didn't care what she thought about me, because clearly she didn't care about what I thought of her and that was nice, because normally, when I liked a girl, I was so tense around her I could barely speak. So this was all nice, because I thought she was cool, in all these different ways, like her hearing thing that made me have to think about what I said, whether I meant it, whether I wanted her to really know it. How she was like this stealth sex ninja, how cool and above-it-all she acted around Tristan at school. And at work, how she underhandedly worked to piss off Kerry with country music and requests from the supply closet and wearing shirts that showed off her boobs. (She didn't realize she was doing that last thing. Probably.)

The one thing I remember from that night in the car, when we just sat there and talked forever, was when I said something about Tristan and how it seemed like no big deal, how they hooked up and that was it, and if guys did that and no one cared, why should she care? I was trying to make her feel badass, better about herself, but she shook her head. Looked me straight in the face, the only light coming from her garage floodlight, and said, "I know. I wish it was. But it just makes me feel so bad sometimes."

# Chapter Eight

It was two days before Thanksgiving. My birthday was the day before Thanksgiving this year, which meant we always had a cake with our turkey. But in the past, this had often been forgotten in the holiday shuffle. Especially when my dad was still around.

But this year I didn't care, because it was snowing like crazy, the first big snow of the season, and I was at Neecie's house, eating a giant plate of fudge that her little sister Melanie made me. A pre-birthday treat, she said. Melanie was sort of crazed about cooking. She was also sort of crazed in general. But I didn't care. I loved being at the Albertsons' house and was happy to not be at home. My mom was talking community college all the time and didn't I want to tour the one where Steven-Not-Steve taught (he taught accounting, which wasn't a surprise), and was my "little friend" Neecie coming over again anytime soon, and it just made me want to laugh and also start yelling but I couldn't do either, because I was signing up for the Marines in secret and if she knew, she'd lose her mind. She was also kind of losing her mind, it seemed like, because my dad was out of the rehab in Arizona and living in this halfway house thing now. Or he'd just left it. He had some job now, doing something outside. It was all part of the expensive treatment thing Grandpa Chuck had paid for. It was like his eleventh rehab. She kept bugging me to call my dad at this one number, between these certain hours, but I kept putting it off.

"Try this kind, Sean," Melanie said, pushing another plate across the counter. Neecie's kitchen had a little breakfast nook thingy, with stools, and Melanie liked to stand there and feed people her stuff. Melanie had some kind of eating issue, according to Neecie, and it wasn't exactly an eating disorder, I guess, but something like it, though mostly it looked to me that Melanie was that awkward junior-high skinny where the girl looks like she's a newborn deer or whatever, all shaky-kneed and stuff. That, along with her braces, and her tendency to do yoga or Pilates in the TV room whenever I came over could have been something pathological or something totally normal. But I never asked; Melanie loved to make food for me to eat. I didn't really see any reason to probe too deep into the exact reasons why.

Neecie was somewhere in the house, dicking around. This sometimes happened when I'd come over. She'd get a call and then kind of slip out of the room and ditch me with Melanie or Jessamyn and then come back, like, a half hour later, all showered. Or wearing different clothes. Like, pajamas. Or just a different outfit. Like, she'd sometimes do yoga with

Melanie, and then I knew she wanted me to leave, which was fine because, knowing Melanie, I'd get pressed into doing yoga, too, which I'd done a couple times. But I didn't want to stick my ass in the air while counting my breaths and hoping my hands would unstick from the purple yoga mat if Mrs. Albertson came home suddenly with her boyfriend, Gary, who was nice and everything, but like, a real dude who worked for the telephone company, a guy who climbed up the poles and shit, and while he loved Mrs. Albertson, clearly, from all his touchy behavior with her when he thought no one was looking, I was pretty intent on Gary never seeing my softer side.

Jessamyn walked in then, stretching, like she'd been asleep. Jessamyn was the sister with the big boobs. She looked older than thirteen, and she didn't talk as much as Melanie, but she always hung out when I was around. Jessamyn was adopted; she was really Melanie and Neecie's cousin, but her mother died in a car accident when Jessamyn was six and then her father went crazy or something, couldn't take care of her, so Mrs. Albertson adopted her. Neecie said it was great to have another sister, but Melanie had a hard time with it, because of being the same age and everything, a sudden twin in life, and going from being the baby to being the middle kid.

"Why do you always make the most bad foods?" Jessamyn asked Melanie.

"'Most bad' sounds wrong, Jess," Melanie said.

Jessamyn sat on the stool by me, picked up a hunk of fudge, and ate it in one bite.

"It tastes good," Jessamyn said, taking another slab. Jessamyn totally ignored her sisters like that all the time. "I like the kind without nuts better."

It was sort of cool, though I'd never admit it, these girls hanging around me like I was big deal. Even if they were both thirteen. Sometimes I thought Neecie's sisters liked me more than Neecie did. But then Neecie was always so relaxed about things at her house. She was different than at school. At school she always had her School Face on; in Global Studies, she barely looked at me. But after school, she'd come and talk to me in the parking lot and we'd walk to my car, and the next thing I knew we were going somewhere or we were in a gas station and she was taking a hundred years to pick out which giant can of iced tea she wanted to drink. Then she was all normal.

"I think I should have put in less butter," Melanie said, pouring Jessamyn a glass of milk in a little Snoopy glass. "Do you want more milk, Sean?"

I shook my head. Melanie pushed the milk at Jessamyn and started wiping down the counter.

Then they started talking about some TV show they watched—the Albertson sisters watched tons of TV shows, in big long marathons, where they set out deliberate, matching snacks and invited people over and made a big huge deal about it, and I didn't want to admit that we hadn't had cable in a while and so I mostly avoided discussions about TV. Then I got up to use the bathroom off the kitchen, which smelled so unbelievably good, I barely wanted to piss in there. It was also nicer than my whole house, this bathroom. I mean, not really, but it was like every room in Neecie's house was designed for you to sit down and relax and grab a home decorating magazine and whatever. This bathroom had a chair in it, next to the shower, and a magazine rack full of issues of *House Beautiful* and all these little shelves with vases and candles and strange weird things, like a pile of foreign coins in a glass dish or a broken antique telescope thingy and a black-and-white photo of a dog in an old washtub splattering water everywhere. Above the mirror, big blue letters spelled out the word DREAM. There were the same letters in Hallie's bedroom, only hers said LOVE.

"Sean?" I could hear Neecie calling for me somewhere in the house. "Sean, are you still here?"

I flushed, and then my phone buzzed in my pocket from a text. Probably Eddie. He was on fire with the dirty photos lately, since he'd found my Marines crap in my car, so now I got all this gay dude porn where the guys wore dog tags or Army uniforms. I kind of wanted to kill him.

"Sean?" Neecie banged on the door.

"I'm in here already! Jesus!" I yelled.

"Ivy's here now," she called through the door. "We're in the living room."

"Okay, just a sec," I said. You never knew when anyone came over at the Albertsons' because they didn't have a dog. It was kind of weird; though there were more people, the lack of dog made everything seem kind of sparse and empty.

I zipped up and then checked my phone. And almost dropped it in the toilet. Because it was from Hallie:

home 4 break.

I felt instantly dizzy. Nervous. And horny. And like doing a million things. For the first time, I wanted to answer this text. Maybe because she was here and it wasn't just long-distance bullshit? All I knew was that right now I wanted to be in my car, flying to her house. Also I wanted to be brushing my teeth.

I wanted to ask Neecie what I should do. But not with stupid Ivy there.

"What's up," I texted back. Hands shaking.

*You pussy. What happened to leaving and never coming back?*

I set the phone on the sink counter. Checked out my hair. It looked messy, but not in a dumb way. Checked my teeth; they were fine, no fudge. There was a zit on the side of my nose, but I'd dealt with it and it was just red. And I'd shaved. And luckily just cut my fingernails, by total coincidence. Hallie had a thing about guys having long fingernails; it grossed her out for some reason. I mean, I guess it was gross, but it hadn't been a thing I'd noticed until she brought it up.

The phone buzzed a little on the blue counter, like it wanted to jump off it and crash on the floor.

I want to see you

In the living room, Ivy and Neecie were eating fudge and reading magazines. Mrs. Albertson seemed to spend shitpots of money on magazine subscriptions. I said hi to Ivy and then sat down uncomfortably on the same sofa as her, happy that there were a million cushions between us. Ivy's hair was now normal-colored, but she had it in weird little knobs all around her head and it made her scalp look tortured. I was glad Neecie never did anything with her hair like that. Neecie just wore her hair all long; I think she wanted her hearing aids covered, but it always looked pretty nice, anyway.

"I don't see the point, really," Ivy was saying. "I mean, I don't even know what I want to do next. Why should I spend the money on the application fee, you know?"

"You're saying you want to live with your parents? What

the hell is there to *know*?" Neecie said. "You apply to college to get the hell out of your parents' house. Not because of college. Not because you're all excited about *learning*. I'm a nerd, and even I know that."

"You like *learning*, though," Ivy said, smacking another page of the magazine down across her thigh.

My phone buzzed again. I kind of jumped.

hurry parents home soon . . .

"I gotta go," I said, standing up. I must have looked crazy.

"What's going on?" Neecie said. She was suddenly alert, all tense now. The School Version of Neecie.

"Nothing," I said. "I just . . . I forgot something I had to do. I'll come by later? Maybe?"

Ivy said something to her magazine that sounded bitchy like, "Wow, lucky us." Ivy and I didn't hang out much, but she didn't like me and I didn't really like her, either. Neecie appeared to not have heard Ivy, though.

"Okay," Neecie said. But she sounded like she knew something was up.

I drove to Hallie's at pretty much light speed. Parked a block away, then walked around her stupid development, through this little park no one ever used that overlooked this ditch that was filled up by accident, as if it were a real lake or something. The whole place smelled like duckshit in the summer, but now it was covered in snow, everything still as the sun went down early, November-style. I cut through a bunch of backyards to Hallie's deck and sliding glass door. She'd texted to come through the back. We'd done that before, when she'd snuck out to meet me a few times.

The house was dark. Quiet. I looked at my phone again. I thought for a terrible minute that maybe she'd meant the text for someone else.

I knocked, then. Just lightly. And then I heard footsteps. And the door opened, and the room was dark. It was the TV room; I'd sat here a million times waiting for her parents to go to bed while we watched movies together. Me waiting. Dying to touch her.

"Get in," Hallie said. "Quick."

I couldn't see her, but I could smell her, her same Hallie smell. Her same lotion or shampoo or whatever.

"Let's go to the basement," she said.

"Why?"

She grabbed my hand, tugged me through the dark.

"The back walkout's there," she said. "If anyone comes home, you can go out that way."

I didn't ask why we didn't just do it in the TV room. I could go out the sliding door, too. But I was too freaked and turned on. Plus I didn't actually care. We got to the basement and finally she turned on the light. She was wearing yoga pants and a T-shirt. Her hair down. She looked great. She hopped up on the dryer and stared at me.

"You're still wearing your hoodie," she said.

"Yeah," I said. I took it off, put it on a pile of laundry.

"Come here," she said.

I looked around the basement. I'd only been in it once or twice. There was a cement floor, a drying rack covered in clothes. An ironing board leaning against the wall. I realized— too late—that I didn't have any condoms. I'd gone over to Neecie's to hang out, not get laid.

I walked toward her on the dryer. I wondered what I was supposed to do now. There was about a foot of space between us; I didn't know how to go about grabbing her and taking her clothes off anymore.

"So, how's college?" I said.

She laughed. Not a fakey laugh. Or a surprised laugh. But not really a real laugh, either. This was a snotty, oh-hell-no laugh. "We can talk about that later," she said. She put her hands on my shoulders, and then, when we were close enough, she kissed me.

●

Then I was driving home.

The whole thing hadn't lasted more than fifteen minutes, and now I smelled like fabric softener sheets, which kind of gave me a headache. That and Hallie's words kept piling up in my head. The few ones she said.

I stopped at the light before the turnoff to my house. I was the only car there. Sitting at the light, my car wasting gas.

"Touch me there," Hallie said. "Like this."

The light kept being red. A truck roared past me.

"*Not like that*," Hallie said.

I did what she said, but I hadn't been sure about what I was doing, or even how it was that different from what I ever did before when I touched her down there. She wore a pair of panties that I'd never seen before. They didn't match her bra, but that was maybe because it was a sports bra.

The light changed and I turned, heading down the freeway toward my house.

*"Thanks for coming over."*

My house was dark. Dark as hers had been. My mom's car was there. I heard Otis bark as I climbed up the steps.

My mom didn't get up when I came in. Normally, she liked me to come in and say goodnight to her, and usually I did, unless I was too wasted or something. Then I'd just holler from the hallway that I was home. But now, completely sober, I couldn't stand the idea of seeing my mom. Felt like I had Hallie all over me.

Hallie sitting on the stupid dryer, saying *oh god* and I don't know what it was, but I just felt crazy and I wanted to go down on her, something she'd never allowed before. The dryer, of all things, made this the perfect access, too, with my height, but when I ducked my head down, she wasn't having it.

She pushed off the dryer and then we were on the cold concrete floor and I was a little pissed.

Another goddamn rule.

But I was on top of her now, and she was grabbing me through my jeans and I didn't care.

*"That's good."*

My head totally spinning with that. What had I been doing? Was she talking about my boner? I didn't know what was going on. But she'd just handed me a condom and that was that.

Then, when I was about to come, she said, *"Don't stop."* Like she knew it was almost over. That I couldn't stop. And I didn't know if it was still good. I couldn't ask her, either. But I didn't stop. Then her eyes closed and it seemed like something important was happening, but by then I was coming anyway and it was all so much, so awesome and feeling so good and she was so beautiful and everything felt better than I remembered it so I couldn't stop myself from saying it, again, words I hadn't said in weeks:

*"God, I love you so much."*

Then I squeezed her so hard, in case she didn't get it. That I'd said it. But she didn't say anything. Her eyes were closed. There was a pink sock right by her head, curled into a ball.

I lifted off her a bit. Felt the grit from the concrete on my palms. Hallie's eyes still closed, like she was pretending to be dead or something. The second I pulled out of her, her breathing start to get back to normal, and then I noticed how cold the room was. And quiet, except for my words echoing in my head: *"God I love you so much."*

Just remembering saying that made me feel sick.

In my room, Otis jumped on my bed. Too tense to sleep, I took off my shirt and did some push-ups. Laid there again until Otis jumped down to lick my face. Waited to hear my mom call for me. She sometimes did that, after all my moving around woke her fully up.

But tonight, nothing. The whole house was still. I could hear the water heater shrieking down the hall from me.

Hallie, putting her clothes back on. Me, tying the condom in a knot over the utility sink, then wrapping it in the dryer sheet she gave me. Hallie, slipping the whole white ball into my hoodie pocket. Like it was a souvenir. A present. Like it was Tupperware I'd brought to a party and she wanted to make sure it went home with me.

Then she handed me my hoodie.

*"Thanks for coming over."*

I stared at her. A bit of hair was caught in the neck of her T-shirt. I wanted to pick it out, but I couldn't move. Because I hated her so much. Loved her so much. Wished I had her naked boob pictures, so I could send them to everyone I knew in the world. But she'd been too smart for that, which made me hate her more. Loved how she smelled, how she felt. Hated the little white ball of cum in my pocket.

"My parents could be back any minute now," she said. "They don't even know I'm home yet. You should probably go."

Dumb as a dog, I walked back through the dark house, following her as she turned on a few lights here and there. Then I slid open the glass door, not even saying good-bye, and stepped into my own footprints in the snow on the deck, half full of more snow now, since it was snowing again, thin streams of flakes as I reversed the trip, cutting through the same backyards, the same little park, the duck ditch covered in snow. Before I got in my car, I chucked the dryer sheet condom into a snowbank. It didn't even make a sound, and the little dimple where it landed filled up soon enough. Little condom-print, vanished.

Pushing Otis away, I went into the bathroom. Brushed my teeth, looked myself over in the mirror. Same old self. You couldn't tell I'd just gotten laid. You couldn't tell I'd broken my best friend's nose. Couldn't tell that my father was a fuck-up. You couldn't tell one thing about me. I looked like any other boy, a little zitty, a little skinny, farmer tan fading, just like any other white guy in Oak Prairie. In America.

I took off the rest of my clothes and got in bed. Shoved Otis to the side, curled toward the wall. I wondered if Hallie was asleep, now. If her parents had come home and found her in her old bed, her stuff all unpacked on the floor.

*Thanks for coming.*
*Don't stop.*
*We can talk about that later.*
*That's good.*
*God, I love you so much.*

I listened to Otis harrumphing and snoring down by my feet and felt like the only person left on earth still awake, the only person who knew the secret that not a single thing in this world was worth a damn.

# Chapter Nine

I was at the Marine recruiter's office, the next day. My birthday. All my crap in my backpack. Paperwork scrounged up on the sly, while avoiding my mom, who was upstairs cooking and getting ready for Thanksgiving.

I'd had to go through about ten boxes she hadn't unpacked to find it all. There'd been a stack of them by the furnace, a ton of stuff Brad had packed. My mom had been methodical about packing; even when I'd caught her crying while she was doing it, she still wrapped things in newspaper, still organized things by room and type.

But the boxes Brad packed were full of a little bit of everything. Old mail, legal shit from the bank and the lawyers, bills from the hospital and the detox unit, an old collar of Otis's that was missing the tags, a box of macaroni and cheese, a pile of catalogs and magazines, the knobs from an old dresser my mom

116

ended up throwing out, the glass pitcher for our blender, but not the rest of the blender. Random shit, all tossed in with zero thought. At least, in the hospital crap, there were other medical bills, so I found my doctor's name and clinic, which would at least give me something to go on.

Finally, in a box that had nail polish, paperclips, and a tin of nasty old caramel corn from Christmas, I found my school files and folders. Crummy faded pictures I'd made in grade school, my name in all caps: SEAN N. Report cards that repeated the same things: "seems distracted" and "often doesn't finish his work" and "talks out of turn." There, next to a half-filled-in baby book of my photos, was my vaccination record and my Social Security card, my birth certificate, and a little thing with my blood type.

Sergeant Kendall was meeting with someone when I got there, and I was impatient. He wasn't expecting me, so it was all my fault. But I couldn't get it out of my head, Hallie's laundry room. It just replayed, over and over, the good parts and the bad parts. Mainly the words I'd said.

I studied the list of things my mom texted me to pick up from the store. Krista was bringing food too. Grandpa Chuck had venison. My mom had bought a cake from the store this time; it had been sitting on the counter when I'd walked through the kitchen on my way out. It would have been better if she had forgotten this year, though. I felt guilty. For a whole bunch of things.

*I love you so much.*

Fuck.

"Sean?" Sergeant Kendall in front of me. "What can I do for you?"

I stood up. We shook hands.

"Got that paperwork," I said.

"Great," he said. "Step back to my office and let's get started."

●

I normally loved Thanksgiving, and not just because it was my birthday. I loved it even when my birthday got lost in it, because it was all about food and there was no church service involved or gifts you had to remember to buy and then you could take a long nap or watch football or both. But this year, I just sat there, feeling tense. Feeling like it was everywhere, all over my face. Filling out the forms and Sergeant Kendall making copies of my birth certificate and driver's license and Social Security card and Hallie and me in the laundry room and all of it. Brad especially wouldn't stop staring at me, asking me to pass this or that dish.

Plus everything everyone said reminded me of the Marines thing.

Steven-Not-Steve talked about credit cards; I thought about the credit check Sergeant Kendall explained they needed to do. To see if I owed money or defaulted on loans or hadn't paid child support. I laughed at that, but he didn't blink.

Krista mentioned that one of her servers was filing a workers' comp claim and it was getting pretty ugly; I thought about how the whole "any falsifications or omissions on medical history" was grounds for instant dismissal.

Grandpa Chuck tossing some turkey to Otis and Krista acting all freaky about eating, asking what was in everything, like she didn't want to blow out her wedding dress or something—all of that brought up BMI and running and whether I'd be able to hack it in boot camp. I was barely able to finish my birthday cake, which, of course, made my mom ask what my deal was.

The next day, I went in early for my Black Friday shift at the Thrift Bin. Still feeling like the secret, the lie, was all over me. Hallie and the Marines, both. But as I walked around, doing all the opening jobs, I also felt a little proud. Smug. Like I was getting away with something.

And that was dangerous, because I was dying to say something. Do my blurting thing. But damned if I'd ever tell Kerry one thing, even if it did involve getting laid. So Neecie it was. And it felt easy, to tell her about Hallie. To explain why I jumped up and left her house like I had. To write it off like a booty call. Which it had been. Only I hadn't known it, I guess. God.

"Oh, Sean," Neecie said. "I can't believe you did that."

I looked at her. "It wasn't just *me*."

She rolled her eyes. "I know, but, god! Have you learned NOTHING?" She kind of yelled this, and Wendy, from over in the collectibles processing area, looked up at us.

Neecie was tagging Christmas-y stuff, sweaters with Frosty the Snowman on them and aprons covered in poinsettias and tiny red velvet dresses for little girls to wear to church and fuzzy Santa hats and crap like that. I was leaning against the clothing table with a box cutter, breaking down cardboard boxes.

"What do you mean?" I asked.

She looked down, her skin going all red. She wasn't wearing her Thrift Bin apron now, just a little thermal with a low neck under a red hoodie that she'd found in the pile of Christmas clothing. The hoodie had little jingling bells along the sleeves and green ribbons all over it, some amateur crafter's attempt at Christmas-ing up a boring hoodie. It was horrible, but she and Wendy got into moods like that sometimes. Wendy wore giant angel earrings made out of tinsel and a sweater covered in reindeer.

Then she said, out of the side of her mouth, "Me and Tristan," and went back to being really absorbed in the work-ings of her tagging gun. As if Tristan had spies hiding out in the back room of the Thrift Bin.

"Oh."

"Be careful. Might become a bad habit."

I shook my head. Neecie had no idea; I'd gone and made the future happen with the Marines. I couldn't be a habit with anyone. "I won't be that lucky. I can't believe it even happened *once*."

Neecie looked doubtful, but she didn't say anything.

"Christ, Sean, do you ever do anything but sexually harass people around here?" Kerry, coming up from behind me.

I pictured, not for the first time, stabbing him with my box cutter. But then Kerry did something totally weird.

"So, Neecie," he said. "You guys should come out tonight. I'm having people over."

Neecie turned super red. But she just said, "Really?"

"Yep," Kerry said, smiling now that he had her attention. "Real festive gathering. Homemade hot chocolate and everything."

"Shut the fuck up," I said. Blurted. "You're so full of shit."

Kerry was staring at Neecie like she was something

delicious he wanted to eat, but he just said, "Oh, yeah? You weren't here last year, so you don't know the whole tradition. Just ask her! Wendy always comes to my Black Friday thing. Hey, Wendy!"

Wendy looked up from the pile of pottery she was squirting with Windex.

"Sean here doesn't believe me about the Black Friday party," Kerry said, all snotty. "Tell him."

"Oh, yeah," Wendy said. "Kerry and I always do that on Black Friday. He makes homemade hot chocolate and everything."

"Hot chocolate?" Neecie said. Now she was smiling. "Seriously?"

Kerry said yes and smiled at her again. He looked like a shark. A shark with a black and ginger beard.

"It's my secret recipe," he said. "You can add a little Hot 100 to it, just for flavor, if you want, too . . ."

"Okay," Neecie said. Before I could say anything. "But I still don't have my car. I'll need a ride."

"I can give you a ride, no problem," Kerry said, looking very satisfied with himself and walking off. Like he'd just totally rooked the dumb girl into some joke. Or worse. I was thinking worse, given the Hot 100 comment. Though he couldn't think he'd get her loaded and try shit with her. Not with Wendy there. Or me.

"I'll take you," I said.

"Whatever," she said.

"Since when do you want to hang out with Kerry?"

She shook her head, and then the donation door rang and Kerry yelled for me, and I spent the rest of the night dealing with this stupid donor who had three carloads of crap from her dead uncle's house and who told me and Kerry about the tragedy and the coincidence of someone dying right around the holidays, when all these bags and boxes of shit could be given to "those in need." Most of it was garbage, I could just tell, looking at the woman, who looked like the kind of lady who saved yogurt containers and the foil that butter got wrapped in and whatever. She was wearing a Christmas sweater too. Which appeared to be contagious, because by the time we were closing, even Kerry was wearing a Santa hat.

And Neecie wouldn't even drive over to his house with me, because Eddie texted me a bunch, wanting to hang out, but when I told her we needed to stop and get him, Neecie, putting her own Santa hat on, said that she'd go straight to the party with Wendy, who was getting a ride from Kerry too.

●

"What's Libby doing tonight?" I asked Eddie as we drove to Kerry's. I sounded kind of like a dick. But neither of us had hung out much this year. He was always with Libby, and I was always with Neecie. Or up my own ass.

"She's at her relatives' in Iowa," he said. Sounding like he was sorry for it, and sorry for ignoring me, and I felt sorry back, too.

"You think he'll sell me some weed?" Eddie asked when I parked in front of Kerry's house.

"Don't bring it up," I said. "He's all touchy about who he sells to. Plus my manager is gonna be there; I don't know if she knows he sells weed. And Neecie Albertson is gonna be there too."

"That deaf chick from school?"

"Fuck you, she's not deaf."

"Are you, like, hooking up with her now?" Eddie asked. "I thought she was gay with that Ivy chick."

"No," I said. "We just hang out sometimes. She's actually pretty cool. And she's not gay, either."

"Whatever," Eddie said as we walked up to the door. Kerry still had his Beware of Dog sign tacked to the door, though his dog Trudy was sweet as pie and came running the second we opened the door, smelling our hands and letting us pet her before dashing off somewhere else.

Eddie was not prepared for Kerry's house. He looked around nervously, took in the general sad state of things, which mostly looked like a tornado had happened to a Dumpster full of paneling and shitty old-grandma furniture. Structure-wise, it resembled our rambler. Though bigger. Surprisingly, it didn't smell like pot, as usual, but chocolate. And peppermint. And there weren't that many people. But it was festive, as promised. There was actual Christmas music playing, not the vomit rock Kerry normally blasted.

As if he hadn't realized what he was getting into, Eddie pulled out a little pint of vodka from his coat.

"You want some? I don't have anything to mix with it, though."

I shook my head. I just wanted to find Neecie. Eddie seemed hypnotized by everything; the camo coats hung up on the rack and the shotgun in its case leaning against the front hall table and the old dudes in the living room watching football. I could tell he was rethinking his pink V-neck sweater.

Passing through the living room and down the hall, we found everyone in the kitchen, Neecie standing beside Kerry and Wendy. Kerry, still wearing his Santa hat, was stirring this gigantic black pot full of hot chocolate, and Wendy was drinking hot cocoa and had a cocoa-mustache and was smiling, and it was all weird.

"Hi Sean!" Neecie said, her face very red. Her Santa hat on the counter beside her. I wondered if Kerry's witch cauldron was full of Hot 100 too.

"What's going on?"

"Kerry's showing us his secret recipe," Wendy said. "You need to try some."

"Does it have Hot 100 in it?" I asked.

"Keep your pants on already, we're not there yet, Sean," Kerry said. "So, anyway," he continued to Neecie. "I bust up like six chocolate bars too. This is none of that Swiss Miss bullshit. Then I add some heavy whipping cream. That really makes it thick and good . . ."

"Nice sweaters," Eddie said to Neecie and Wendy. Probably because he needed some support, clothing-choices-wise.

"Thanks, Eddie!" Neecie said. All happy. She seemed drunk. Or maybe she'd smoked some weed. She just seemed too happy to be here. Wendy looked all cheery too, now that I thought about it. Or maybe she just didn't laugh that much at work because she was all stressed out and stuff. Both of them were definitely the Non-School Versions of themselves.

Kerry looked at Eddie like he wished he and his pink sweater would die, but he gave us mugs of the cocoa and then let us dose them with the stuff on the counter: Hot 100, Rumple Minze, something with no label that smelled like burnt dirt.

Eddie was sniffing at the no-label bottle when Kerry came

over and glugged a bunch in Eddie's cocoa. "You'll like it; it's good stuff. It tastes way better than it smells."

"What's it called?" Eddie said, but he drank obediently, like he thought Kerry would get mad otherwise.

"It's homebrew. It's from Wisconsin," Kerry said. "My housemate Shane gets it for me when he goes back home."

"We should go out back, you guys," Wendy said. "Shane's making a fire."

Even though it was November, and there was snow piled up, the last few days had been weirdly warm. So we all followed Kerry through his shitty house, past the football-watching old guys, past the bathroom where someone was taking a piss with the door open—nice—and went downstairs, past a very sad-looking couch and a weight bench with a cracked vinyl seat and a million-year-old washer and dryer and out to the back, where apparently Kerry spent the bulk of his home decorating energy, because he had made this half-enclosed deck space with a fire pit and chairs and whatever. It was actually pretty nice. Shane, the other housemate, was feeding the fire with twigs and sipping from a bottle of Jack Daniels.

"This is really nice, Kerry," Wendy said, leaning back in a chair. "You added the little trellis thing, huh?"

Kerry nodded, started talking about how Shane was growing some vines this spring and whatever else, and then Wendy said that Mary Clare wanted to do the same in their backyard and then Kerry asked where Mary Clare was and Wendy said she was at her mother's house, but her mother didn't believe in gayness and so they always spent holidays apart.

The chair I was sitting in had a cracked armrest, which snagged on my coat when I leaned over to Neecie, who was sitting between me and Eddie, and asked her how much she'd been drinking.

"Just one cup before you got here," she said.

"How much booze did you put in it?"

"Why does it matter, Sean?"

"Just curious," I said.

"You get that hoodie at the Thrift Bin?" Eddie asked Neecie.

"Yes," she said, all proud. I noticed Eddie talked straight to her face, too. Maybe he instinctively knew this? "Wendy and I both picked them out."

Wendy looked up from her conversation with Kerry. "Yes, mine's more a classic bingo lady sweater. Neecie's is crazy-cat-lady-does-crafts."

"You get that sweater at the Thrift Bin?" Kerry asked Eddie, pointing too, as if it weren't clear. Shane, silent until now next to his bottle, laughed, this kind of *hughhughgha*-sound, like he was an old crappy machine coming unplugged.

"No, Goodwill," Eddie said right back, no stumbling or anything. Sometimes Eddie got that way. Like, if he answered your questions fast enough, maybe people would forget what they asked? It sometimes worked, actually. "But it was on sale. I was just looking for a record player," he said to Wendy, as if she'd be insulted that he visited the competition. "You guys didn't have one."

"Record players, stereo systems, speakers," Kerry said. "I don't take that shit when it comes through the donation door." He grabbed Shane's Jack Daniels and glugged some of it into his hot cocoa.

"Bummer," Eddie said. "Because I would totally buy *that*

*shit.*" Now Eddie leaned back and propped his feet up on one of the big-ass logs Kerry had lying around the fire pit.

Wendy sat up now, straightened herself. Like she could tell, like me, that there was something going on between Kerry and Eddie. Which was not going to happen, I mean, Christ! Eddie? Eddie was like some dude from Abercrombie & Fitch. Eddie shaved what little body hair he had every season during swimming sectionals. Eddie had no chance with getting riled at Kerry. Kerry probably cut his toenails once a year with a butcher knife or whatever. It made zero sense.

But then Kerry turned to me and said, "Some Marines guy came into the store looking for you the other day."

"He did?"

"He said he wasn't there on official business or anything," Kerry said. "Just knew you worked there and wanted to say hello."

Wendy blinked at me. "You're thinking of joining the military, Sean?"

I shrugged. I didn't want to say it, not now.

"Oh, come on, Sean," Neecie said, kicking my shoe with her boot. "It's not just an idea," she told Wendy.

"I didn't know that," Wendy said. "That's . . . interesting."

"Interesting, fuck," Kerry said. "Dumbassed is more like it. Might as well hand over your nuts to the Man and be done with it."

"Hey, shut the fuck up," Shane said. "My brother's a Marine. He's been out a few years now. Freedom isn't free, you know, asshole. Somebody's gotta do it."

"Do what?" Kerry said. "Buy into the government's bullshit that we need all this protection? That our economy must keep churning out shitty crap by the ton so I can bale it and toss it in a goddamn Dumpster even though it's barely used?"

"You're fucked up, man," Shane said, swigging some more Jack.

Kerry grabbed the bottle from him, swigged himself.

"My brother's in the Army," Kerry said. "He went in, just a regular guy. Pretty cool. Came out a total fucking prick. Even his wife can't stand him. Rigid motherfucker. You really want that? Just so you can go be a fucking hero, Sean? Save some people who don't even want you around? Go to some shithole and get your arms and legs blown off for no reason?"

I swirled my cocoa around, drank some. It tasted like ass. I wanted to get up and, I don't know. Something. Punch Kerry? No, leave. Leaving sounded pretty good.

"You know them guys have DNR orders on them if they step on something that blows their nuts off," Kerry said. "You gonna do that? Get your nuts blown off? Before you barely get a chance to use them?"

"Kerry!" Wendy said, like she was his mom. Or my mom.

"Well, it's true," Kerry said. "I heard a whole story about it on the radio."

"They pretty much kill everyone they want dead with them drones now anyway," Shane said. "It's all different now."

"Someone has to control those drones, though," Wendy said. "It's not like they fly themselves."

"Sometimes fighting's just unavoidable," Neecie added. "It sucks, but it's unavoidable."

"You're fucking romantic about this shit," Kerry said to Neecie. "They let women on the front lines now; wait till some of them come home all shot-up and one-legged. Then see how you chicks feel."

That Kerry would sweet-talk Neecie earlier, and now be such an asshole to her made me want to clobber him. I clenched a fist, then unclenched it. Pulled the snagged thread from the sleeve of my coat. Clenched a fist again. Wished I wasn't such a pussy, that I'd not think twice about punching Eddie but had to rein it in when it came to Kerry.

But Neecie barely shrugged. Didn't say a word. I wondered how she did it. Was it a matter of not hearing?

"Quit jacking my Jack," Shane said to Kerry, who was adding more to his cocoa. "Drink that pussy juice you got up in the kitchen since you love it so bad."

Then Neecie laughed. And then Shane looked at her, and he laughed, too, and the look on his face was surprised. Happy, too. Like he was thinking, *Damn, right! You know what: I AM funny. And you're a cute girl. Ha! I'm just noticing these things.*

I thought Neecie would be creeped out. Shane was a million years older and was wearing this ancient thermal shirt and no jacket and his chest hair poked up around his neck and he had long hair and a stupid goatee. Shane looked like someone who would only get laid if he paid a woman to do it. Neecie looked like a little piece of candy he'd like to slurp up. It made me really tense. And kind of sick, thinking about how she didn't even see this.

But then Neecie stood up. "I'll refill yours, Kerry," she said, grabbing for his mug. Like he hadn't just yelled at her like a cockface. Like she was all cozy and at home in his shitty house now. Kerry smiled and thanked her, and Shane looked at her ass the whole time, but Wendy didn't notice because her phone rang, and Kerry asked about whether we'd been hunting, and

I had to tell him about the three deer I'd shot, and he couldn't believe it. I'd just started explaining everything, because it actually was a good story, and Eddie jumped in, too, which made Kerry irritated, I could tell, when I saw Shane follow Neecie, holding open the door for her, both of them going inside together.

I wanted Wendy to do something, but she was on her phone, standing up and talking a few feet away, and Kerry was adding wood to the fire and Eddie was talking about field-dressing stuff, like he wanted Kerry to be impressed. I felt like punching someone again. And leaving. I stood up, like to stretch, but if I couldn't take on Kerry, there was no way I could pretend to handle Shane. Shane was way too big. Just—a really big guy. I was tall, but I didn't have a chance. I grabbed the log Eddie's feet were on and added it to the fire, which pissed off Eddie and made Kerry bitch about how I'd added a log when we clearly didn't need one, so he had to get up and stir everything around until it was just right. Then I couldn't sit down. Just stood there. Looked at the dark backyard, listened to the sound of traffic from the highway in the distance. Cracked the two knuckles on my left hand that always cracked the loudest and best. I wondered if Neecie was scared. I wondered about the rest of the guys in the house. I moved toward the basement door.

Eddie asked, "Where are you going?" all panicked, like I was ditching him, which I was, but Jesus. That would teach him to think before he put on a pink sweater again.

"Be right back," I said.

I ran the shitty basement and then back up through the living room, down the hallway. The bathroom door was shut

130

now, at least. And no one was in the kitchen. Though there was a hallway off it that led to somewhere and I could hear people talking and I didn't pause for a second to look.

It was Shane's bedroom, and there was Neecie, sitting cross-legged on Shane's bed, wearing a giant pair of headphones. The expensive kind that asshole kids went around wearing between classes in the hallways, like they were actual deejays and couldn't live one second without music.

She waved at me, Shane behind her on a chair, staring at me. I realized I had nothing to say. No reason to be standing there.

"I'm listening to this band Shane likes," Neecie said, talking in that loud way people do when they are wearing headphones. "What's up? You leaving?" She pulled off the headphones, and they messed up her hair.

"No," I said.

"Okay," she said, looking at me funny.

Shane lit a cigarette, blew the smoke toward me. It reeked, and I couldn't imagine smoking in the same room you slept in.

Neecie stood up, set the headphones on Shane's bed. "Should we get another drink?"

Shane said, "I'm good. I don't drink that cocoa shit." But he was behind her and she couldn't see his face and so I nodded, said yes.

It was awkward, but only for me, because Neecie breezed out and then we were in the kitchen and there were Kerry and Wendy and Eddie.

"Took you long enough to bring my drink back," Kerry said, touching Neecie's back in a way that creeped me out. But she just smiled and said she forgot and hopped up to sit on the counter and started scrolling through stuff on her phone.

Kerry ladled more cocoa into mugs and filled them with Hot 100 and Rumple Minze and passed them around. Wendy opened a cupboard and took out a package of cookies and passed some to Eddie, who shook his head. I wondered if Kerry had smoked her out. I wondered if her wife knew she was doing this, hanging out at this gross coworker's party. It seemed like it was beneath her, to be around kids like us.

Shane came back into the room, still smoking. He ashed into the sink, stood beside Neecie, who looked up from her texting to talk to him. I wished I could hear them, but Kerry had turned on his shitty seventies rock so I knew it'd be hard enough for her to communicate with Shane face to face. I slammed back my cocoa, then. Feeling annoyed and pissed off. For no reason. Eddie nudged me.

"Is she gonna get with that guy or something?" he asked.

"Dunno."

"He's like, way older."

"I know." I drank some more, and Kerry and Wendy came over.

"You guys want to smoke out?" Kerry asked.

Eddie's eyes got wide. "Sure."

"It better be that mellow shit, Kerry," Wendy said, biting into a cookie. "I have to work tomorrow."

"It's mellow shit. You've smoked this stuff before."

I was shocked about Wendy. You had to be piss-tested to use the baler and probably the forklift, too. Did Kerry have someone else pee in the cup for him? Maybe Wendy did it for him? I was starting to feel like everyone had weird secret relationships now. It made me feel paranoid as hell.

Of course, it wasn't mellow shit; Kerry never had mellow shit and I knew it, but five minutes later, I was with everyone all circled up and claustrophobic in Kerry's bedroom, smoking out of Kerry's little red glass bong.

"I'm good," I said after two passes, knowing I'd be destroyed with another.

Eddie was coughing his head off, and Wendy was laughing at something Kerry said, but they passed it around some more and then I just knew that Eddie was going to be a total disaster. Wendy and Kerry seemed totally normal, which was something I never understood, how people could smoke pot and not act high. It seemed like a superpower. Or a waste.

●

After that, though, as if by magic, or marijuana, the party got fun. Some girls showed up—adult women, really, Kerry and Wendy's age—and that seemed to make everything less grim and shitty and just kind of loose. Having girls around always makes any party better. Kerry hugged and kissed a bunch of them hello, which was weirder still. One of them hung off him, too, which was strange, but her name was Brianne or Brianna or Deanna or something, and she was teasing him and he was laughing and suddenly, everything was fun, all mixed up and loud and people down by the bonfire talking and smoking and someone playing Christmas carols again and Neecie and Wendy were laughing their heads off, wearing Santa hats, and it was all good.

Kerry introduced Brianne/Brianna/Deanna to me and Eddie, and she was funny; she had this tattoo of a fish that was saying, "I'm hooked!" and it didn't make any sense but she was telling us the story of how she got it and I wondered if she and Kerry were fucking and figured they were. Or had. Or might yet tonight. And somehow that didn't make me depressed or anything, just kind of, like, all right. Resigned. Everything going along, nothing stopping, sometimes you were up, sometimes you were down, nothing you could do but just roll along and accept it. I knew this was the pot, of course, but it also seemed true, down-to-my-balls *True*, and I wished I could call Hallie and tell her this, with my mouth, though, not in a text, because I couldn't explain it in short sentences. I'd need to talk it all out.

I went inside, then, to do it. Call her. Just tell her that it was okay, and we didn't even need to hook up again, and it wasn't because we had, either, and I could take back my whole *I love you* thing because I understood her now, what she had meant that night before she left in the weird un-breakup breakup we had, how there was possibility and it was all so good and we shouldn't stop, we shouldn't rule it out, we should just follow our ideas, and plus, that was how I knew the Marines would be good for me, it was my thing, it was where I was supposed to be, where I would fit. Because it felt right, no matter what people said, it felt like the story I would tell about myself, I would be like Shane's brother or Kerry's brother, but not a prick; I would be in the Marines, I would know things, I would go there and then I'd come back and still be me, but better, because that was how life worked, if you just fucking let it. I would tell Hallie this and she would say something good and then I'd tell my mom, too, and she'd get it and then it'd be okay and I was leaving and never coming back but maybe I would come back, after a while, eventually, and everyone would see, then, how it was okay, how I'd done it, and you just never know what a person can do with their life and themselves, really, which was fine because everything, all of it, was fine. Good.

But there was a loud ping-pong game in the basement. And upstairs in the living room people were eating kettle corn out of one of those giant holiday tins and watching *A Christmas Story*, which was sort of lame, but still festive, I guess, since they were laughing and stuff, but it was still too loud to talk on the phone and organize my mind around what I wanted to say so I went into the kitchen, where Neecie was sitting on the counter and Shane was kind of standing between her legs, his hands on her knees, talking to her, super close, like they'd been kissing. Or would be, soon. Either way, I just stood there in the doorway and stared at them. She couldn't see me; her long hair was around her face and Shane was talking in her ear and I felt like throwing up for some reason, but I couldn't move, because she was sitting right next to the sink where it'd be best to barf and I didn't want either of them to see me, and I knew the bathroom wasn't far away, but I couldn't move, because what the hell was happening to her and everyone else? What was making Shane think he could rub his big gross hand on her thigh like that? Her girl-sized thigh, his old-man hand: his losery, braindead-from-Jack-Daniels smoking-in-his-bedroom-and-living-with-Kerry-in-a-shitty-house hand?

And what was making Neecie think that was a good idea? That was the real question.

But then I had my answer, because her phone beeped and she grabbed it and checked it and then there was a gap in the music and I could hear a horn honking and she jumped from the counter, away from Shane's old-man hands and his greasy goatee, and rushed right toward me, where I stood like a statue.

"Move, Sean," she said. "I gotta go."

"Where are you going?"

She stopped and then just slithered around me. "Tristan's here," she said. "I'll see you at work." And then she grabbed her coat from the hook where all the shitty camo coats were, and before Shane could even say one word, to her or me, she was gone.

# Chapter Ten

Hallie, again. Tuesday night. Early December. She was back again for winter break.

In the laundry room. Again.

She wore jeans. A sweater. Smelled good.

The concrete floor. Again.

Her saying *don't stop*. Again and again.

And me not knowing if what I was doing was what she liked. Again.

All I knew is that I liked it enough for the both of us.

She had gone down on me, this time. That part of things went on for a really long time, and it was good and I didn't realize it until later, when it was over, but that was the best part, really. The part where I didn't have to think. Or wonder about what I was doing.

But then she handed me the condom, and then there was

sex and me wanting to say all sorts of blurted-out things when I came, but I held back, and when she got off me and found her clothes, I peeled off the condom and tied it over the utility sink. Again.

"What were you doing when I texted you?" she asked. She handed me a dryer sheet for the condom, handed me my coat after I got my jeans on.

"At Eddie's." Not mentioning that Emma and Libby had been there, too. Eddie'd managed to finally do it with Libby, after a million weekends of her dithering over birth control and timing and if she was "ready," until Eddie was ready to rip his hair out. Fuck: *I* was ready to rip my hair out just hearing about it. I'd been sitting in Eddie's basement, in the dark, eating cookie dough out of a bowl with Emma, the bowl between us on the sofa like a referee, watching television while Eddie and Libby ate each other's faces off and whatever else. Not sex, because Eddie's parents were upstairs. It all felt super lame. Babyish. And I had signed up for the Marines and still hadn't told anyone, not even Eddie or Neecie, because it was like I wanted to be a man and have secrets that were mysterious and keep my business private. Like, if Sergeant Kendall could see me, being all nuts and proud and braggy about things, he'd think I was a pussy or something. Like, when you were a Marine, you had to act like it was nothing big. You couldn't just go around blabbing about your plans. Especially when you hadn't even done anything yet. You had to wait until it was the right time. You had to be calm. You had to be cool about it. And the longer I held it in, the cooler it became to me. The better the secret became, the longer I held it in. Me being the only one to know felt really good.

But I'd been really quiet, and not just because Emma seemed embarrassed, either about being around me or Eddie and Libby being so touchy and gross. I'd just sat there, eating and watching television, until Hallie's text, when I had no problem standing up and saying I had to go, no explanation, just saying "see you" and not even looking back.

"Was he having a party?" Hallie asked.

"No, just hanging out."

She flicked off the laundry room light and we headed upstairs. She went into the kitchen and drank a big glass of water.

"You want any?" she asked, holding out the glass. I shook my head. "My parents are at some Christmas party thing," she said. "I was supposed to go, but I didn't get back in time from Madison."

"Oh."

"I don't know how I'm going to stand it now," she said. "I don't want to back to school. It sucks."

I would have asked her why it sucked, but honestly? I didn't really care. It was pretty petty of me. But I thought, since she didn't want to talk the other time, why pretend now? I didn't have to be her boyfriend anymore.

I couldn't be anyone's boyfriend anymore.

"I have to be back January twentieth," she continued. "I don't know what I'm gonna do. What the hell is there to do *here*?"

She sounded whiny, kind of desperate, but damn. If she couldn't think of anything to do, Jesus Christ, I sure could. Just the thought of it filled me up, like money in my pockets. It just felt so fucking badass. Like, maybe I really deserved whatever I wanted now. I'd made a sacrifice, and even though it was secret,

139

it still counted. So I didn't have to wait for say-so. I could just leave someone's cookie-dough-basement-make-out session to go get my dick sucked and get laid. Get whatever the fuck else I felt like too.

So I took the glass of water from her hand, not in a nice way, and I gulped it. All of it. Then set it down on the counter and got my keys out. Didn't look at Hallie at all.

"You can always just text me if want to hang out in your laundry room," I said. "That passes the time decent for me at least."

Then I walked out the back deck door. Same footprints in the snow, same stupid roundabout route to her house, through backyards of people I didn't know, to my car, which was still warm.

●

I've never understood how girls always like guys who are total dicks, but after I said that to Hallie, all assholey and bossy and whatever, instead of her being, like, *fuck you dick*, it was the reverse. The laundry room thing kept happening. Not all the time, but just enough for me to always feel up for it. My mom and Krista bugging me about what did I want for Christmas and me shrugging. What else do you want for Christmas besides that?

●

Christmas Day, I sat in the living room with Grandpa Chuck and Brad and Krista and my mother, eating cookies and drinking eggnog and everything seeming really boring and slow, like we'd all gone into some shredded wrapping paper–induced coma, surrounded by boxes of new sweaters and gift bags of socks and some books I'd never read. Sergeant Kendall said he was flying to Jamaica for Christmas to meet some buddies. He had a few days' leave. I thought about Jamaica. Rum and the beach. Chicks in bikinis. Surfing. Who knows if they surfed in Jamaica, but there was an ocean and Sergeant Kendall had grown up in California and talked about surfing as a kid. It made me feel jealous.

And made me think, for the hundredth time, that this was when I should tell everyone. Before Brad gave me shit about living with Mom until I was forty and Grandpa Chuck asked me about my future plans—had I thought about veterinary school at all, since it was a kind of the family business, ha ha—and Mom started in about Steven-Not-Steve's community college.

My mother poured everyone eggnog. It made a thick, slow, glooping sound that made me want to take a nap. Grandpa Chuck loved eggnog and asked my mom for a refill. Then he said he had some news.

"Todd called me this morning," he said.

Todd = my father.

"He's got a ticket for Brad's wedding," he continued.

Everyone immediately got tense; you could just feel it.

Except for Krista. "Oh, how nice!" she said, all happy.

"He must be doing well," my mom said in this sort of dazed robot voice.

And then I didn't want to say anything about anything, least of all the Marines. Another reason to put it off: I should wait until everyone was here. All formal-like. But also, *of course* my dad would be back for Brad's wedding. Not for my graduation a few weeks before, though. Pretty much what I'd come to expect from my dad.

And I thought of Sergeant Kendall. How dry and smooth his handshake was. How he never seemed to sweat or pause or hesitate. How he always said just enough, like he planned his words; how he moved the exact amount necessary, like he meant every step and gesture.

Then I felt guilty. I'd told him I could run the mile and a half in under thirteen minutes. I told him, and I hadn't done shit. I looked at my family, still in their Christmas coma, and said I was going to take Otis out. Though it was freezing cold. I needed to stop thinking about screaming and hitting and acting like a two-year-old. I needed to *mean* what I was doing.

Otis ended up ditching me five minutes into it, cutting through the snow back to the house, the pussy. But I walked at least an hour, down the highway, until I was back to normal. Numb with cold and calm. But slow and steady as eggnog sliding into the glass. Secret safe for another day.

●

By New Year's Eve, I was ready to eat rocks, I was so sick of my family and doing nothing. When Hallie texted that we only had a little window—her parents were having dinner with her grandmother at the nursing home—I jumped.

But this time, when it was over and she tried to lift off me, my hands clamped down on her hips.

"They'll be back soon," she said.

"You said the nursing home's in Chaska. And it's not even close to midnight."

"Yeah, but they won't stay that long. The old people don't stay up until midnight, you know."

"Just wait," I said, squeezing tighter.

She folded her arms across her chest. Like she was cold. Or pouty. She looked both. But she also looked beautiful. There was something about being pinned down by her this way that I liked, that made her more beautiful. I mean, she was always beautiful, that didn't go away, even on days when she claimed she looked like shit. She always looked the way she looked, which was beautiful in a way that sort of made me feel panicked and jealous and maybe I needed to be the one who was on top, holding her down. But I didn't. I wanted her on me, just like this, us together, and me being able to look at her as long as I wanted.

"What are you doing tonight?" I asked, since she was letting me get my way. At least for a few minutes.

"I don't know."

"You're going to do something, though. You're going out."

"I don't know yet. Maybe." She looked down at her fingernails for a minute. She had polished them, a silver-grey color with sparkly glitter. I thought about that for some reason. I hadn't noticed her polishing her nails before. Had she? I didn't remember it from before she left for college. This was another reason I needed to look at her. Though not noticing probably meant I'm a terrible boyfriend.

Am. Was. Had been. Whatever.

*God, I love you so much.*

"So, let's go out together. Get drunk or something."

"I'm tired of getting drunk."

"Okay, so, then, not get drunk. Something else."

"I don't want to smoke pot, Sean."

I barely had any pot left, and I didn't want to smoke it anyway. I didn't see why bringing that up would help, though. Still, I was pissed at why she couldn't just do something with me. Instead of just sneaking around. I felt like telling her about the Marines. Saying something like, *I'm going to boot camp. Then who knows where. Deployed, somewhere far from here. And you'll wish you'd been nicer. You will.*

"My knee's falling asleep," she said. All cold. Pissy.

Her rules. Always. I fucking hated her rules now. Her too. Hated that she'd called me to come over and we'd done this at all.

*I am leaving. And never coming back.*

I took my hands off her hips and she stood up, separated herself from me, a little huffy, stepping into her clothes. Pajama pants. And a UW–Madison T-shirt.

Usually, I went and did my bit at the utility sink with the condom, but this time I watched her get dressed like a total perv. It was dickish. Nasty. But I didn't even hide it.

She turned away from me to hook up her bra, and I got up, put my boxers and jeans on, tied the condom in a knot.

She handed me the dryer sheet then. But I wouldn't take it.

"You deal with it for once," I said, smashing the tied-off condom into the middle of the dryer sheet, making her flinch.

She made a face, all disgusted. Which pissed me off more. As if it were really any grosser than her letting me put my dick up in her.

"Fine," she said, the dryer sheet unsteady in her palm, like it was radioactive.

I put on my shirt and hoodie. I felt like shaking her. Hitting something. Her? I wanted to do something like that so bad that I couldn't look at her. I was afraid she'd be able to tell it, just from my face.

"See you," I said. "Happy New Year." Stomped upstairs.

She rushed behind me, all the way to the sliding glass door.

"Sean, wait . . ."

I turned around.

"I mean, I'm not trying to be, like," she started. "It's just not . . . I mean . . ."

"Fuck, Hallie! Just fucking say it already!" I yelled.

She backed away, put her hands on her hips.

"God. You don't have to be such an asshole about it."

"What am I even being an asshole about?" I said. "Tell me." I put my shoes, my old shitty Adidas, flakes of Grandpa Chuck's patio cement falling everywhere on the Martins' perfect carpet. I didn't bother to tie them.

"I don't want to fight with you," she said.

"Oh, are we fighting?" I said. "We're not fighting. What would we have to fight about? See you. Happy New Year."

"Sean . . ."

Then I stepped through the glass deck door. It was dark; it'd been dark since forever. My watch glowed that it was 8:02. I went through the same footprints as before, snow crusted and established. I wondered if her parents ever went out there, noticed the size-eleven prints, asked her who was coming and going through their back deck in the middle of the winter like that.

I wasn't out of her yard when I started running. Running like I hadn't been. Running like I'd promised Sergeant Kendall

I would that day in the recruiting office. I was lucky I didn't wipe out, my untied shoes full of melting snow.

By the time I got to my car, I wanted to just, I don't know. Cry. Break something. Choke the goddamn life out of someone. My hands in fists. Wishing to just SMASH.

Then another text.

"FUCK YOU!" I screamed into the interior of the Mercury.

But then I looked at my phone. Because I was always going to look at it, because that's how I rolled, no matter if it was Hallie wanting to talk or something. Or Eddie sending some goddamn sex picture for the millionth time; the last one had been a picture of a buck's balls.

But this time it was Neecie.

can you come get me?

•

"Whose house is this?" I asked as Neecie got in the car. Though I knew exactly whose house it was. Been down the long windy drive toward the lakefront to a couple of parties here. Tristan Reichmeier's house on Prairie Lake. The gate was open, and there were a bunch of cars parked there, in the driveway and in the muddy snow.

Neecie didn't say anything. She just put a stick of gum in her mouth and rolled on her lip gloss.

"Neecie?" I touched her arm, made sure she saw my face when I asked again.

"Can you just drive?" She shook my arm off her.

"Can you just answer the question?"

"It's Tristan's, okay. Which I know you know. Will you just drive?"

She glanced toward the door of the house, where a light had just gone on.

"What," I said. "Did you guys have a fight?"

"No."

Then the door whipped open and there was Tristan. No coat, but with his shoes on, and it looked like he might come out. Until he saw me. Then, beside him, stood Ivy Heller. Her hair was blue again. Then Neecie said, "Will you fucking drive already?"

I pulled the car out of park. But not before Tristan and me had a nice long stare-down. I'll admit it; I enjoyed him looking uncertain about whether to come and mess with me.

Getting back on the county road from the lake involved paying attention, so Neecie was lucky I didn't ask her anything for a while. Then I asked where she wanted to go.

"Just to my house, if that's okay."

"So, are you all right? I mean, is Ivy . . . was he having a party?"

"Yeah."

"Hey. Are you all right? Did he hit you or something?"

She laughed that fakey laugh again. "No, of course not. God. It's just . . ." She turned toward me. "Do you really want to hear all this crap? Because it's totally fucked up. I mean, I could go on for a million years about it, probably. I don't want to depress you."

"Why didn't Ivy come with you? I thought she hated Tristan."

Neecie pressed her hands to her eyes. I thought she was

crying. I hoped she wasn't. I didn't know what to do when girls cried. My mom cried so much before my dad left. My favorite part about him leaving was that my mom's crying was reduced by like 95 percent.

"I didn't know he was having people over," she said. "He just texted like normal. Said to be ready, whatever. He picked me up at home, even. I didn't even ask him about anything. It's usually like we don't have a lot of time. Like, someone's coming home. Or he has to be somewhere. Or I have to be somewhere. So it's kind of like, walk in, strip down, do it, leave."

I tried to keep my face normal. But I hated Tristan Reichmeier even more now.

"But sometimes, he doesn't have anything going on afterward," Neecie went on. "Like, he'll want to hang out. Watch a movie or something. Usually never on weekend nights, though. Usually weekend nights he's got stuff going on."

"So, why exactly is that bad? You don't like the movies he likes or something?"

She laughed. Not a fakey laugh. A surprised one. "God! No! I don't know what movies he likes, actually. It's just, I used to do that stuff with him. Hang out. But I won't do it anymore. It's like, he can't have both things, you know? He can't ignore me in school and then expect me to snuggle with him on the couch whenever he's bored or lonely, you know?"

"So, you're the one who doesn't want to be with him?"

"No," she said. "No, I do. I would do that stuff with him. I have. It's just that it makes me want it every time. And he won't do it every time. The only thing he'll do every time is . . ."

"It?" I interrupted.

She laughed again. This one was a real laugh. I liked that.

Not just because it distanced things from crying.

"I just feel like shit when he talks me into more," she said. "More than *it*. And then I swear I'll never see him again. And Ivy will come over and I'll cry and she'll yell at me and then she'll cry and we'll make a plan. Swear off him. And then he'll text a week later . . ."

"And you go."

"Yeah. But this time, Ivy was already out at his house. And some other people, too. And she was drunk. And he . . . he's been bugging me, okay? For a while. To do that."

"What?" I said, though I already knew.

"To be with both of us."

I didn't say anything. And there were too many things to ask.

I guess she could tell I was upset, because after a minute she asked me what was going on.

I laughed. "You mean, with *me*? Nothing's going on with me. I'm totally boring."

Neecie shook her head. "You're not talking. Usually you say things."

"Yeah."

"Well, just say it, won't you? Ask me what I know you want to ask."

I sat with that for a while, drove. Considered the millions of ways to ask, all the shit rolling around in my head, all the questions and how mad I was and how jealous I was and how everything was stupid and unfair and made no goddamn sense.

"What I don't get is why he won't just hang out with you all the time? Like, normally? Where everyone can see. I mean, it's been so long now. Obviously he likes you."

"Wow." She laughed. "I didn't expect you to say that."

I shrugged. I was still trying to stop imagining punching the shit out of Tristan Reichmeier. The worst part was that thinking about that felt good. Also, bad. Guilty-bad. And then there was The Horn. Too many things going on in me, as usual.

"But he doesn't *like* me," Neecie said. "*Liking me* is not the issue."

"That's stupid," I said. "Of course he likes you. If he wants to hang out with you, you know, afterward, even a little bit, even sometimes . . ."

"He just can't be alone. That's the main thing, Sean. He's kind of spoiled and he's kind of dumb and he can't handle being alone . . . It's not really that complicated . . ." She leaned back in her seat, started combing her fingers through her hair. "God. I'm so tired. It doesn't seem like New Year's Eve, does it?"

I nodded. For a few minutes she was quiet, and I just drove. Thinking all my things and not knowing which to pick from, not knowing what thing to say would be right, wanting to be able to say them, all at once. Too bad you couldn't do that.

But when Neecie turned on the radio, I snapped it off two seconds later. She looked surprised at me.

"Not to be an asshole, but if you're just interested in sex, you'd never want to just hang out, okay?" I said. "That's the shitty truth, really. For a guy, if he wants to do anything besides, well, *it*, then that means something." Then I wanted to barf. Because: *God, I love you so much.*

"Thanks for saying that, Sean, but don't worry about trying to make it nicer than it is," she said. "I'm okay with the reality."

I turned on the radio, then. I couldn't talk. I couldn't listen.

I couldn't say all the things in my head. And I was trying not to speed or plow off the road right now. Trying to think about nothing, all the way back to town.

"Is anyone home at your house?" I asked.

"My sisters, probably. I don't know about my mom. Do you want to come over?"

●

We went to her house, and it was like any other time we'd hung out, Neecie's house all white and bright and colorful. The giant old washtub full of hats and mittens in the front entryway, the mat full of smooth stones where Neecie set her boots. Neecie's house was definitely a Shoes Off house. You could tell by how it smelled—like strawberries and cake or something.

In the TV room, Jessamyn was packing a duffel bag, and in the kitchen, Melanie was wrapping up plates of cookies.

"Where's Mom?" Neecie asked.

"With Gary. They're at some deal for his work."

"Is it going to be late?"

"I don't know, she told Jessamyn, not me. I was in the shower."

"I thought you had a thing over at the Dobranaks'?"

"We do; we're just packing. Jess didn't want to go at first. But then I called Tasha and she said Gwen wasn't coming and so then . . ."

Neecie nodded, and I could tell she didn't want to hear more, but she stood there, listening to this big long pointless story, being all nice about it. She was way nicer to her sisters than me and Brad were to each other.

Finally, Melanie stopped talking, and she and Jessamyn put their coats on, started collecting up their bags and stuff. Neecie got a giant can of iced tea—peach—from the refrigerator and yawned, asked me if I wanted anything to drink. I said no, and then she asked if I'd drive her sisters down the block, because they looked like sherpas with all their shit.

In my car, Jessamyn asked me if I liked Neecie.

"Yeah," I said.

"But as friends, right?" Melanie interrupted. "You don't *like*-like her, do you?"

"Jesus," I said. "We're friends."

"Who's the guy with the red truck, then? Is that her real boyfriend?" Melanie said, very suspicious.

"We saw him come get her tonight," Jessamyn said.

"It's right here, on the left!" Melanie yelled, pointing, and I hit the brakes.

"Wow, you're kind of a bad driver," Melanie said. "So who was that? In the red truck?"

"You have to tell us, Sean," Jessamyn said.

"I don't know anything about anyone," I said. "Seriously."

"Well, you need to find out," Melanie said. "It's weird."

"Neecie's weird in general," Jessamyn said.

"No, she's not," Melanie said. "Move your stuff, Jess, god!"

When I got back to the Albertsons', Neecie was nowhere to be seen. I took off my shoes, went to look for her. Into the living room, with the old-fashioned stereo with big foamy speakers and a record player, all stuff Kerry would have bitched about getting at the donation door. Two couches in a bright flaming orange. A giant piano with a tower of books on top of it (Nancy Drew and the Hardy Boys, which we always sold at the Thrift Bin in dusty boxes by the lot) and a plant that looked like a bunch of green beads dribbling down the side of the pot. Which wasn't a pot but an old ceramic milk bottle. I mean, it looked like Neecie's job working at the Thrift Bin was all according to the plan of whoever decorated this house. Still, it was a nice house. Like, intentionally nice. Like someone gave a damn. Someone who said, "Let's have a milk bottle with a plant in it! And not just any old plant. Something weird that looks like it's from Mars or the Amazon or whatever!" I liked it, though. I liked Neecie's house. It was a good place to be.

I found Neecie in her room. She was flopped on the bed, which wasn't made, and the floor was covered in clothes and books and crap. She was sometimes messy, sometimes clean; either way it was nice. She told me to toss the crap off the chair in the corner, which was all gooshy and pink and covered in clothes. She seemed her Home Self, all comfortable, asking if her sisters got to the party okay and thanking me for doing that.

"And thanks for picking me up," she said. "I mean it. I really like that we're friends, Sean."

"Sure. Okay. I mean, no big deal."

"Ivy thinks that guys and girls can't ever be friends, but I feel like she's just pissy that I spend time with you and not her. I don't think she gets it, how we're not like that. We're normal. We're really friends. There's no weird sex thing, you know?"

"Right."

"God, I'm so glad to be out of there."

"Was it . . . bad? The whole . . . thing?"

She rolled to her side, looked at me.

"No," she said. "I was the only one sober, though."

I wanted to know what they did so bad I wanted to rip the strings out of my hoodie. Which I was gripping and picking at like a psycho. But I didn't talk about sex details like that with Eddie even. That was need-to-know information, if you were having sex or not. And then, it was only if you'd done it, not all the details. The only guys who talked about sex in long gross detail were generally total douchebag liars.

"It was terrible," Neecie said. "Like, he expected us to know what to do. Like Ivy and me should have studied up on the same porn he's been watching or something. I figured Ivy might bail, say something, but she was just looking at him and not me and then he just kind of started things and it was so uncomfortable and stupid. I couldn't stand it. I'm telling you, it was totally unsexy, Sean! So I just kind of left. We were in the bathroom and someone was banging on the door, anyway. I kind of hate him for the whole thing. Hate me, too, for even going along with it, you know?"

"Whoa," I said.

She flopped on her back, turned on the nightstand light. "Will you turn off the overhead light, Sean? My eyes are killing me. It's just so bright."

I got up, flipped off the light. Sat back down. Tried not to imagine Neecie with Tristan and Ivy in a bathroom.

"I think I should just stop it," she said. "I've never thought I should before. But I think I should. It makes me crazy. It makes me feel so bad."

I nodded. This was twice she'd said that—*It makes me feel so bad*—and I couldn't stand it. It made me feel so bad, too. For her. For myself. For the world, where nobody normally said things like that out loud. Not without losing it or breaking down.

I wondered if she'd ever lost it or broke down in front of Tristan.

She wasn't going to lose it or break down now, though, thank god. She just looked tired, lying there on her bed, with her legs in the air, tugging off her socks.

I wondered if she put her legs in the air when she fucked Tristan.

Hallie never did that.

God, The Horn. It was a good thing no one could see into my mind.

She sat up, stretched. Opened a drawer in her dresser, pulled out a little bottle of nail polish.

"I'm gonna paint my toes. Want me to do yours?"

# Chapter Eleven

If I had to map it out, when it was, it was probably then, that night when she made it clear that we were just nonsexual friends. That night she painted my toenails. She painted them blue— "to match your car," she said, laughing—and she was grossed out by my toenails and the hair on my feet and that was when it was, when I knew it wasn't just friends with us, that I'd crossed over without her, somehow.

Because, The Horn.

Because I felt embarrassed by her looking at my feet and touching them and touching me in general.

Because now she was cute to me in a way I wanted to hog all to myself and not let anyone else have, because she smelled really good, kind of like cake, and something else, like the candles they kept in the bathroom and her hair was all shiny and long and she moved around in this completely unaware way, in a way I don't think she saw at all, or anyone else did, maybe not even Tristan, but I could see it now, her little boobs denting out the top of her shirt, the straps of her bra were yellow and sticking out the neck of her T-shirt, and her body, too, I could see how she had a little curve going there, and how it might feel, my holding onto her hips and ass, how you did when you were fucking, which made me wonder if she shaved down there too and if it was blond or darker or what, and did he go down on her, Tristan? Did he make her come? Did he know how to do that, or was it just silent between them, and he just got off, alone? Or could she get off *with* him? Because he was so hot or because the whole thing was all secretive? Or maybe she told him how to get her off? Because maybe Neecie knew how to get herself off? And wasn't afraid to say it to him, to show him? She wasn't afraid to go in sex stores or try a threesome, after all. Or say how things made her feel so bad.

You'd think that it would have been a good thing, us alone, with no parents, on New Year's Eve, in her bedroom. Privacy. But I was so panicked, I almost left. I felt like a dope, maybe it was the nail polish fumes, maybe it was just the niceness of the whole thing, the naïve way Neecie was acting, like I didn't have The Horn or any shitty suspicious motives. Like this was just another cookie-dough-in-the-basement situation. Less than that, even.

I just needed to get through this dumb year of school and ship out to boot camp and be done with it—*I am leaving and never coming back*—maybe I needed to be done with it too, where Hallie was concerned. But thinking of Hallie and The Horn and all of it just seemed impossible. I couldn't say no to Hallie. But I couldn't tell Neecie that. So, then, when I should have left or said anything else, probably, I just asked her if she wanted to smoke some weed.

"I've never done it," she said.

"Really?"

"Sorry," she said, her neck and face getting all red. She took a handful of her hair and shook it behind her back, like it was bothering her. Like it was alive or something. I tried to not be fascinated by that. I really did. But I was staring, and she assumed I was judging her about the pot.

"I'm not that cool, I guess," she added.

"It's not a big deal. It's just an idea."

She looked at her fingernails for a minute, which were freshly painted this weird yellowish color that reminded me of the spray paint Kerry used to mark the parking lot lines at the Thrift Bin.

"Will you do it too?"

"If you want, I won't. In case you freak out."

She looked a little panicked.

"But the stuff I have, it's nice," I said, real quick. About this I wasn't lying. This wasn't Kerry pot; it was some stuff Eddie got from his sister's boyfriend. "It's mellow. It'll make you laugh. You'll laugh about weird stuff."

"Okay, let's do it," she said. She got up then and started brushing her hair. Neecie was always brushing her hair, too. It sounded weird, but her hair was just this long blond sheet all the time, but she never really did anything with it, so it didn't seem overly vain, her brushing it constantly. She even kept a hairbrush in her purse. But I didn't want to watch her do it now; now it seemed like something different than before.

"You've got me kind of concerned. You know how I'm all

uptight and tense sometimes."

"You'll be fine."

"What if I lose my mind and you have to take me to the emergency room?"

"That's not going to happen."

"It happened to this girl Ivy's cousin knows. Her parents found out and it sucked."

"That's not gonna happen to you," I said. "I promise."

She kept brushing her hair, so I went out to my car and got the weed, and when I came back in, Neecie was standing in the hallway.

"I put a pizza in the oven," she said. "For eating, like you said. Where do you want to do this?" That made me laugh, how prepared she was being. Like getting high was a quiz and she was going to bust out the flashcards any second now.

"Somewhere with a window we can crack," I said.

"The bathroom?"

"Sure," I said.

We went into the DREAM bathroom. Neecie opened the window and the cold started streaming in. While I was getting my one-hitter ready, she sat down on the wicker chair beneath the window. I always thought having a chair in the bathroom was weird. I mean, if you're going to sit down in a bathroom, isn't the toilet the main place? Who wants to, you know, *lounge around* in a damn bathroom?

"Okay, so have you ever smoked a cigarette?" I asked.

"Yeah."

"This is kind of like that. Suck in the smoke, but don't exhale it right away. Just hold it. Maybe try to swallow, even. Then, when I tell you, exhale it out the window."

"You should turn on the fan," she said.

"I will, but I want to make sure you hear what I'm saying." Background noise was always a bitch for Neecie.

She smiled at me, patted my hand. "You're so nice. You're my marijuana doula."

"What?"

"Doula," she said. "Assistant. The lady who stands by you while you're giving birth. Ices your head and massages you and tells you what's coming next. My mom had one with Melanie."

"Okay," I said, trying to not focus too much on that comparison. Neecie said things like that all the time, though.

I handed her the one-hitter, then lit it.

"Inhale," I said and she did, her eyes going big. "Keep it in," I said.

She did, sucking her cheeks in, her mouth a perfect little O like in a lipstick ad.

"Okay, okay: hold it. Hold it! Now, exhale!"

She turned and shot the smoke out the little window, just like I'd said, and then I whipped on the fan.

"Good job," I said, looking straight at her. She smiled.

"It tastes terrible," she said. "Like burnt alligator skin."

"How would you know what burnt alligator skin tastes like?"

"I don't know," she said, her lips curling in a grossed-out way. "That's the first thing that went through my mind. Do I do it again?"

"Yeah, but wait a second," I said. "You want some water or anything?"

"No, I'm good. Let's go again," she said, all business.

She ended up doing two more hits, and then I told her to stop.

She slid down in her chair, making the wicker squeak, and stared at toilet paper roll for a minute. The old thousand-yard stare.

"You okay?" I said.

"I don't know," she said. "Everything's kind of . . . slow. But it kind of feels like nothing."

"Yeah," I said.

"Maybe I should do more?"

"Just wait."

We went back to the kitchen, and I took out the pizza, which had sort of burned, but given that I am a human garbage disposal, I didn't care. Neecie didn't want any pizza; she just drank a giant iced tea (mango). She seemed the same, except less chatty. Not that "chatty" was how I'd normally describe her, but she definitely seemed more deliberate. Slow.

"How you feel?"

"Good," she said. "Kind of lotion-y."

"What?"

"Liquid-y," she said. "But, like, a *slow* liquid. Like lotion. Toothpaste-like. Is that normal?"

"Yeah," I said, though I'd never felt lotion-y or toothpaste-like while high. I laughed.

"What's so funny?"

"You are," I said. "Let's go listen to music in the piano room."

"Why?"

"I think you'll like it."

"Okay."

The piano room at the Albertsons' was small and mostly taken up with a shiny black upright piano that I always wanted to touch but never did, thinking my greasy paws would fuck it up.

Neecie sat at the piano, played a chord that sounded pretty choppy.

"You know how to play piano?"

"Yeah. But I quit lessons a long time ago. Only Jessamyn takes them still."

"You should play something."

"No way. I feel mentally retarded," she said, getting up from the piano. "I mean that literally. Not in the dickish way. I feel *so slow*. Actually *delayed*. Like my words are taking forever to reach you, through space. Like, I could grab them after they travel out of my mouth and take them back. I couldn't play anything. Aren't you going to put on some music?"

Mrs. Albertson had a ton of music. Dance stuff, which Neecie said she used for teaching fitness classes at the Y—Mrs. Albertson was kind of a health fiend—plus a bunch of old records. Classic rock, hippie stuff, disco, a mix of everything. I found a mix CD that Jessamyn had made called "Waiting Music" and put that on.

We sat down next to each other on the floor as the music started.

"What is this? Is this one of Jessamyn's?"

"Yeah."

"She makes good mixes," she said. "Jessamyn's always so secretive and sad about things. You never know what she thinks."

Kind of like her older sister, I thought. Older cousin. Whatever.

She sighed and rested her head on my shoulder. My whole body tensed up.

"I feel kind of syrup-y, now," she said. "Even slower."

"Yeah," I said. Still tense. My hands around my knees in a panicky grip.

"Is that how I should feel?"

"Sure," I said.

Her head moved the other direction then, and I breathed out in relief.

"I feel like I could fall asleep," she said. "Why don't I have the munchies?"

"I don't know," I said. "You don't *have* to have them. It's probably better you don't, actually. It kind of destroys your high a little."

"Makes you feel shitty?"

"No, just dilutes it. Makes it go away sooner."

"Oh."

She laid back on the carpet, then, which I approved of, as that meant no more head-on-the-shoulderness. But then she dumped her bare feet into my lap, bright yellow toenails and all. I told The Horn I would kick its ass if it didn't stop it already.

"Did you want to be a pianist when you were little?" I asked.

"What? A penis?"

"No," I said, pointing at the piano, turning so she could see my mouth. "A pianist. Piano player."

She laughed, then, and I knew it was good, her being high, because she couldn't tell I was tense. That I'd turned The Horn on her and was thinking all kinds of shit that I shouldn't be thinking. She was high and it was okay, she was oblivious, she couldn't stop laughing. Laughing like birds flying over us, tumbling around the whole room. Which made me start laughing, too. Then we were laughing at each other for laughing. Which is the kind of thing that happens when you're high, really, except I was sober as hell. Fucking weird.

"No. I didn't want to be a pianist," she said, finally, when we stopped laughing. "Or a penis."

"God, you're fucked up."

She laughed. "I'm not into music like Jessamyn is. I like it, but I'm more into other things. I like science. I like writing. I like reading. I don't know. Maybe I'm just going to be one of those academic people. A professor, maybe. That's what my mom always says."

"So, is that your future? Is that what you're gonna do in college and everything?"

"Who knows? It's not worth discussing. Can you even hear me? I feel like the words are so slow, traveling to you . . ." I shook my head, told her it was fine.

"I get kind of blank when I think about the future," she said. "There are so many things, you know? How do I know what to pick, when I haven't seen any of the things out there?"

That sounded suspiciously like Hallie's breakup talk.

"Whatever," I said. "You're going to college. You've already picked that. That's one thing, at least."

"I guess. But really, college is like my ship out," she said. "I'm going to just get on it and see what happens after that. It's just the vehicle. To find out what I really like to do. I can't get really specific. Especially now; I'm all lotion-y, you know. My words are even like lotion. Or pizza cheese. Stringy. Like spiderwebs. Weird . . ."

I laughed. I didn't want to, even though she sounded completely wasted and crazy. I knew what she meant, I guess. I'd never heard anyone describe getting high like that, actually. But I could see it.

"Plus I like a lot of things," she said. "But a lot of them I just know about in books, you know?"

"Not really."

"Because you don't read."

"I do, too. I read school stuff."

"That's different," she said. "That's being forced. What are you really *doing*, Sean? Doing on purpose? Doing on your own?"

"I'm doing the Marines," I said.

"Oh, whatever. You are not."

"I am too," I said. "I signed everything."

"Shut. Up."

"I'm serious."

"When?"

"On my birthday. Back in November."

She sat up, slowly. Like a submarine rising out of the water, cautious, and it would have been funny, but I didn't laugh. Because it all came gushing out of me, the whole story.

"I signed the papers, I gave them all my documents," I said. "I have to take this test, the ASVAB? It's for deciding where to place me, jobs-wise. I should get my boot camp assignment this summer probably. It's happening."

She was staring at me, but I didn't care: telling had felt so good! The words had been the opposite of slow, like Neecie thought her words were. Like I was trying to prove a point about it.

She crossed her legs beneath her, pretzel-style, like in kindergarten. Raked her hair out of her face, tucked it behind her ears a million times.

"Sean, my god," she said. "I can't even. I mean . . . So, you're going to, like, go to war?"

"Jesus," I said. "That's not the only thing. There's a lot of other . . ."

"And jobs?" she said. "That sounds super weird. Like, it's not a *job*, really. Not how I think of it . . ."

"There's many forms of service," I interrupted, repeating line for line how Sergeant Kendall had explained it to me. "Communications, logistics, psy ops, supply chain, IT, mechanical. So it's not just infantry, you know."

"Infantry?"

"That's what you're thinking of," I said. "Being in a tank, a foxhole. Front-lines stuff."

She laid back down. Her hair covered her face. When she talked again, it was like the words were being sent to the ceiling.

"You are very brave, Sean. I couldn't do that. I hate making my bed. And I can't do one single push-up."

"I bet you could do *one* push-up. Look at you. You probably weigh like a hundred pounds! That's barely anything to lift up!"

"I weigh more than a hundred pounds, idiot. I'm like one forty-five. And don't look at me like that's a lot. Nobody weighs a hundred pounds unless they're sick or something, Jesus. And plus, men have bigger things. You know?"

"Things, huh? What things, exactly?" I was smiling like crazy. "I, personally, have so many *things* on me."

"You know what I mean." She motioned to her own shoulders. "You know. Muscles."

I laughed. "Come on, do it, it's easy."

"No."

"Yes," I said, lying beside her. "Roll onto your tummy."

"Tummy!" she said. "You just said 'tummy'!"

"So?"

"Do they call it that in the Marines?" She laughed.

"Oh, shut up," I said. I felt that bossy thing again, like I wasn't gonna fool around. "Now listen to me. Put your arms like this. No, ninety-degree angle . . . No, you're gonna do it the boy way. Not on your knees, that's the girl way in Phy Ed. Use your toes."

"I *am* a girl, you know," she said. "Don't girl Marines get to do it the girl way?"

"All Marines do it the boy way," I said, though I didn't honestly know.

"Now, just pretend you want to lower your body to the floor, like you're pressing something down with your belly," I said.

"With my tummy, you mean."

"Jesus! Yes, fine. Press it down with your tummy."

"You sound like the biggest dork when you say 'tummy,'" she said. "Boys should not ever say the word 'tummy.' Or the word 'panties' either. There should be a law."

"Whatever. Just do it."

She lowered herself down, and I could see a little of her bra through the armhole of her T-shirt. Part of her boob, too. God.

She did one push-up, then another, then one more. Then she collapsed on the carpet.

"See?" I said. "You could totally do it."

"How many can you do?"

"I'm up to fifty," I said, trying to sound low-key and not braggy.

"Jesus," she said. "You have to do that to just get into the Marines?"

"Not specifically push-ups. Pull-ups and crunches. And running. And that's just to prepare for boot camp."

"Are you running now?"

"Not yet. I need new shoes."

"Why?"

"Mine suck."

"But you'll have to run in combat boots, anyway, stupid," she said.

"How do you know?"

"Come on, Sean! Haven't you ever seen a movie in your whole life?"

I rolled my eyes. But I knew I'd have to ask Sergeant Kendall. Because, really, that could save me a big hunk of money, not buying new running shoes.

"You should join track," she said. "Melanie does track. I think that would be funny. You'd get to wear those gross cutaway short shorts. And those man tank tops and stuff. I bet you'd look just *fabulous*." Then she laughed at her own joke for a long time. Another hazard of smoking pot I should have warned her about.

But I laughed too, and then we just laid there some more, the music changing into some trance-y stuff. Both of us and our secrets. Kind of. Her with her secret sex-ninja life; me with the Marines. Maybe I was being stupid, with the Marines: it crossed my mind a couple times since signing everything. But mostly I'd been thinking, yeah, the Marines was a good thing. Which was what I focused on, lying on the piano room floor with Neecie.

A little while later, Neecie decided to eat some of Melanie's Christmas cookies, and I watched her devour them. I'd never seen her devour anything before. It was pretty worth it, all the non-high babysitting, because she was like Cookie Monster, at least the way Cookie Monster was before they made Cookie Monster only eat carrots. She had crumbs on her boobs, eyes closed, saying how much she liked them, how awesome they were, until I told her why didn't she just marry her cookies if she loved them so much, and she laughed and laughed and swatted at me, and I laughed, and she kept eating, crumbs all around her mouth.

Then she said she wanted to watch some TV, and she laid on the sofa, and I sat on the floor, her hands brushing my hair a little, telling me I was her pet and did I use this one kind of conditioner, which Melanie used, which didn't have some chemical in it? Because my hair was so soft, like a girl's.

"I can't stop touching it," she said, her fingers chopping around the back of my neck, all awkward and grabby, which freaked me out and made The Horn get all excited again.

But luckily, then she stopped petting my hair and fell asleep. Way before midnight. And I was glad, because I didn't want to be there when her mom and Gary came home. Didn't want to keep liking hearing her breathe. Didn't want to keep liking her, either.

I stood up, nudged her arm a little. "Neecie, I'm going home, okay?"

She opened her eyes, looked up at me in the half-dark of the TV.

"What?"

"You okay without me?"

She yawned. "Yeah. I think so. I think I'm just going to go to bed," Neecie said.

"Okay."

She followed me to the door, watched me put on my shoes and jacket. I was about to open the door when she crossed her arms over her chest—her little boobs popping forward—and then she said, "I'm gonna do it, Sean. If you can go in the Marines and run in combat boots and wear those cutaway track shorts, then I can do it, too. No more Tristan. New Year's resolution. You'll hold me to it, right?"

"Sure," I said.

"Good," she said, then stepped toward me and kissed me on the cheek. Her mouth was soft, smooth. Like all the other girls' mouths I'd ever kissed. Like Hallie's mouth. Was my mouth like that?

"Thank you," she added.

"Yep," I said, trying to keep cool. The Horn was all freaked out, of course.

I drove home, trying to be steady. It was only after I'd talked to Steven-Not-Steve and my mom in the living room, who were watching the ball drop while they tied up little ribbons to some crazy thing that had to be for Brad and Krista's wedding and drank wine and ate crackers and cheese and whatever other crap Steven-Not-Steve thought made good snack foods, after me and Otis toppled into bed, that I saw Hallie had texted me. I had left my phone in my jacket pocket all night.

I did some push-ups. I looked at the phone. I thought of Neecie, all lotion-y, petting my hair.

And then I wondered, how it would work, to be done with Hallie too? I laid there for a long time, thinking of how to tell her.

# Chapter Twelve

Brad's not the sharpest tool in the shed. I know I'm smarter than Brad—I know it—and not just because of grades. It's like Brad never thinks or something. He just goes around and DOES things and that's it. He's very simple. But Brad was always golden, always good, always doing the right thing, even if the right thing was something dipshitty like getting his truck stuck in the mudflats or getting in trouble for fighting at Homecoming or something idiotic like that. But with me, the one who didn't get caught, the one who didn't usually fuck up, my mom was always sighing. And my dad? I don't know what he was doing. He would ride Brad's ass a lot, but that was because he was older and more into the kind of sports my dad liked: football, baseball. By the time it was my turn for that stuff, my dad was too fucked up to notice.

I was trying to tell Neecie this, not in those words, really, but trying to explain all the shit in my head, in order for her to get it, why we were up at the crack of dawn on a Saturday morning in early February, but she just sat in the passenger seat of my car, holding her coffee and sausage biscuit on her lap. Neither of us had to work for once, and I'd picked her up at her house and got her McDonald's for breakfast ("My mom thinks McDonald's is the devil!") while I explained what I wanted to do.

"Why do you have to do this now? It's freezing cold!"

"I've got to be able to hack it in boot camp," I said. I'd said that so many times, I was sick of hearing myself saying it. Then I told her about the timing, the whole thing. I was looking her right in the face and everything, too, but Neecie wasn't very athletic; she seemed to think I was being excessive, that I was out of my mind. It bugged me having to explain, but she was the only one who knew what I'd done, so there was no one else who could help me.

"Okay, so where do I meet you?"

"Just drive to that little shitty road behind the school and then go three more blocks to that park. That's four miles."

"I thought you needed to do just one mile."

"A mile and a half. But this is for general conditioning and stuff. I can't just do the minimum and think that's enough. You run every day in boot camp."

"How do you know?" she asked. "Did you actually ask your recruiter guy what happens in boot camp?"

Of course I hadn't. I hadn't even watched the videos of how to do correct pull-ups. I was just assuming, but I didn't want her to know that.

"Yes," I said, then put my hat on and my earbuds in so we

could be done talking.

"You shouldn't wear those kind of earbuds," she said.

"Why?"

"At elevated volumes, they're bad for your ears."

"Oh, really?" I asked, sarcastic. "Is that how you got the way you are?"

"Shut up," she said. "I was born with this shitty problem."

"It's not shitty," I said. "People have to look at you if they want to lie to you. That's really genius. Plus, anything you don't want to hear, you can just ignore it."

Neecie bit into her sausage biscuit. The smallest bite, Jesus. I could eat one of those things in two bites. She looked really tired, though, and I felt instantly shitty about how good she was being about this. It wasn't even seven a.m., and while she'd agreed to this, I hadn't realized maybe she had other things to do. Like be asleep for a couple more hours.

"Go," she said. "Let's get this over with."

"You're not even the one running!" I said, handing her the keys and turning on my music. "I'll see you in a little while!"

Maybe some people think about really great things while they're running. Like maybe they come up with new inventions or whatever. Solve math problems. Meditate on the nature of the universe. Or maybe even cook up excuses or lies, elaborate stories for why they needed to dump their girlfriend or quit their job or whatever the hell.

But I'd found, since I'd been running for a few weeks, that after the first few hellish minutes, during which my body basically screamed at me internally to JUST STOP STOP STOP WHAT ARE YOU DOING STOP FOR FUCK'S SAKE, I thought of pretty much nothing. I just saw things. Noted them.

Like, "Burger King." Or "patch of ice." Or "Shitty house that looks like the rental."

So, after the last mile, when I saw Neecie sitting in my car, and I had to walk to cool down, and she popped out to accompany me, sipping her coffee and asking me how was it, I really had nothing to say, unless I wanted to say "Burger King. Patch of ice. Shitty house." Also, I was coughing a little and spitting, which I couldn't help, but if Neecie thought that was gross she didn't show it. She just sipped her coffee, and we walked around the little park where I'd mapped out the finish line until I got back to normal.

"You know, I want to be able to hear it though," she said.

"What?"

"What you said, before you left? About not having to hear shit? I don't like that. I *want* to hear what people are saying. Know what's going on. I mean, I don't want to have to talk back, always. Or have a long discussion about stuff. But I want to have the chance. To at least know what's being said."

"Oh."

"I was just thinking about it, that's all."

"Okay."

I was trying not to be all huffy and puffy with my breath, but it was colder now than when I'd started running. Or maybe *I* was just cold now that I'd stopped running. I didn't even have a coat on, just windpants and a hoodie and a couple of old thermals.

"I didn't mean . . . I was just saying, you know, like . . . Never mind."

"I know what you're saying," I said. "I get it." We looked at each other for a long time, and then she nodded.

"Are you cooled down enough now? How much longer can that take? It's freezing out here."

Back to the car, she said, "Can I drive again? I really like your car. It's super dreamy and smooth. Like butter."

I said I didn't care; I was tired and cold. Could feel my sweat rolling, cold, on my skin. Neecie drove to my house because I needed a shower pretty bad, and we didn't talk at all because she had the radio on and had to face the road, anyway, and it was weird, being the passenger in my car, with her driving. It could have been that we'd been married a million years. Or that we didn't know each other, either, like I was some sweaty, red-faced hitchhiker she'd picked up out of the goodness of her heart. Or some other third thing, where it could have been awkward, but wasn't because, well, it just wasn't. The song on the radio was Springsteen's "I'm On Fire," and it was old as fuck and Neecie wasn't singing along or anything but I could tell she liked it from how she had this little twisty smile on her face and her fingers tapped the blue leather of the steering wheel and she just seemed awake now, happy, just happy, and then I realized it, what I was thinking, and it was that it was like she was my girl-friend, that was the third comfortable feeling, as if Neecie was the girl I was *with*, like, *together*-with, the girl I liked, or maybe even would love soon enough, because we weren't far from it, and that was how it was when you were in the car together, and when you let someone drive your car for you, and when you knew they'd be there, four miles down the road, after you'd finished running on a 22-degree day in February, the month that has Valentine's Day, which hadn't happened yet, but was coming up next week, we'd been hearing about it on the morning announcements at school every morning, about the stupid carnation sales in the cafeteria at lunch, how you could send one to someone with a message for a dollar, secretly, even, and how goddamn annoying that was to me, had always been, both because I hated how girls would get all squeally about getting flowers, and because I never ever had the nuts to send any to anyone, even anonymously, even girls I really liked, and maybe that was why I'd gotten so mad last year and broken Eddie's nose, though I knew it wasn't the whole reason, which was my dad and all that shit no one would ever know and I was fine with that.

Neecie stopped at a light. Turned to me.

"Tristan's been texting me," she said.

"What else is new?"

"So. I texted him back. Twice. Both times were to tell him to stop it, though. So that shouldn't count, right?"

"Right."

The light turned green, and Neecie turned onto the highway, guiding the steering wheel through her hands, driving slower and more safely than I ever did. She was precise when she drove. Precise and certain about Tristan, too. She was done with him. She had made up her mind, she said. She told me when he texted; she even showed me the texts he'd sent at first. She was honest.

But I was still being a shithead. I'd gone over to Hallie's the night before.

And it had been bad. Because it was bad with Hallie now. Hallie, who'd not gone back to college. Hallie, who was having some kind of mental breakdown and looked like she was dying and never wore anything but pajamas now, who cried the last couple times after we had sex, and who told me all this shit about why she hated her life and college and couldn't go back and didn't want to stay here, either. Hallie, who didn't make me use condoms anymore, since that time I'd smashed the used one into the dryer sheet in her hand, and who said she was still on the pill, so that was good enough.

Sex without a condom? Like I was going to put up a fight about *that*.

When Neecie pulled up the gravel drive, my mom's car was still there.

"Shit," I said.

"What?"

"I just thought my mom'd be gone by now."

Neecie went into my house first, petting Otis, saying hello to my mom, who was in the kitchen filling the dishwasher. Neecie liked my mom. She liked our house too. And Otis. There wasn't much she didn't like about my life. I felt like she wasn't getting something. Like, if she really understood everything, she'd stop petting my dog, who licked his own asshole twenty times before breakfast, and stop talking to my mom, who always gave a little sigh whenever she saw me. She'd not fall into a chair at the kitchen table and start fiddling with Krista's piles of ribbon that were going to become something unspeakable romantic for the goddamn wedding.

Neecie and my mom started chit-chatting, my mom offering tea—my mom being very big on tea, the more stanky and herbal, the better—and by the time the explanations about the ribbon on the table came up, I had slipped downstairs to shower and get dressed and figure out a quick exit. I didn't like being alone with my mom lately. I didn't want to tell her about the Marines thing yet, but it was so close to my mind, my mouth, I was worried it'd just spill out. I wanted to wait until my dad was back. When I got my boot camp assignment, at least. When everything was solid. No debate. Just, I am leaving, and here's where I'm going, and that was it. The never coming back part I'd leave out.

But just as I was putting my shoes back on, my mom asked if she could talk to me for a minute, alone.

"I'll be in the car," Neecie said, her face getting all red like it did when she was nervous or uncomfortable.

"What's going on?" I said, trying to be all unconcerned.

"Two things," my mom said. "First, your dad called. He'd like you to call him."

"Okay. Why didn't he just call my cell?"

"He didn't have the number; they didn't allow him his cell phone at the place he was, so I just canceled it, anyhow."

"Oh."

"Second, all the papers for the divorce came yesterday. I signed them and sent them back."

"Okay," I said. Not really getting why she was telling me. I knew that she'd filed; I'd wished for it long enough, and I'd seen the papers after the shit with my dad finally forced the issue. Last year at this time, in fact. Perfect timing.

She kept looking at me, as if she was checking for signs of distress or drug use or something else I was hiding. Which just pissed me off.

"What? Why are you staring at me?"

She shook her head. "No reason. I guess I expected a different reaction to that news."

"Well, I'm glad," I said. "It's good news. And he's not my husband, he's yours, so what do I care, exactly?"

"Come on, Sean," she said. "He's still your father."

"Barely," I said, putting on my coat.

"Don't be like that," she said. "Brad doesn't see it like that."

"I'm not Brad."

"I know that . . ."

"And what does he want me to call him for?"

"Well, you know, the divorce stuff, for one thing."

"Which I don't care about."

"And he just wanted to talk to you, in general, I think." She handed me a piece of paper with his number on it.

"Can he get calls there? Or is it a pay phone like the other places?"

"It's his new cell," she said. "He's out of the halfway house now. He's living in a kind of group space. A kind of recovery community, too, but not like the halfway house. Well, he can tell you all this himself. Just call him."

"You, like, talk to him now? Why would you *talk* to him? You're *divorced*, Mom. You don't have to talk to him at all."

"Sean . . ."

"And neither do I, you know," I said, opening the door. "I'm eighteen. There's no visitation, no custody."

She looked at me like I was a total piece of shit then. Like I'd done something bad by admitting I was grown and not a minor.

"I knew you'd be touchy this time of year," she said. "Anniversaries are hard."

"I don't know why you're making this such a big deal; you even have a boyfriend now."

"Steven is not my boyfriend. We're just friends."

"Whatever. I don't care, either way."

"Will you please just call him? Just once? I think he has some things he'd like to say to you."

I could have argued. I wanted to. But I didn't want her getting more therapeutic and didn't want her giving me that shitty look again. So I said yes and tried not to run out the door, where Neecie was waiting for me in the passenger seat.

"Is everything okay? Where do you want to go?"

"Anywhere you say," I said.

⬤

We went to the gas station. Neecie bought a giant can of iced tea and some Sour Patch Kids; I bought corn nuts and nachos and donuts because I was hungrier than shit. Then Mrs. Albertson texted Neecie and said we had to pick up Jessamyn, so we picked her up from someone's house and then dumped her off at someone else's house. We went to the bookstore, where she bought a bunch of books and crap. We stopped at the YMCA to look up the indoor track hours. Eddie had scored some free passes for me; I figured running indoors might be better than going in the subzero. Then we went to the Thrift Bin so Neecie could buy some junk she'd put aside in the donation room and somehow, from me looking through racks of old T-shirts, Neecie talked me into buying some jeans, making shit out of the ones I was wearing being so crappy and old.

"As if *these* jeans aren't old, either," I said, coming out of the dressing room in a pair of Levis she'd found for me. She'd insisted I try them on and show her, like she was my mom. They were okay jeans, but they had a stupid button fly. I hate button flies.

"Levis are well-made denim. They'll last you forever. Unless you get fat."

"Fat? Who just ran four miles, huh?"

"I'm not accusing you of fatness. Just stating facts."

"I don't need a lot of clothes, you know. They'll be giving me a uniform. You can't bring a ton of stuff to boot camp."

"You can't bring *any* stuff to boot camp," she said. "Nothing. Didn't your guy tell you that?"

Your guy = Sergeant Kendall.

"Well, yeah, but . . ."

"Nothing," she repeated. "You don't get your own stuff back until you complete boot camp. I've been reading all about it."

"Where? What have you been reading?"

"Just the stuff online, military websites. It's all there. You didn't read any of that before you signed everything?"

I shrugged.

She rolled her eyes. "Those look good on you," she said. "I'll even buy them for you. A going-away present."

"Big spender. All of $5.99."

"Don't forget my employee discount."

Neecie bought the jeans, so I bought her another can of iced tea (pomengranate) when we stopped at another gas station so I could get some gas. We'd picked up our checks at the Thrift Bin, too, and I'd deposited mine at the ATM outside the gas station. I kind of had to do things like that the second I got paid, otherwise I'd spend everything and end up on an empty tank. I was kind of a dope about money.

"Where now?" I asked.

"Just take me home, I guess," she said, yawning. "I totally

want to take a nap."

"Okay," I said. Not wanting her to know how bummed out I was. I mean, I was tired, too, but I didn't feel like being alone. Or going home either.

I drove toward Neecie's, a little slower than normally. Not that she noticed. She just sort of lolled around in the passenger seat, talking about dumb little things.

"This is why I like being friends with you," she said, out of nowhere.

"What?"

"Just, that you don't take it all personal if I want to be alone," she said. "And you don't care if we do dumb little things. You know?"

"Right."

We drove in silence for a few more minutes.

"I can't believe you're doing that Marines thing," she said, out of nowhere. "God. That's gonna be weird. I'm totally gonna miss this. Who will get your car? It's not like you can drive it to boot camp."

"What?"

"Well, you can't. You get flown or bused to boot camp. Depending on where you are in the United States. West of the Mississippi, you go to California for training. East, and you to Parris Island. That's where you'll go. Parris Island, that's where they go in *Full Metal Jacket*, you know?"

"What?"

"You know? That movie, with the drill sergeant screaming about how he's gonna skullfuck the recruits and stuff? That guy who does all the shows about guns on the History Channel? It's a famous movie. Stanley Kubrick directed it."

Skullfuck? "No idea what you're even talking about."

"Wow, I can't believe you haven't seen that. Like, every guy has seen that. Tristan quotes from it all the time."

I shrugged. Because, fuck Tristan. "Fuck Tristan."

She stopped talking, then. Stared straight forward. I didn't know if she was pissed off. Or had been seeing him again.

"What?" I said, after I parked in front of her house. "Is it surprising I don't like the guy?"

"No."

"Well, what, then? Did you want to see him again or something?"

"Do you still see Hallie?"

It caught me, I had to admit. I was quiet.

"Fuck you!" she said, pushing at my shoulder. "You're still doing it with her, aren't you?"

"Did you do it with Tristan?"

"No," she said. "No, but . . ."

"But . . . ?"

"Almost," she said. "I wanted to tell you earlier. He came over last night. If my mom hadn't woken up just when I could have slid out the back door, I might have."

"Wow."

"I know." She was quiet a minute. Then she turned back to me, mad. "I can't believe you! What's your problem? How can you be all judgey of me when you're still with Hallie?"

"I'm not *with* her."

"Technicalities. She's at college, big deal. You have a car."

"She's not at college," I said. "She didn't go back after Christmas break."

"What?"

I mumbled through the details. Neecie looked shocked. More shocked that Hallie had quit college than that I'd been doing it with her.

"Was it, like, too hard for her or something? College?"

I shrugged. "I don't know. All I know is she's depressed or something."

Neecie was quiet for a minute. Then: "So, that's why you go fuck her, then? Because she's so sad and pathetic?"

"Jesus!" I said. Because saying it that way was blunt. And pretty much true.

"Or because *you're* so sad and pathetic?" she asked.

"Jesus! Is that why you fucked Tristan?"

"Obviously."

"You're not sad and pathetic, Neecie."

"Whatever."

Then she wouldn't look at me, so I had to stop talking if I wanted her to hear me right and I thought it was a pretty sweet system she had for controlling and cutting off conversation. Until I realized she was crying. Oh god. Crying girl, in my car. I wanted to hit the eject button.

"Neecie. Neecie, come on. Neecie, it's okay . . . Okay?"

My words being feeble and probably hard to hear as I was almost whispering and she wasn't looking anyway.

I touched her knee, and she looked up.

"Hey," I said. Then I couldn't think of anything to say.

She wiped her eyes a little, her makeup getting smudgy. It was the first time I'd noticed she wore makeup. She didn't seem like a very make-uppy girl, I guess.

"I didn't think you believed me at first," she said. "That we were doing it, me and Tristan. Because, you know. I'm me, and everything. And he's, like, Tristan."

I hadn't believed her, really. But there was no way I'd ever tell her that.

"And he's not, like, you know, always a dick to me," she continued. "Sometimes he's really nice, Sean. Plus, I know a lot about him. Not on purpose. But it's been, like, you know, like half a year. He doesn't get why I wouldn't text him back. He was so mad! And, like, whining. Sad. But what did he expect me to do? Start crying? Start fighting with him, like I was his girlfriend? Be all crazy and possessive? I mean, he's gone out with like four other girls since all this started. So, what was I supposed to do? I mean, I know all these *things*. All these little weird things about him. Like, he's only ticklish in one spot. And he loves country music. I mean, how geeky is that? Like, not just the cool alt-country stuff. I'm talking Taylor Swift and Tim McGraw, all the shitty new stuff. And all the twangy old stuff. He knows all the words, too. He's kind of a good singer, actually. Sometimes he sings along with it, when we're in his car alone. He has tons of it on his iPod. No one knows that about him but me, because, you know, he doesn't really advertise. I mean, country music sucks, right?"

"Well, *yeah*."

"And he has this cat? At his mom's house. He misses that damn cat so much when he has to stay with his dad. He sits and cuddles with that cat. He talks to it. The cat stays in the room, on the bed, while we're doing it, you know? Because he feels bad closing the door on her. I mean, what do I do with all that information, Sean? I can't do anything with it. But I can't really forget it. And I can't really break up with him, either."

"It sounds like you tried."

"Yeah, but I think Tristan thinks . . ."

"Hey, who cares what he fucking thinks?" I said, a little loud. "Him and Hallie both. I mean, it's fine, I guess. Just to be hooking up. I mean, obviously both of us think it's fine or we wouldn't do it, right?"

She nodded.

"And so, what?" I continued. "It feels good. That's fine. I mean, not gonna argue with things that feel good, right?"

"Well . . ."

"Does it not feel good, Neecie? Tell me it did, at least little. Because, otherwise, why would . . . ?"

"God!" she shouted, and laughed a little and covered her mouth. "I can't believe you. I mean . . . yeah. It felt good," she said. "We got good at it. I'll say that for the whole thing." Then she got all red and laughed some more. "God."

"Well, that's a fucking relief," I said. Though I didn't feel relieved. Not at all.

"It wasn't good at first, though," she said. "It was, you know. Boring, a little. For me, at least. Then, later, it . . . wasn't."

I couldn't look at her for some reason, then. She was kind of smiling, and red, and she had tears, and it was like, I didn't want to hear the sex stuff when there were tears. Or maybe I did. But I didn't want to hear it and then pretend everything was normal and there wasn't The Horn or that I wasn't insanely curious to know every last detail. Every last one. Because I was curious. And jealous. Because it was Tristan. Just, too many things.

"I mean, too bad if he's sad or Hallie's gone mental or whatever," I continued. "Tough shit, right? I can think of a whole lot worse shit than Tristan not getting laid or Hallie failing out of college."

"Hallie failed?"

"No. I don't know. She wasn't getting along with her room-mate or something. Who cares, that's not the point."

"Right. What *is* the point, then?"

Shit. What was I trying to say?

"The point is that we did it and we enjoyed it and that's good enough. Like, just fuck the whole thing, you know? Don't worry about it."

I had no idea what I was talking about anymore. This pep talk had just been aimed at stopping the crying. Beyond that, I didn't really know what the point of anything was.

"Okay," she said. "Okay, okay, okay." She wiped her eyes, wiped her hands on her jeans, shook out her hair.

"Now go take a nap. And I'm gonna . . . I don't know. Do something."

"You should take a nap, too, Sean," she said. "All that running. Aren't you tired?"

"Yeah," I said. "Kinda sore, too."

"Take a bath," she said.

"A bath? No way."

"Good for sore muscles, my mom says."

"Guys don't take baths, Neecie."

"Whatever. You're just being an idiot about it. All the pro athletes take hot baths and stuff. I've seen it on ESPN. It's like you don't watch television, I swear. You need to take care of yourself so you don't get injured. I mean, is this our new Saturday tradition? I get free breakfast and then pick you up miles away from the starting point?"

I sighed. "I don't know. It's kind of a whole big pain in the ass."

"Look, you can't flunk out of boot camp, Sean! You've got to keep up or the gunny will humiliate you and you'll blow your brains out in the latrine."

"What?"

"*Full Metal Jacket*," she said. "You need to see that movie."

"Oh."

"Or just join track," she said. "Then all the workouts are figured out for you. Like, the coach'll do it all."

"But I don't want to compete and stuff. I mean, I don't want to . . ."

"Just join for the workouts. Who cares if you compete? Even if you just run with the B squad, it'll be easier. And over with. Just think, every day, you'll be done at 5:30. No weekend bullshit." She unclicked her seat belt. "I can't imagine you with no hair, Sean."

"What?"

"They shave your head, you know. You'll be all bald. I can't even imagine you like that. Like, what if your skull is all lumpy? Or covered in moles or something?"

"What are you even talking about?" I ran my hand over my head, though. Like I was checking for lumps already.

"You know they shave your head, right? How can you not know that?"

"I know that. But, just, who has *moles* on their damn head?"

"I don't know; I go to the dermatologist a lot. They have some pretty weird photos on the walls there." She started gathering up her Thrift Bin bags and stuff. "See you at work tomorrow?"

"Yeah, okay."

"Sean?"

"Yeah?"

"Thanks for cheering me up. I mean, sorry for crying and stuff."

"It's okay. What . . . what are you doing tonight?" I said it all casual. Didn't want to sound date-y. It was Saturday and everything, but we weren't like that.

"I said I'd go out with Ivy," she said.

"Okay."

"But I'll text you if that's boring."

"Text me if it's fun, how about."

She laughed. "I will."

And there it was, again, us, friends. But The Horn, man. The Horn was all over Neecie Albertson's shit. The Horn didn't know what he was doing. I swear, though, it was The Horn that texted Hallie before I could drive away.

# Chapter Thirteen

Valentine's Day at school was more than a day. Since the actual day landed on a Wednesday, it dragged on all damn week. Nothing but announcements about the flower and candy sales and girls fluttering around the student council table at lunch getting all insane about who they were sending stuff to and a few cases of swaggering guys doing it too. Like buying one-dollar carnations made you some kind of romantic badass.

Neecie was home sick most of the week, which was good, I guess, because then she wouldn't have to watch that Hannah chick Tristan went out with lose her mind about her cheap, assy-smelling carnations that she got in the middle of our goddamn English class. I kind of wanted to clock her, to be honest, the way she was acting all fake-surprised and all "OH MY GOD WHAT IS GOING ON" like she didn't know damn well what was going on.

Two days after Valentine's Day, Eddie and me were eating lunch in the cafeteria. He told me he'd gotten Libby a candy bar but she hadn't really seemed that into it.

"I think she's pissed," he said. "Maybe she wanted flowers?"

I didn't say anything. Mostly because it a no-brainer: go buy her some flowers, then, too. Or a whole box of candy. Or some other thing she liked. Mostly, though, buying stuff for people in order for them to know you liked them seemed like the creepiest thing in the world. Prostitute-y.

Obviously, I was kind of salty; I'd gone over to Hallie's after school the day after Valentine's Day and she was also in bed, sick. I wondered if she had the same thing Neecie had.

Whatever it was, she was sick enough to not even want to go down to the laundry room. And though we were in her bed, she didn't seem into it. I mean, she was the one who texted me, so I guess she was. But mainly, it was just me doing my thing. A little too fast, probably.

"Now I've gotten you sick," she said, when I coughed while getting dressed.

"I'm just clearing my throat," I said.

"Mine started with a cough," she said, pulling her sweatshirt over her head and coughing herself. No bra. Hallie seemed uninterested in wearing underwear lately. This might have been sexy, if not for the fact that she seemed so dull and sad since leaving college. Even when we had sex, I felt like she was about to sigh the whole time.

It would have been okay, beyond the fact that she never had anything to say anymore, because she said she just sat around in her old room in bed all day watching movies on her laptop. We walked out to the TV room and she flopped on the sofa. I started putting my shoes on and then, out of the blue, she just started crying.

It was real crying, too. Messy. Like she'd been holding it in for a long time, and while I felt like escaping through the sliding glass door onto the deck, I just couldn't. Neecie had cried in front of me, and I'd managed to deal with that.

"Hallie, what's . . . What's going on?"

She didn't talk for a long time; she blew her nose, she sniffled, she gasped for air, she shook her head. Basically, she was more animated than she'd been with my dick up her. Which made me want to cry along with her. The both of us were so shitty. I went to the bathroom and got her a wad of toilet paper, hoping that would help, that she'd wipe her eyes and get over it.

But she kept crying. It went on so long, I didn't know what to do or say. I'd never heard anyone cry that long before. And I was running out of patience, which was shitty to admit. I was starting to think it was all an act. Nobody could cry that much. Not in front of another person who was standing there looking concerned and handing you toilet paper, at least.

I tried to interrupt her crying, asking her what was wrong again, but the only things she would say was that everything sucked and she hated her life and nobody even gave her a Valentine except her mom and dad and they didn't count and why the fuck did this happen to her? Why did it feel like everyone hated her?

"Why, Sean?"

I didn't know why. I kind of hated her, too, at that moment. And then her mom came home with a bunch of bags from Walgreens and she looked at me sitting by her sobbing daughter on the TV room sofa like I had fallen from the sky into her house.

But she didn't seem surprised by the endless crying, and I just handed Mrs. Martin the wad of toilet paper and she nodded and hugged Hallie, and this time I went out the front door because I didn't want her to connect me with the footprints in the snow on the back deck, since obviously she had enough problems.

●

Since he was in trouble with Libby, Eddie and me decided to hang out one Friday. We spent the first bit of it in his basement playing video games and eating dinner (Eddie's mom made the best food, I swear). Then we decided to go to this party he'd heard of, even though I thought it'd probably be a bunch of sophomores, from the sound of it.

But it wasn't; it was a pretty great party, some dude he knew from lifeguarding's house. And strangely enough, Neecie was there, with Ivy. And Ivy was drunk and hanging around Neecie's neck, and Neecie looked super happy and a little buzzed and her face was all red, down to her neck and the top of her boobs and she wore this shirt that was really low and I wondered if she got red like that all the way down under her shirt. And then Ivy started hanging off Eddie, after a while, and Eddie and her went into another room because he wanted to smoke his little bit of weed and Ivy was all about that so it was just me and Neecie standing next to each other in this cram-packed party when the cops showed up and everyone bolted in a million directions.

Running from a house party when the cops come is a stupid thing to do. They're looking for you to run, really, which is why you should just stay put until you know the situation. Like if they're more cops out on the street or if it's just a warning or whatever. But Eddie and Ivy freaked and with a bunch of other kids, shot through the back door, right into the snow drifts and started running.

But it was just a cop responding to a noise complaint, wanting everyone to leave, not to bust anyone. That's all they wanted, really: to make the fun end.

I explained this to Neecie, because she wanted to run at first too. Then we played pool in the basement for a while. The kid whose house it was hung out with us; with most everyone gone, he shut off all the lights and music and sat on the little built-in bar thing and smoked weed out of a pop can and told us about how he was going to college in North Dakota and it was boring as hell, but I knew Neecie wasn't paying attention anyway, and I was mostly paying attention to her low-neck shirt and her pink bra sticking out at the shoulder and wondering again, now that her skin was all calm and pale again, what her boobs looked like and thinking I was gross, because it'd only been like a week since the Hallie crying thing had happened, and it was like I had some kind of addiction with The Horn or something.

"I have some pretty good news, Sean," Neecie said when we'd left the party. The kid who'd been smoking out finally passed out on his sofa watching Cartoon Network. Neecie and I sat in my car; I was spitting sunflower seed shells into an empty bottle of Amp while she kept checking her phone for texts from Ivy.

"What's that?" I asked.

"I got into Carleton," she said. "I just found out this afternoon."

"Really? You're kidding! That's awesome!" I wanted to hug her, but it was awkward in the car, plus I didn't want to spill the sunflower seeds everywhere.

"I know," she said. "It's expensive as fuck, though. My mom's making me work with Gary's brother's company all summer, plus the Thrift Bin. She's sort of crazy about all the loans and stuff."

"Well, but still, that's great, Neecie. I'm really happy for . . ."

"Oh!" she said, as her phone beeped. She scrolled through the text. "They're going to the King Pin. She says to meet them there."

"For what? To go bowling?"

"Yeah, I guess. They got a ride from someone Eddie knew. And Ivy's car is still parked over here, so, I don't know how she's gonna handle that shit."

"But, bowling?"

"It'll be fun," she said. "We gotta go. She said they'll get us a lane."

"I hate bowling."

"Everyone hates bowling. Just drive."

●

The King Pin was past its prime. Seriously. You went to the bowling alley connected to the movie theater if you wanted something decent, because that place had cool games and shit to do.

But the King Pin was for people who actually still bowled competitively, and not for a joke like kids did. Though the King

Pin had probably been a hopping joint back in its day. It was still all kitted out with gold walls and bright orange plastic seats, the kind that looked like the old version of spaceships, in what people thought was so cutting-edge back then. There were still ashtrays built into the curvy seats, and you know the million-year-old score machine that looked like the overhead projector our Global Studies teacher still used must have been considered pretty fancy too.

But I was feeling a little shitty. Because I was supposed to be happy for Neecie, celebrate her going to college. Instead I was just thinking about my own dumb self, how I didn't have a good answer, still, when someone asked me what I was doing after graduation, because I couldn't tell my mom because I was a giant pussy about everything. Neecie was the only one who knew about me, and now if anyone asked what she was doing after graduation, Neecie could pop up like toast and chirp, "Going to Carleton!" and everyone would smile and be impressed and think she was super smart—which she was and which they should be.

But I still didn't have an answer. Not one that I could say, at least, because I didn't want it to get back to my mom. And I didn't know when I was leaving, either. And that sucked, too; I wanted to know, because I wanted to have something to say. And keeping secrets from my mom made me feel like a little kid. Like I'd stolen money from her purse or jacked the last piece of cake—though this wasn't that kind of secret. The longer it went on, the worse it was.

The King Pin was wall-to-wall kids. Kids from our high school and from St. Albans, the Catholic one that some kids I knew in elementary went to, and the whole place was jammed.

Kids playing pool, standing in groups around the restrooms, smushed into the lanes next to all the hardcore bowlers, some of who wore those wrist guards, too, as if bowling was a dangerous sport that required equipment. One dude I kept staring at. He was sitting there, his face half covered by his VFW trucker hat, all covered in pins and crap, and the number of his unit back in Korea or whatever, and he was spitting chew into a Styrofoam cup and it looked like he didn't have any teeth, but it was hard to tell because he had the biggest mustache ever. It was kind of funny, seeing him spitting into his cup and probably talking shit out of the side of his mouth to his friends about all of us dumb kids. But then he took off his hat, and he was bald. Totally bald. And his head was *lumpy*. Not covered in moles, though. Just those dark, ragged freckles that old people get. Also his head skin wasn't smooth and tight, but sort of saggy around his ears. I couldn't help it; I had my hand in my hair instantly, feeling around everywhere, especially my ears.

"What is your deal?" Neecie asked, handing me my rental shoes. "You keep scratching your head."

I ignored her, took the shoes. One of my socks had a big hole in it. "I can't bowl for shit."

"It'll be fine. Everyone sucks at bowling."

I sighed, nodded. Tried to not be so tense. I just wanted to go home, check my scalp for moles. But there was no point to acting like an asshole. Especially on a night when Neecie had something to celebrate.

Eddie and Ivy were drunk and bowling and acting like best friends. I wasn't sure if they'd actually hung out before; maybe they had? But it didn't matter. Eddie wasn't that kind of dude; he didn't care now that he was loaded and spinning around in his bowling shoes to boy-band music, or that the lights got all pinkish and low and hearts started swirling around the walls as a cheesy voice announced the "Glitzy Midnight Bowl." Nope, Eddie was the kind of dude who just grabbed Ivy and started tangoing all over the place until her turquoise bowling ball popped back up out of the machine. Seeing that, I decided to stop being mopey and sorry for myself; I had to be happy for Neecie and try to just have a good time already.

But then I turned around and saw Tristan Reichmeier standing by Neecie and he had his hand on the back of his neck and was looking down at her and she was smiling and shrugging and then he laughed and she kind of shook her hair, in a totally non-Neecie way, and they kept talking and then he grabbed her by the elbow and they ducked behind one of those dumb machines where you can try to pluck a stuffed animal out of it with those little pincher claws, the kind that are impossible to win at, and I couldn't see them anymore.

"Can you do Neecie's turn, Sean?" Eddie, poking my shoulder. "Where'd she go anyway?"

"To the bathroom," Ivy said, but then she was scanning around just like I had been.

I almost slipped getting up on the lane and then Neecie's ball had just tiny finger holes so I couldn't even use it normally; I just sort of granny-shotted it down the lane and turned around, and Ivy and Eddie were shouting, "Sean! You just did a strike! First crack, too!" and "Holy shit, dude!" but I didn't care. I couldn't see Neecie anymore, and I was feeling headachey, and I couldn't stand it.

But I rolled Neecie's turn like a million more times, and even when Eddie bought another game, I went along, holding her tiny-holed ball and not getting any more strikes and wondering why we were celebrating Neecie's good news if she wasn't here. But I didn't want to be a downer, because it seemed pretty likely that Ivy and Eddie were into each other; I'd never seen Ivy so happy and smiling.

"What's your problem?" Eddie said once when Ivy was up bowling her turn.

"Nothing."

"Ivy thinks Neecie's with some guy. Ivy's pissed off about it, I think."

"You seem to attract girls who get pissed off, you know that, Ed?" He smiled, but then quit right away. Because then Libby was standing just two feet away from us, with all of her friends, Emma, too, and everyone's good time really screeched to a halt.

"Who's that?" Libby asked me and Eddie, nodding toward Ivy up in the lane.

"Ivy Heller," Eddie said.

"I know who she is."

"Then why'd you ask?" I said. "Jesus Christ."

Eddie looked at me like, "Dude, don't," and Libby's eyes were all squinched and teary, and then Ivy came back and the girls all had this uncomfortable stare-off and I couldn't stand it anymore. I took off my bowling shoes, left them beside a plate of half-eaten French fries and put on my own shoes. I looked everywhere for Neecie; I even went outside, scanning the groups of kids waiting for rides next to the hardcore bowlers smoking cigarettes. No Neecie. No red truck in the parking lot, either.

She'd gone and done it, hadn't she. Another disappearing act. I couldn't believe her.

"You owe me fifteen bucks." Eddie, at my shoulder.

Then Ivy was behind him, on her cell phone, super mad.

"Well, if your mom calls, I'm not fucking lying to her again," Ivy yelled. "I'm not. And I don't fucking care. No! No fucking way! He's a total dickhead and full of shit and you totally fucking know it."

"Dude, just get us out of here," Eddie whispered to me when we got in my car. "Libby's in there, crying. All her friends are going to kill me . . ."

"They're sophomore girls, Eddie," I said. "They can't kill anyone."

"They're juniors, Sean," he said. "And they're freaking me out. Let's get out of here."

He buckled his seatbelt and rapped his fist on the dashboard. "Chop chop," he added. I started driving, but Eddie kept checking the rear-view. Like we were being followed.

Ivy was in the backseat, but not the phone anymore. When I glanced at the rearview mirror, she was crying. Awesome. The night was turning out just great.

It wasn't the bawling-loud crying like Neecie and Hallie had done, but just the movie-scene crying where the tears just slopped up under your lids and slid down your face. Given that Ivy went overboard with her eye makeup, it was more dramatic than it had to be. I didn't think she'd meant it be dramatic, though; it was just a coincidence. I kept looking at her in the rearview the whole time, though it was probably dickish to stare. Eddie must have seen it, too, because suddenly he was looking straight ahead, like he was pretending it wasn't happening. Which probably more dickish, really. But all of us stayed silent, until we dropped Ivy at her car over by the busted-party house; then Eddie asked her if she was okay to drive. Ivy didn't say anything, just slammed the door, and Eddie sat there looking at the texts on his phone, saying, "Fuck" over and over and the whole way home, I had the image of the bald guy in the King Pin and had to grip the steering wheel tight so I wouldn't be tempted to feel around for lumps again.

# Chapter Fourteen

I didn't talk to Neecie the rest of the weekend. She didn't text me; I didn't text her. She called in sick to work, too. Monday during lunch Eddie and me went to a meeting for track, so I didn't see her, then, either. I saw Tristan Reichmeier, walking with his set of douche hockey players. It made me pretty damn salty, her talking me into going bowling and him talking her into leaving with him. All of that pissed me off to no end. By the time Global Studies rolled around, I was wondering what the fuck was up.

But, in Global Studies, Neecie was all, "Hi, Sean!" and passing back the handouts and sweeping her long hair over her shoulder, and for the first time, that move, her slipping her fingers behind the sheet of blond hair and tossing it out of her way, instead of looking nice and pretty, it looked bitchy and snobby to me. So I didn't say anything to her, not that I normally did;

Neecie had to concentrate in class on what was going on, if she wanted to hear properly, so she always shut me down if I poked her or whispered to her—"I hate whispering, Sean. Say it, or don't say it, but don't fucking WHISPER."

But after class, she turned around and kind of looked at me like always, like normal, like next we'd start talking as we walked to our lockers to collect our shit. But I couldn't look at her. I couldn't, because of her now-snobby hair flip move and because of Tristan who gave shitty carnations to his dumb girl-friend and Neecie ditching me at the King Pin to be with a guy who wouldn't even give her shitty carnations. So I just hustled out the door, fast as hell to my locker and when I got to the parking lot my phone rang and it was Sergeant Kendall.

"Sean, how are you?"

"Good. Good, sir. I mean. I'm good."

"Good. Hey. I'm calling because I have a MEPS appoint-ment set up for you. It's short notice, but I want to get you in as soon as possible. It makes for faster boot camp assignation."

"Okay. When?"

"Tomorrow, oh-eight-hundred. I can drive you. And give your school a note, excusing you from class."

"Right," I said. I turned around and saw Neecie, at the top of the school steps, holding her books across her chest.

"We went over this, but let me remind of you of what you'll need, okay?"

"Okay," I said, and he launched into a list of shit. Medical history, Social Security card, driver's license. Told me to take a shower the night before, wear underwear—"Nothing too flashy: trust me, you won't want to stand around in anything out of the ordinary"—and remove any jewelry, piercings, and earrings; hats were not allowed, nor was any clothing with profanity or offensive imagery.

"Right," I said. Listening, watching Neecie approach and stand in front of me. Waiting.

"Make sure whatever you wear is clean and loose," Sergeant Kendall continued. "And again, not unusual. You're going to be poked and prodded and asked to do some stretching, and so you want something that'll be easy to show full range of motion. Jeans and a T-shirt and a sweater or hoodie over that are what I'd recommend. So, any questions?"

"No. I'm good."

"Great. Pick you up at school or home?"

"School," I said. "Hey. I have a question. Should I wear running shoes? Will I be running?"

"No," he said. "No PT for this portion. But you should be running anyway, like we talked about."

"I just joined track for spring," I said.

"Good. That's awesome. Okay. Well, I'm excited about this. This'll be great. Tell your parents you should be home around dinnertime. But I'll get you dinner, anyway; traffic'll be bad that time of day, okay?"

"Yeah, great. Thanks."

I hung up and then said to Neecie, "You always listen in to people's phone conversations?"

"Yeah," she said, frowning and pissed. "Especially conversations where you keep saying, 'yeah' and 'okay' a million times. Those are so fascinating."

I shrugged.

"Why are you avoiding me?"

"I'm not avoiding you," I said. "Just got things to do."

"Right," she said.

And we stared at each other, and I could tell she was going to just wait and be quiet until I couldn't stand it, because I was about to blow, the whole thing with the MEPS appointment was huge and I was freaking out, thinking about it, how there was an oath and all these medical tests and health questions and I was going to have to just hope I knew all my shit well enough, though there hadn't been that much wrong with me in my life, besides a broken arm back in third grade when Eddie and me jumped down the staircase onto a pile of couch cushions and I landed funny. And once I got pneumonia after snowboarding all weekend in junior high. But nothing else. Except that I was shitting my pants—something happening, something to tell people about! Except not my mom!—but it was good and bad, because this was HAPPENING and I hadn't really studied for the ASVAB and my strategy was that I shouldn't because I might as well just show them what I was capable of, instead of cramming and inflating my score and then having it seem like I was fit for something really complicated and technical, which I didn't want, anyway. I was an okay test-taker, at least; Sergeant Kendall recommended practice tests if I was a bad test-taker. Neecie would have helped me with that, if I'd asked her. But I didn't ask her, though. I forgot. Or didn't want to remember. Or I wanted to do other things with her, not involving tests.

But when I looked at her, I just saw her snobby hair. Her snobby yellow hair, all over Tristan's bed. Her pink bra. Him over her. The cat he loved more than anyone else. And him wearing the stupid black cap that hung off his head like he was some kind of Rasta. A Rasta listening to goddamn country music.

"See you tomorrow," I finally said. And she said nothing, but I knew she heard me because I was, obviously, looking straight at her when I said it.

●

On the way to the MEPS, Sergeant Kendall tried to draw me out and talk, but I was nervous and I couldn't get into it. Couldn't follow what he was saying. Felt like sleeping, but that seemed lazy and rude, too. I was wearing jeans and a button-up shirt (I figured why not go one step further than the hoodie and T-shirt) and I had clean underwear on—boxer briefs, grey. And I'd shaved my weak-ass stubble and put on extra pit-stick. I even flossed my teeth. Except for my running shoes, I looked ready to go to church. Or court.

When Brad did his maybe-I'll-join-the-Army thing in his senior year, it had been pretty low-level stuff. Certainly he'd never ridden in a car with a recruiter for an hour. All it had taken for my mom to lose her shit was finding an Army recruiter's business card in Brad's pocket. Of course, Brad never intended to sneak around about it, so he just told her he was thinking about it. She did her whole freakout thing about killing and peace and shit, but after a couple days, she got practical. She knew how to work Brad. This was before things really went to shit between my parents, before all the bankruptcy and foreclosure stuff, so my mom told Brad she'd give him the down payment on a used pickup if he'd go on a weekend visit to where she went to college in Moorhead and tear up the Army dude's card.

My dad drove Brad to Moorhead, where Brad ended up getting shit-faced at a frat party and Dad probably did the same in some crappy hotel room and that was the last we ever heard from Brad about college or the Army. He still runs his tree-trimming business out of that truck, though.

●

The Military Entrance Processing Station was in downtown Minneapolis, where I'd only ever gone for Twins games or once to some play that my mom wanted us to see at Christmastime. It was in an old marble-looking building that looked like a museum. When we went in, we had to go through a screening thing like at an airport, and my backpack was searched and all that shit. Then Sergeant Kendall nudged me toward the Marines liaison and said he'd pick me up later today.

The liaison gave me and a bunch of other dudes a big speech. That we needed to listen to instructions and realize we were being watched and that there was no spitting or listening to music and cell phones, that we had to put our bags in this cabinet and take out any necessary ID and forms now and not give them to anyone who wasn't a medical doctor and there would be no bathroom privileges until after the medical exam had been completed. It was kind of hardcore and freaky, and at one point a Marine walked through where we were all sitting and told the guy next to me sit his ass up proper, and the idea that I could have been that guy made me feel like my hair could start on fire.

Then we did a pile of paperwork. A whole bunch of instructions from this woman who had her hair pulled into a tight ponytail that was painful to look at. I fished out my medical forms, and Tight Ponytail came over, her huge ass bumping the other little tables and butted in to ask what I was doing and I told her and she was like, Okay, go ahead, like I was a complete idiot and every inhalation and exhalation needed to be approved by her.

After I finished my paperwork, then there was another bit of waiting and then Tight Ponytail Lady gave us all Breathalyzers, which just made me feel guilty, though of course I was completely sober. The little tube thing she handed me looked like something you'd suck up pot smoke through, except way more clinical and sterile. So we did that, and they collected them, and then we were shuffled to another room for the ASVAB test. Which, while technically a test with math and crap on it, was the first thing I didn't mind doing, because finally I had something to actually do instead of being yelled at and sitting and waiting.

But then I finished mine first. Which meant more waiting.

The medical part was at least with just a normal doctor, and just like the normal doctor's office, including more wait-ing. Only difference was, once the doctor showed, it was like the longest exam ever. Eye exams and blood being drawn and peeing in a cup. By the time I got in front of him, the doctor said I was lucky because the physical exam was usually with a fuckload of other people—yes, he actually said "fuckload"— and then he asked me to strip down to my underwear so he could do a physical survey, and I didn't see how this was lucky, being alone and naked in a room with a dude I didn't know.

But he just stood there and looked at me, asking me to do all sorts of stuff, like rotating my foot at the ankle and bend-ing over to touch my toes and stuff and follow his finger with my eyes and walk this way. Then the bend-over-and-cough move, which, gross. Then this weird-ass duck-walk thing, which he actually demonstrated, and I wanted to laugh but I was too scared. I guess I did the duck walk right, though, because he just nodded and sent me along. God. I could never be a doctor.

Then, I got dressed. And—shocker—more waiting. Finally, there was a hearing test with this really cute nurse chick. She had nice boobs, too, and she smelled good, and being all dick-conscious from just being in my underwear, I was glad we were sitting down with a table between us because I totally got wood. Typical of The Horn.

Listening to all the buzzes and clunks and peeps with those heavy-ass headphones, I wondered how Neecie did on a hearing test like this. Or did she just flunk? And then I felt shitty. I'd been kind of shitty to her. But I still had a boner. And now I was thinking of Neecie naked with my boner while raising both arms every time I heard a buzz or a clunk or a peep.

Then they told me to go have a break because the doctor was eating lunch, so I went to this shitty lounge area where there were signs everywhere yelling in all caps to do things or not do them:

NO SHAKING VENDING MACHINES
THERE IS NO CHANGE GIVEN AT FRONT DESK
ALL VANDALISM WILL BE PROSECUTED
THIS LOUNGE IS A PRIVILEGE DO NOT ABUSE!

My lunch situation wasn't great. A sandwich made by a robot inside a vending machine. Luckily, then Sergeant Kendall showed up and handed me a bag of McDonald's to eat, which was, like, the greatest timing ever. And I almost wanted to get down on my knees and thank him and kiss his feet because it felt like I'd never see anyone normal or nice again (cute hearing-test nurse being the exception).

"How's it going? Did you bend over and cough already?"

I laughed, and we chatted, and a Marine guy walked into the room and Sergeant Kendall popped up and saluted and I sat there with my mouth full, unsure of what to do, and then when the dude said, "At ease," Sergeant Kendall smiled and introduced me and I stood up and wiped my hand on a napkin and then the guy was nice and cracking jokes and asking me if I regretted that nutsack tattoo now and I was like, huh? but laughed anyway, because Sergeant Kendall was laughing, and then the guy smacked me on the back and said good luck and some other junk and I was all, Thank you, sir, which I hoped sounded good and polite enough.

"Okay, I'm out of here," Sergeant Kendall said, balling up his trash and my trash and putting it in the little garbage can, which had a big sign over it, too (PLEASE THROW ALL TRASH INTO RECEPTACLE! TRASH ON THE FLOOR IS NOT TOLERATED!) and then he said he'd be back to pick me up.

"I'll text you. But don't be checking your phone unless you've been dismissed," he said. "Some of the Marines get pissy with recruits at MEPS acting sloppy."

"Okay," I said. Not knowing what "sloppy" meant but not wanting to ask, either.

He walked off. I admit, I kind of wanted to run after him.

So, more waiting. In this awful yelling-signs lounge. I could feel my phone in my pocket buzzing, but I didn't dare touch it. It was probably just Eddie sending me porn pictures. So I just sat there, looking at the signs and wishing I wasn't here and thinking that if the real Marines was a tenth as stressful as this, I would never survive.

But after all that, there was just an interview with another doctor, a different one from the dude who felt up my balls. (Why do doctors feel up your balls and make you cough? Why do guys just submit to that without asking why?) This doctor went over the medical records I had and was going down a checklist, asking me a whole bunch of questions, yes or no. When he asked if I ever drank alcohol or used illegal drugs, I said No and my hands were all sweaty where I was gripping onto the seat of my chair. Lying. I knew I was lying. But I figured, who the fuck would they ever find to be in the goddamn military if they were expecting complete law-abiding citizens like that? Everyone must lie. But the doctor didn't even look up, just asked the next question.

When that was done, then I had another long waiting session in the yelling-signs lounge. But by then I was feeling okay. Like, none of this was anything I had to do but get through. Answer the questions. The waiting turned into something I was outlasting. Because I didn't have to do anything but answer and react. None of it was my idea, and a lot of it didn't make sense, but I felt like I was getting somewhere. Closer to the end. Like it was all a test and I was going to pass.

I got out my phone, then. But made sure I was sitting up straight and not looking "sloppy" while I did it. And I was basically texting with Eddie, not even acknowledging his pictures of some pregnant chick getting it from behind, but asking him what I missed in school and him asking where I was and me avoiding that question. I really wanted to text Neecie with some dumb excuse, like asking for the Global Studies assignments, but I didn't. Maybe I was feeling crappy for being a dick to her, still? Maybe I knew I should apologize. That pretending everything was okay was babyish. She deserved something direct, face to face. Maybe I knew I wasn't ready yet for any of that, though.

Tight Ponytail Lady came back. "We're going to the job selection review now," she said. Her voice sounded rusty. Like something in her throat was scraping on something else rusty. I stood up right away, slipped my phone into my pocket.

"You can't have phones in there," she added, then explained that like nine more times in case I was deaf and mentally retarded, and I think she was just huffy that we had to reroute to the storage lockers where all our backpacks were stored.

We went into a little room to go over our ASVAB results, which I guess were good and which meant I was probably going into infantry/rifleman or communications, and I just said "Yes, sir" a million times and the guy repeated how much of this was subject to the demands of the Corps, and I just said "Yes, sir" some more, and finally, he handed me everything to sign and then Sergeant Kendall came in and said, "You're ready for the oath now?"

And I nodded. "Sure."

And he looked at me funny. So I said, "Yes, sir," but he'd already turned and maybe didn't hear me.

As if I wasn't already a sweating mess. Jesus Christ. Sitting there waiting for everyone to be quiet and get set up and whatever. And it was all stiff and important and there was a flag and a dude in full serious mode and the other dudes beside me looked as blown-out and hacked-off as I was, but you could tell we were all tired from duck-walking and blood tests and lying about smoking weed and feeling shitty and tense all day about everything and now we just wanted to do this part, get it over with. Though it felt like a wedding. A wedding with dudes. A dude wedding with no party afterwards.

*"I, Sean Alan Norwhalt, do solemnly swear that I will support and defend the Constitution of the United States against all enemies, foreign and domestic; that I will bear true faith and allegiance to the same; and that I will obey the orders of the President of the United States and the orders of the officers appointed over me, according to regulations and the Uniform Code of Military Justice. So help me God."*

I didn't believe in god. But I repeated it. And then, there was hand-shaking, and my palms were clammy but I shook hands with every guy in there, even the dudes I didn't know, and then I just wanted to, I don't know. Collapse. Run twenty miles. Jump off a pier into the ocean. Get completely fucking drunk.

Sergeant Kendall hit the Burger King drive-thru and we ate in the car, Sergeant Kendall driving and eating fries from the bag, me just spreading everything out on my lap. Normally I don't like people eating in my car, so it was hypocritical of me, but it felt good to just be able to eat as fast as possible. And everything tasted extra delicious for some reason.

"Bet you're tired," he said.

"Yeah," I said. "Don't know why, though. There was so much waiting and sitting around."

Sergeant Kendall sipped his Coke, wiped his mouth with a folded napkin. I needed to start doing that more. When I even bothered to use napkins, I just bunched them up into a greasy sticky ball.

"Waiting and sitting around constitutes most combat situations, actually. It's kind of funny that this is your first experience with MEPS. Because there's going to be more. There always is."

The rest of the drive home, he just put on the sports talk radio thing. I mean, I could have asked him a lot of questions, beyond the running in combat boots thing, which was only half true; Marines ran in both, and I should bring my normal running shoes to basic training. But after that, I didn't know what to say. I didn't want to blurt out a bunch of shit. And now I had these lies on record and I had to be careful. I felt like going home and scrubbing out my sock drawer of all the weed shake and condoms and whatever the hell else illegal I had. Felt like apologizing to everyone for everything I'd ever done, too. Wiping everything clean.

# Chapter Fifteen

The beginning of the spring was mostly me and Eddie at track practice. Though there was some drama with Eddie and Libby and their breaking up and him hanging around with Ivy and all sorts of other shifting around. And a few wedding chores, tuxedo fittings and special dinners and tours of the Kiwanis camp out at the lake where the whole thing was happening. Steven-Not-Steve offering me endless streams of community college literature. Lots of shitty melting snow and mud. Lots of sore muscles and shin splints and mornings where I wondered if my body was ever going to stop hurting and get used to this.

But there was no Neecie. No telling my mom. The hollow in my chest still empty, no matter how far I ran or how many push-ups I did or how perfect my pull-up technique got.

And then, in April, the first of April, April Fool's Day, to be specific, though I hadn't planned it, it just happened. We were all having a dinner at our house on a Thursday night, because Krista had to do some more wedding things.

"Set the table, Sean," my mom said, whisking through the kitchen, pushing a stack of plates into my arms.

"Are we in the kitchen? Or back deck?" Brad was grilling hamburgers on the deck, so I figured we'd just eat out there, less formal.

"Deck's all wet and dirty," she said. "We'll be inside."

Krista walked in then and set her purse down. "How can I help, Tabitha?" she asked my mom, and my mom had her stir some lemonade while I set plates around the table.

"Oh my god, will you get out of here," my mom said, shooing Otis, who had parked himself in the kitchen, lying on his big fat beefy side in the middle of the linoleum, as if that was a natural place to relax when all the humans were making dinner.

Right in the middle of me setting out the plates and my mom mixing up a bowl of salad and Krista carrying glasses to the table, my phone rang: Sergeant Kendall.

I ran downstairs to my room and shut the door before I answered it.

"Sean? It's Anthony Kendall. Sorry to call you so late."

"No big deal," I said.

"Good. I've got some good news for you. There's a slot open for an upcoming class at the MCRD at San Diego and I want to verify that you will graduate by June tenth."

"Yeah, no problem. Commencement is June third."

"Okay. Well, it looks like we can set you with the class that begins June eighteenth," he said. "I just found out about this and wanted to double check before I call them back and confirm your spot."

My hands started shaking. "All right."

"Great. I will have a confirmation for you, but for now, you're slated to stay at one of the hotels we use by the airport on June seventeenth. Puts you on the yellow footprints about noon on the eighteenth."

"Yellow footprints?"

"Yeah, I didn't tell you about those? Every Marine ever born never forgets them."

"No."

"You'll see. It's your first time in formation. It's the first introduction to the Corps. It's . . . well. It's intense. But good. It'll be good. So, I'll be arranging your flight and overnight hotel accommodations. I'll call you when I have everything set."

"I can get myself to the airport."

"We arrange for that, Sean. So you'll be right on time and everything. No delays."

No excuses. No options. No more secrets.

"Right. Great. Okay."

"So, I'll have more specifics soon, but know that's your date. June seventeenth. Get it on your calendar."

"I will."

"Congratulations, Sean. This is very exciting news. I was worried you'd be delayed until November, but this turned out to be very lucky, timing-wise."

"Yeah, cool. I'm really glad," I said, trying to sound more

upbeat than I felt, and a minute later we said good-bye and hung up.

Then I sat on my bed.

Thought for a minute.

*Just tell her.*

*You are leaving. For boot camp.*

*Just tell them you are leaving.*

*You are leaving (and never coming back).*

*No delays.*

I could hear everyone upstairs, Otis barking and his claws clicking on the kitchen floor and my grandpa's voice and my mother murmuring. My hands were shaking still. Then Krista called my name and I went upstairs.

●

Uncomfortable dinners in our family were rare. When we all lived together, my dad worked late. Or my mom had school. Or Brad and I had sports. So we didn't do a lot of circling around the table pretending to love each other a lot. Which was good, because when my dad was home, that was when he liked to get shit-faced. He wasn't a bar-goer, really, and he traveled around for work selling farm equipment, and so he had to be sober on the road. He was pretty strict about that. So the second he hit the front door, he was done with being sober.

Sitting at the table, eating hamburgers and fried potatoes—my mom didn't consider potato chips food, even though this was basic picnic shit we were having—my mother and Krista and Brad and Grandpa Chuck and everyone was all clueless and acting like they'd been born for nothing else but to sit here and pass the ketchup bottle and pour each other lemonade and talk about the groom's dinner, which was going to be at this restaurant that one of Krista's friends managed, and there was going to be a big chocolate cake, Brad's favorite, and wasn't that so fucking awesome?

"Sean, can you pass the potatoes?" my mother said.

And I looked up, looked right at Grandpa Chuck and Brad and Krista and my mom and said, "I am going to boot camp. I joined the Marines. I leave the day after Krista and Brad get married. June seventeenth. I just talked to the recruiter." Then I passed my mom the potatoes.

No one said anything. No one moved. Except for Brad. He kept eating. Shaking his head, smiling.

Still no one said anything.

So I kept talking. "He called just now. I did my MEPS appointment a few weeks ago. That's kind of like an intake thing. So I'm all set up and everything. But, it's lucky. Sergeant Kendall didn't think I'd get in with a class until next November. But anyway, it's a sure bet I'll get in with that class. It's in San Diego."

No one said anything.

*I am leaving and never coming back. And no one says anything.*

"Shouldn't it be Parris Island?" Grandpa Chuck asked, finally. "Because you're east of the Mississippi?"

"Sergeant Kendall said it was San Diego."

"Is that Camp Pendleton?"

"What does that *matter*?" my mother shrieked.

"Just commenting," Grandpa Chuck said. He sounded a little miffed. At me or my mom, I couldn't tell.

My mom looked at me, tipping her head to the side. Laying

down her fork very specifically and slowly. "Well," she said. "I guess I just don't know what to say. Mostly I'm surprised."

"Me too," Brad added, shoveling potatoes into his mouth.

"Sean, I just can't... I'm so sad you're leaving the day after!" Krista squeaked.

"Well, aren't you going on your honeymoon, anyway?"

"Not for two weeks," Krista said. "I couldn't get the time off."

"Oh," I said.

My mom pushed back in her chair, ran her hands through her hair so that the top part stuck up weird and you could see all these little greyish/white hairs sticking up on top, like little wires or bolts of lightning.

"San Diego's a better place. Weather's hotter than sin at Parris Island," Grandpa Chuck said. "Humid. Sticky. Southern weather. And the bugs are supposedly fierce."

"They've got bugs in San Diego, too, I bet," I said.

He nodded, pushed back from the table, rested his hands around his plate a little, his hands big and wrinkly. He still wore his wedding ring, though my grandma'd been dead for years.

I stared at his wedding ring hand. I didn't want to eat anymore. My mom looked like someone had told her somebody had died. I knew she was going to cry next. I could feel it. I couldn't be with these people. But I couldn't be alone. So I stood up and headed out to my car. Not in a huff or anything, no door slamming. Just, like, escaping, slowly, like a slow leak from a tire.

I dialed Neecie. When she didn't pick up, I texted that I was coming over.

Then Grandpa Chuck, in the driveway, calling for me.

"Sean? Sean! Where you headed?"

"Nowhere," I said. Then I thought I'd joke. "Or San Diego."

He didn't laugh, of course.

"You know you launched quite a bomb there, son."

"I know."

"Just so you realize, we're not upset or anything. We're just surprised."

"You speaking for everyone, Grandpa?"

He stepped back. I was never rude to my grandpa like that. Because he was old. And also nice. I never wanted to be a dick to him.

"No. No, I'm not. I shouldn't be."

"What's the big deal? I'm eighteen," I said. "I don't need anyone's permission. Or approval."

"I understand that, Seany," he said.

"I gotta go," I said.

"That's probably a good idea. Give your mom some time to absorb this."

"Right."

"Remember when Brad wanted to join the Army?" He scratched a hand over his bald head; it wasn't quite warm out yet. The breeze picked up across the highway, and we watched a plastic cup fly into the chainlink fence.

"Yeah."

"Keep that in mind, then. You've got some explaining to do, Sean. This isn't the easy way out."

I nodded. But I didn't agree with him and it bugged me, him saying that. He had no idea how hard it'd been, the whole thing. Easy was the last thing I'd call it. But I didn't want to get mad at him. He looked sad and old, and I loved him, my grandpa. I didn't want to fight with him.

Before he was even back in the house, I was speeding down the highway. Straight to Neecie's house, no detours or stops or regrets. No delays. And she was standing on her stoop, wrapping her hoodie around her in the cold when I pulled up. Waiting for me. Which I had known she would be.

# Chapter Sixteen

I've never really liked being alone.

I mean, I can *be* alone. I'm not incapable of it. But it's harder. There's just too much going on in my head when I'm alone; being around other people sort of quiets down all the noise. I wouldn't be alone in the Marines, either. Especially boot camp. It was something I didn't mind about it, when I thought about it. So making myself run down the frontage road, in the not-quite-warm spring air, seemed temporary. Something I'd get through. Outlast.

One night, though, it was the end of April and the world was getting warmer and greener, I kind of felt it. Felt the point of running. Why people like Eddie's dad did marathons and trained by themselves all the time. Because I was running down the frontage road, two miles from home, and the moon was out and it was cold, but there was something so good about it too.

Like, I was a man and no one told me to go running, but I had, anyway, all on my own, and it was like the Marines secret had been. All mine, and fuck you for thinking you know me.

Fuck you, Hallie and Brad.

Fuck you, Grandpa Chuck for saying it was the easy way out.

Fuck you, Mom. Well, not her, directly. Just her *I accept your decision. I am proud of you* robot voice, with her eyes looking like I killed something already.

Fuck you, to everyone, in general, really.

Well, not Krista. And not Otis. And certainly not Neecie.

Who was sitting in her Blazer in the gravel drive when I came up, sweating and panting.

"What are you doing here?" I said when she jumped down from the Blazer.

"Waiting for you," she said. "Go take a shower. Let's go do something."

"Okay," I said. She followed me in and told me to hurry and so I went into my room and stripped down but it was weird, because she was there, and I was naked and she was upstairs somewhere, and that normally never happened, and then I was in the shower, with The Horn, and thinking I was pretty fucking great, for no good reason, except for the running under the full moon thing.

When I came upstairs, I grabbed a bagel and some juice, but she was gone. In the driveway, she had already started the Blazer. Hair dripping, I got into the car, turned on the heat so my hair wouldn't freeze into gel-icicles.

"There's a party at the river trestle," she said, pulling out of the driveway.

I couldn't say anything, either, because her car was so damn noisy, even with the radio off. I had no interest in going to the river trestle. The last time I'd been there was the weird break-up with Hallie.

But I didn't want to bring that up. Not because she would mind; I just didn't want to think about it, really. But Neecie didn't mind if I was silent, especially in the car when she had music on. And I was just glad we were friends again. It sort of killed me, when I thought how long we'd gone not talking. How dumb that was. How I could have fixed it with just one text, too.

Once we got there, it didn't seem like much of a party. There were a few cars down there, but the people were all seniors from St. Albans, no one I knew or gave a shit about.

"I thought Ivy'd be here by now," she said.

I shrugged.

"Let's get cups," she said.

"I don't have any cash."

"I'll get you one," she said. Jesus. She really must have wanted to get wasted. So we got out and got cups. But it was weird. We stood by each other and looked around. It was muddy but a little too cold for a party outside. I felt like a baby for being cold.

"See that guy, there? The one with the green jacket?"

"Yeah."

"I made out with him once. At a party."

I stared at the guy. He was drinking something from a water bottle. He looked completely forgettable. A regular guy. Just sitting there, not talking.

"What was his name?"

"Aidan. I can't remember his last name. It was a boring

last name. Something like Smith or Anderson? He was cousins with the kid whose house the party was at. Ivy and I went with some people she knew from St. Albans. I wonder what he's doing back here. I thought he lived somewhere else, I guess. I never thought I'd see him again."

"Oh."

"He was the first penis I ever touched."

"Jesus, Neecie!"

"What," she said, crossing her arms over her chest and shivering. "It was."

"But . . . why? Why are you telling me this?"

"No reason," she said. "It's not like I expected him to be here. I'm just noting it. It's a strange coincidence. Strange coincidences get talked about, Sean. Like your mother's sudden happiness with you and the Marines."

"I wouldn't call it happiness."

"Acceptance, then."

"Whatever."

We didn't talk. I tried not to look at that guy whose dick she'd touched. Failed.

"Was it big? That dude's wang?" Blurting.

"How should I know? They all seem about the same size to me, really."

Jesus. How many had she touched?

"How many have you touched?"

She laughed. "You think I keep track?"

"I know you do. A guy would."

"I'm not a guy."

"Still."

"Six."

"Wow."

"You think that's a lot. But really, you should probably touch the dicks that go inside you first, don't you think?"

"You've fucked six different guys?"

"I didn't say that."

"You're annoying the shit out of me, you know that?"

"No, you're just in a pissy mood. You want another beer?"

We refilled a couple more times, and though she seemed buzzed, seemed up for some kind of adventure, I just felt bored. Which quickly turned into feeling annoyed. Especially because I couldn't stop searching out that Aidan kid she'd pointed out.

Then, when she checked her phone to call Ivy, I looked at mine; Eddie'd sent a text of two people in clown masks fucking.

"God," I said.

"What?" she asked.

"Nothing."

"Ivy's still at home," she said. "She just got out of the shower."

"So . . . ?"

"So I'm supposed to be staying at her house tonight."

"Oh."

"So we could stay out all night."

"Oh."

"But this is boring."

"Yeah."

"You're kind of boring, too, Sean."

"Sorry."

"Let's go back to the car. I'm freezing."

"Okay."

Once in the Blazer, Neecie pulled a stadium blanket from

the backseat. White with yellow squiggles. She offered me some of the blanket, and though I wanted to take it—I was still cold and my hair was feeling icy—I shook my head. Finished my beer, set it in the cup holder. Neecie turned on the car so we'd have some heat, and I leaned back and stared at the cracked vinyl ceiling.

I hated that we were here, with all these people we didn't know. That I didn't want to know, either—even though all of them seemed hell-bent on knowing each other. It seemed like all these St. Albans seniors were tripping over themselves to party one last time "while we're still all together"—that kind of thing was pretty common lately. Reminded me of all the parties with Hallie and her friends. It was a waste, though, that Neecie could stay out all night and there was nothing worth doing. I didn't want any more beer. And I couldn't think of anything to say. Anything I really wanted to bring up, that is. I didn't want to hear about the cocks Neecie had touched and now fondly remembered like some a third-grade spelling bee ribbon. All of these people I just wanted to fast-forward through. Though not Neecie. I didn't mind being with her. Around her.

"Will you ever tell me your real name?" I asked.

"No."

"Melanie and Jessamyn won't tell me, either."

"I've trained them well. Put fear in their hearts."

"I could ask your mom."

"She respects my wishes as well."

"Gary?"

"Gary is clueless."

"Why won't you tell me? Why do I get dick stories? The name thing; that's something I've always wondered."

"You don't like dick stories?"

"No."

"Why did you punch Eddie, but you guys are still friends?"

I didn't say anything. I was not expecting her to ask that, obviously, and not expecting her to care about it, or need to have more explanation. Guys hit each other; they did that and they moved on and that was life. Sometimes it was better after the hitting, with some guys. Sometimes not. All I knew was that guys hitting seemed a lot less involved than the way some girls acted with each other, cat-fighting and saying assholey shit and spreading rumors and whatever. Waging constant war on each other in the cuntiest way possible.

I must have been quiet for too long, because she sighed and said, "Fine," like she was bored and tired. "Berniece. Berniece Diane. My middle name's my dead aunt's name. Berniece was my great-grandmother. My mom loved her very much."

"Oh."

"Stop saying 'oh' every second. You sound like a mouth-breather."

"Maybe I am. They call Marines 'grunts,' did you know that?"

"Someone's been on the Internet. Did you watch *Full Metal Jacket* yet?"

"No."

"You should."

"Get it for me, and I'll watch it."

"Did you punch Eddie over a girl or something?"

"A girl?" I laughed. "No. God. Nothing like that. Eddie just said something he shouldn't have said. It didn't have anything to do with him."

"What did he even say?"

I didn't want to say it, because it sounded so lame.

"He just called me a pussy."

*A fucking pussy.*

"Why?"

"Because I wouldn't skip study hall and English with him to go talk this St. Albans girl he liked."

"But that's so dumb!"

"I know."

"I mean him. Not you."

"I was dumb too. Why break someone's nose for them calling you something? Stupid."

"He shouldn't have said that."

"Whatever. He did."

"Wow."

"But, that's not really it. Not the whole thing."

"What's the whole thing?"

"It's what happened that week. Before. There wasn't any way Eddie could have known. I mean, he could have. I just never told him."

"What happened, Sean?"

I sighed. Sighing, not because I was weary or whatever. Though I felt exhausted just that second. Sighing, because it's a way to hold back tears. To try to suck in your sinuses when they're starting to drip down your nose. Sighing, instead of crying. Which I didn't want to do in front of anyone, ever. Especially Neecie.

But she could totally tell. Saw everything.

"Oh, Sean," she said, hugging me, the stadium blanket falling around my shoulders. It smelled like mothballs. And

Neecie. Who smelled like that lotion she put on her face when she got all red. And cake. She smelled like cake and flowers. Or some other plant. Good, though.

I let her hug me and I sniffed up my leaking nose-tears and then I kind of pushed her back, because it wasn't over yet, and I cleared my throat and just explained it.

How that day, the day before I punched him, my mom was going to the after-hours clinic she worked at for extra money and how I had dicked around all afternoon with Eddie, screwing around in my car and him texting this girl he was going to St. Albans with, and it had been fun, because though I was a little jealous, he and I would both go to the dance, this chick would get us in, because their dances were invite-only or something and I hadn't hooked up with anyone in a long time, and besides that, never had a girlfriend to go to actual dances or dates with, for any reason, and how that sounded fun, like maybe I'd meet a new girl, one I hadn't been stuck with since junior high, a new girl, someone who was cool and cute and fun to hang around with.

So I was supposed to be home, but I wasn't because the St. Albans girl was sending Eddie stupid pics of her and her friends and we'd been idiots about it, but it was really funny and good and I didn't want to be home, anyway, because two days earlier, my mother had told my dad he had to move out, go to rehab, or go live with Grandpa Chuck, it didn't matter, she wasn't living with an alcoholic anymore, and we were going to lose our house, since he'd been out of work for over two years, and Eddie knew that part—about the money and no job—but not the alcoholic thing. Or maybe he did, but he didn't know what that really looked like inside our house. And he didn't know what I found, when I came home, which was Otis barking all strange, and randomly, like he was distressed or something, and I knew things were wrong because his bark was wrong. And that's when I went and found my dad, half in the running bathtub, water all over the floor, wasted out of his mind and vomit everywhere and piss in the tub water and him looking basically dead and how I did nothing. Not a thing. Just stood there and calmly reviewed how long, exactly, it'd been, since I'd wished him dead, since seventh grade, probably, when things got really bad, and the fighting was constant and him passing out on the couch was constant and him checking into the hospital rehab to "clean himself up" or "get himself right" was constant, and Brad had to do everything, then, fix stuff and shovel snow and jump my mom's car if the battery died and carry in the groceries and tell me to shut up and go back to my room if I went to his room to ask him if we should do something, and so I just sat there and did nothing but hate my dad. Because I was in charge of hating him. Hating him and wishing him dead.

He was just lying there, in the water. The water spilling everywhere. Piss. Barf. His skin looking blue.

But maybe I hadn't been wishing he'd be dead. Maybe, I was just wishing he'd be gone. He didn't need to leave the earth permanently, I thought, while I turned off the water and started draining the tub. Just leave. Be absent. Not make me listen to my mother cry all night from across the hallway in the house we couldn't live in anymore, because my dad wouldn't stop drinking and broke his whole rule about drinking and driving which was why his job fired him: he needed a valid license and having a DUI, even one, was grounds for dismissal.

I didn't know he took pills, too, before he got into the tub. We didn't find that out until later. Until my mom—by total accident—came back home to get her phone charger and found us, my dad and me, in the bathroom, and she didn't even ask me anything, how long it'd been or what had happened because she knew. She wasn't an idiot like her youngest son. She was on her barely charged cell phone with the 911 dispatcher, pushing me out of the bathroom, saying, "Sean, call your brother, right away." Giving me a job to do. Which I did. I called Brad and told him that dad had passed out in the tub and mom was calling 911 and to come home.

"You mean the hospital?" he said.

"No, we're at home."

"Jesus, what's the matter with you? I'm going straight to the hospital," he said, and hung up.

By then my mom had hung up with the 911 people, but my dad was still in the tub. I could see his dick and balls. He looked grey and horrible. I couldn't tell if he was breathing. My mom was checking his pulse, on that big vein in his neck or whatever, and she nodded at me, like to say, yes, he has a pulse. Then my mom asked me for a towel and to help her wrap him up and we had sort of done that—sort of—when the paramedics came and we had to get out of the bathroom and then they were pulling him out the door on a stretcher, and then she got in the ambulance with them and told me to wait for Brad to come, and I didn't want to say that he wasn't coming, that he was going to the hospital because he wasn't me, he was brave and normal and strong, and so the ambulance jetted off and I stood there, in the dark, though it was just, like, six thirty, and the neighbors were out on their stoops, looking at us, looking at me, while I did nothing. Continued to do nothing but look straight back at them for a little bit longer. Waiting for fuckall. Waiting for nothing.

And then I just drove myself to the hospital, where Brad ignored me and my mother said nothing and Krista, still in her Applebee's uniform, hugged me and said, "Come here, Sean, it's okay, he's stable, they pumped his stomach, you were lucky you found him when you did, oh, honey . . ."

I had stopped talking. Neecie was crying. Also, I was crying. Though I wasn't making a lot of noise about it. It was more like I was dripping. Leaking.

"I'm so sorry," Neecie said. She turned off the car, and suddenly everything was much quieter. "So sorry about all of that. Come on. Come here."

We got in the backseat of her car and she put the blanket on me and then we didn't say anything more, or do anything, either, and that's how I spent the whole night sleeping with a girl for the first time in my life, not even kissing or anything, just sleeping next to her, next to each other, not touching anywhere except maybe my shoulder nudging her shoulder, in the back of her car, sleeping like the dead, fully comfortable and good, though not in a bed, all night, until the sun came up.

# Chapter Seventeen

Kerry tossed another twig into his little fire pit thing. It was drizzling out, but he insisted the weather was going to clear up by noon.

"Can't believe you're doing it," he said. "Fucking military."

"He's doing it," Eddie said.

"I feel like it's all a fucking joke," Kerry said. "It doesn't even sound like you."

What Kerry knew about me was next to nothing, really. Or really, what Kerry thought he knew about me was nothing. He'd been my boss for a bunch of months; this didn't really qualify him as an expert on my life.

Shane came out then. Nodded at me and Eddie. Sat down in a chair, lit a cigarette. He smelled like he'd just taken a shower; he was barefoot, his hair was wet, and he'd shaved off his goatee.

"Going somewhere special?" Kerry asked, in his mean way.

"Maybe," Shane said. Then he started cleaning out his toenails with a toenail clipper. Eddie looked away; Eddie was always squeamish about that kind of thing. He had sisters, so he couldn't freely be disgusting and open about his personal habits. Plus, he was pissed; he only was here because he wanted some weed, and Ivy was waiting for him and was probably wondering what was going on because he kept getting texts-beeps every second.

Then my phone beeped and I checked it. Hallie. Fuck.

Hallie, who was texting me again. Hallie, who said she was better now. Hallie, who I think I almost liked better when she was depressed. I hadn't been responding to her texts. Though once I'd been a dick and sent back a photo of a topless girl milking a cow that Eddie'd sent me.

"Got any weed you want to sell?" Eddie said, suddenly.

"They piss test you before boot camp, you know," Kerry said, looking only at me.

"I'm not the one who asked," I said.

Shane laughed, started clipping his toenails. Clip, Snip, Click, Snap. Fucking gross.

"It's not the mellow kind," Kerry said, to Eddie.

"That's okay."

"All right," Kerry said, staring at me another minute before finally acknowledging Eddie. "You want it, come inside."

Then they went inside to do the whole dirty money-exchange business, and I was stuck with Shane and his toenails. Which he was done clipping, at least. How he'd managed to smoke while clipping his toenails was kind of miraculous. Though still gross.

"When you go to boot camp?" Shane asked.

I told him. Now he was working on his fingernails. The bits were flying everywhere. Christ.

"You going on a date or something?" I asked.

"Why's everyone got such a problem with a guy wanting to clean up? Jesus."

I didn't know what to say. It wasn't like I wanted him to be gross. I guess I just didn't want to look at it, mostly. It seemed really unmanly.

"Hey, tell that friend of yours I finally did download that movie she was telling me about."

"Who?"

"Blond chick. Neecie?"

"Oh," I said. "What movie?"

"*Full Metal Jacket.* Turns out I saw it a long time ago. Good fucking movie, though. You ever see it?"

"No."

"That's a boot camp movie you probably don't want to see," he said. He laughed. "My brother said they can't do half that shit anymore. Can't even touch you. Still. Fucked-up movie. Tell her I liked it, though."

"Why don't you tell her?"

He laughed. "Maybe I will. Haven't seen her for a couple of weeks, though."

A couple of *weeks?*

I stood up and didn't say shit, but I got Eddie from Kerry's room, where they were doing bong hits, and was like, "We gotta leave. Now."

And Eddie didn't get it, but I didn't want to explain it and Kerry just shook his head at us like we were completely worthless, his whole, *how'd I end up with these assholes* routine again, and Eddie was like, "What's your deal, Sean? You're acting like a prick."

"Fuck you."

"No, fuck you," he said, getting in my face. Kerry was behind him, smirking, looking down.

"Jesus Christ," Eddie said. "Been sitting here all fucking morning but once you get something up your ass, then it's time to leave?"

Kerry set down his bong on his dresser, far away from us.

"You think you're so superior or something? For not smoking weed anymore? Because you're going into the Marines or something?"

"I don't fucking think that."

Eddie shoved me in the chest.

"What the fuck, Eddie?" I shoved him back, but not as hard. Just so, you know, he'd know to stay in his own lane and everything. But that's not how he saw it. He shoved me again, right into my chest hollow, and it actually hurt and I wanted to kill him.

But he walked out and I rushed after him, Kerry behind me.

"He's right, you know," Kerry said. "You are being a prick, Sean. It's already starting." He shook his head, smiling a little.

"Fuck you too," I said as I headed out the door, seeing Eddie walking halfway up the street, like he hoped to walk all the way home or some stupid shit like that.

"The hits don't stop with you two girls," he called after me.

"I'm glad you wanted to hang out," Hallie said. "Not just because of the other stuff. I mean, I have so much to tell you."

I nodded at her. We were at this graduation open house for her cousin, who was graduating from college, actually, and why Hallie needed me there, I don't know, but at least the food was good. It wasn't just ham on buns in the garage like everyone else had; there was, like, actual catered food that was hot, everything in steam tables off the back deck, and tons of people and little tables everywhere in the huge backyard.

"I've applied to a couple different places for fall," she said. "St. Kate's is my first choice. I think I needed a smaller setting, personally. Madison's pretty big."

"Right."

"Plus, Carenna goes there. I don't think we can be roommates, or whatever, because she said that stuff might be hard to set up, but at least I would know one person there."

"You didn't seem to have a problem with meeting people at Madison, Hallie," I said. "You were constantly posting pictures of you with people. It wasn't like you were, like, all by yourself all the time."

A little kid came over and told Hallie her mom wanted her in the kitchen. "Tell her I'll be right there," she said, smiling at the kid. Once the kid ran off, she said, "Yeah, but none of them really understood me, you know. For real? Not outside of a party context. It was just super fake. It was all bullshit."

"Oh."

Hallie started picking at her fingernails, then chipping the polish off with her thumbnail, right onto her placemat. Jesus, what was with everyone and their weird grooming habits in my face lately?

Without looking up, still picking, she said, "So, the other thing I was going to say wasn't a big thing, but I thought you ought to know. I mean, I probably should have said something earlier, but then it happened so quick, and I didn't want to bother anyone or anything, because there was really no question about what I had to do."

Then she looked up at me. In a way that made me suddenly want to barf. I didn't know what was coming, but it felt like something big.

"Well, so I was depressed and stuff but that wasn't it. I kind of . . . Well, I was pregnant too. I didn't know then, but after that one day, I kind of put it all together and took a test and stuff."

"What?"

She shrugged. Like it was nothing.

"My mom and sister took me to the clinic and everything. It's all fine now, but I thought you might want to know."

"What?" I repeated.

"What do you mean, what?"

The little kid came back. It was a little boy. He had a big orange stain on his shirt, like he'd spilled juice or something. "Your mom says to come now," he said. "Hurry up!"

"All right, yes," Hallie said, smiling at him, all fake. When he left, she turned back to me, completely normal. "I heard from my mom who heard from someone else that you're going to join the Marines."

"What the fuck, Hallie?" I said. Blurted. Loud, too. People nearby looked at us.

"Lower your voice," Hallie scolded me, all mom-like.

"Why in the hell would you tell me this?" I said, leaning

in and trying to talk lower. "I mean, why now? If you were just going to do what you wanted to do, anyway?"

"Oh, you think I should have had a fucking baby, Sean?" She was hissing, whispering so fierce.

"No, but Christ, you wouldn't even ask me . . ."

"You're assuming you have any say in the matter."

"Hallie!" Mrs. Martin, on the other side of the lawn, waving and motioning for her.

"Just a second, Mom!" she yelled, fake-smiling again.

"I don't have any say?" I asked.

"No, you don't," she said, louder. "No one does but me."

"I don't know how this fucking happened," I said. Set my hands on the table a little too hard and the plates and cups jumped.

"Calm down," Hallie said, through her teeth.

"You said it was okay," I said, trying to breathe out. "You said I didn't need the goddamn condoms . . ."

"You didn't. I'm still on the pill." She stood up, grabbed her plate, crossed her arms over her boobs. Looked pissy.

"Well, then, what the fuck?"

"Sometimes when you take antibiotics, it interferes with the pill, okay? I didn't know that, but I guess it does."

"Oh."

"I wasn't being irresponsible, Sean. God. I can't believe you would ever think I'd just do it without anything . . ."

"Well, I don't know. Christ." I pushed my plate away. She grabbed it, stacked it on top of hers, removed the silverware, the bits of food making a sticky sound as the paper plates suctioned together. Then she grabbed my cup, like she was some kind of waitress, and stacked it inside her cup.

"Hallie!" Mrs. Martin hollered again.

"We don't have to talk about it anymore," she said. "It's done. I just . . . I don't know. I thought you should know. But I guess you didn't have to. I didn't have to tell you. I just thought . . ."

What? She thought I'd like to know about how she had my kid vacuumed out of her?

Which I said. Blurted.

Her face looked like she might cry for a second. But then she didn't. She tilted her head to the side and paused, her eyes narrow.

"Hallie . . ."

"It wasn't just you that I was texting, Sean," she said.

I didn't want to even look at her. I couldn't not look at her, though.

She sat back down, put the plates and cups in a stack. Her mother yelled again, but she didn't turn around. Instead, she reached for my hand, uncurled it from its fist.

"But it was just you that I actually, you know, cared about, even," she said, soft and quiet. "You mattered to me, okay? That's why I told you. I wanted to tell you. We're friends, right? We were at least. We're more than just sex, okay? I know you don't believe me; I can see it in your face, Sean. I know. But that's always been the way it is with us."

She was crazy. She was so full of shit. I had no idea how someone so dumb had actually made it into college. Maybe that was why she'd had to quit, though.

But I didn't want to act weird. I nodded. Her mom yelled again and she said "I'll be right back" and she was gone, leaving me there with nothing on the table, so I felt like an idiot, just sitting there for no reason.

When she came back, it was like the conversation had never happened. And we just said a bunch of polite stuff. Stuff that sounded like the right thing to say. Like, sorry for everything. That she had to go through all that. That I was glad she told me. Even if I wasn't. Even if I wished I'd never come here. Wished her hand would get out of mine. Wished I didn't know about my kid or some other dude's wasted kid swirling around some drain in a clinic.

Finally I told her I had to get to work, so she walked me out, down the street where I'd parked with all the other cars of the party guests, and she said we'd have to stay in touch, for sure hang out a lot before I left, which to me was just another way of not saying good-bye. Another way of not being brave.

●

After I punched in for work later that day, I went straight to Neecie in the break room, where she was tying on her apron.

"Hey, tell me this, will you?" I said. "Did you have sex with that Shane guy?"

"What?"

"Shane. That guy who lives with Kerry."

"Oh," she said, tilting her head. "No."

"Nothing with him, though? You didn't do anything else?"

"Why do you even care, Sean?"

"Just . . . did you?"

"No," she said. "I saw him at Applebee's one night. He came and sat with me and Ivy and some other people. We talked a little. Don't be all weird." She pushed past me, toward the tagging table, where she started filling a rack with hangers.

"I'm not being weird," I said. "I just had to, you know, witness him clip his fucking toenails and tell me to tell you how much he loved *Full Metal Jacket* and whatever."

"What does clipping his toenails have to do with anything?"

"Nothing. I'm just telling you."

"Well, thank you," she said, kind of snobby. "Now I know."

Then she didn't talk to me the rest of the shift. God, I was fucking annoyed.

There were six bins of clothing to bale, too. Some volunteer group had come in the night before and plowed through a ton of stuff, according to Wendy. Now it was my gig to use the baler, since I was old enough and had done the whole training thing on it with Kerry and everything.

The baler was a pretty simple machine. You lined up the twine, then loaded the hole with the unwanted clothing, shut the door, turned the key until the light went red, then hit the button. Then fight the urge to plug your ears as things got louder than hell until the final CLANG sound and the light went green, letting you know you could turn the key the other way and out came a perfectly twined-up sandwich-deck of unwanted clothing that smelled like body odor and mildew and dirt. Easy to stack ten deep on a truck. Nice, neat. And no fucking hassles.

I blew through all the bins and then I stacked bales until Wendy told me to stop, that the rag dealer wouldn't be here until next week and we'd have to wait to get another truck down here before we could store them. I was sweating like a fucking pig and I wanted to tell Wendy that if it was all the same to her, I'd just keep baling forever. I'd stack them to the ceiling, I'd load them up in the truck and tear off to the river trestle and dump them in the water, which was running high from spring rains. Or I'd put them along the property lines of the rambler, like a gunner's nest, stacks and stacks, like a fortified fence. Or take them to the clinic where Hallie had gone, let the nurses use the rags to soak up all the blood before it went down the drain. I knew a million places to put unwanted useless shit.

Kerry looked at me the whole night like he was pissed. Building up to saying something too. Like he was mad at me telling him to fuck off the day before. He kind of huffed around, popping in while I stacked the bales, looking at me funny until Wendy sent me to clean out a storage bin where someone had donated a terrarium full of rancid nasty water. Including two dead turtles. Jesus, could people not even drain the goddamn liquid before hustling their kid's dead pets out the door?

And that's when I found it. The exact thing that I knew Neecie would like for the shelf of stuff in the break room. She might like it for herself, actually, too. It was kind of perfect. Only now I didn't want to talk to her either. Or I wanted to talk to her too much, maybe. And I kept making it so I couldn't and that was all my fault and I was tired of not doing anything right.

# Chapter Eighteen

School was almost done, and it was hotter than hell with no air-conditioning and everyone was ragged and worn-out. Papers all over the floor and kids acting stupid and teachers too tired to deal with it. Like, when I told my Global Studies teacher that my dog had pissed on my homework, he just nodded and shrugged like he didn't have the energy to even be mad anymore, even though Otis actually *had* pissed all over my backpack. Had been pissing all over everything, actually, lately, and my mom was going crazy.

You could feel the let's-just-be-done-already vibe from all the teachers, too, as if they got infected with it by all the seniors, who nobody could touch anymore, really, with graduation in thirteen days and the weather sunny and beautiful and everyone hanging out in the parking lot more than the hallways. Plus all the girls were wearing little tank tops and shorts and I was all

The Horn, all the time, and instead of being annoyed about it, and wanting to leave—*I am never coming back*—I just wanted to make out with every single one of them, even Ivy Heller, even Neecie—who wasn't really talking to me again—and it was disturbing, how everyone bitched about being done and how over high school they were and being ready to graduate and now I just felt like it was all rushed and ending. When people saw in the school newspaper Senior Showcase thing, where they listed what everyone's graduation plans were, that I was going into the Marines, they were all, "Wow, Oh, Cool!" and I felt worse, like *no no no, you have no idea, I am leaving, for real, you have no goddamn idea how real and neither do I so we need to stop, and mark this and never let each other go* and it was embarrassing that I felt that way, since I'd never felt that way about them to begin with.

●

The last track meet of my brief high school track career ended on the high fucking note of my fourth-place finish in the 800.

Or at least I thought it had ended. And then the assistant coach, this cute college girl named Gretchen who everyone had The Horn for, asked me why I wasn't warming up, since I was doing the 4X400 relay, and didn't I know this?

I looked at Eddie, who looked at me like, *dude—keep up already.*

"Okay," I said. But I'd never done a relay in a meet, and doing them in practice always made me nervous. The baton especially; my hands would sweat and I thought I'd drop it. Still, I got up and started shaking out my calves a little, not that I wanted to do that, but just that everyone else did that, so it seemed like the right thing to do.

Then I found out that I was the anchor on the thing, which was even weirder. Usually they put one of the scrawny fast-as-hell kids on that part, but I wasn't going to go up to Gretchen and say, "Hey, I'm your slow-as-fuck lump, remember? Why, exactly, am I closing this race out?"

So the race started and I waited and waited and it seemed like it would never be my turn but finally the baton smacked into my hand, I felt it and didn't see it, which was strange but made it easier to not drop it, and it was like holding a stick of dynamite, I guess, because then it was almost too fast for me to even think. I couldn't get to where I wanted to be in reality fast enough; it was almost like I was still back waiting, even though when I looked to my left, I was in a dead heat with this kid next to me and I was like, *fuck. This can't be happening.*

But then I saw the finish and when I whipped my head to the side the kid wasn't there. And when I hit the finish, the whole team was all over me and Gretchen hugged me. Everyone crazy and yelling and happy. My body was all sparking, too, like it sometimes did in the middle of a longer run, when my mind would finally stop, and then I looked over in the bleachers and saw Neecie, walking along between the seats, not looking at me but just watching where her feet were going and even though she must have missed the relay, I didn't care, because she was wearing a little pink skirt, white tank top, pink bra straps sticking out, her hair long and shiny, and I kept hoping she'd turn, and finally she did, but then Gretchen was calling us over for the little coach speech part and I got tugged along to listen to all the junk about uniforms and great job and the end-of-the-season banquet and whatever.

I could barely listen. I worried that Neecie would leave before I could talk to her. Stood there jiggling my leg up and down and being annoyed. Finally everyone dribbled off to the locker room to shower and stuff.

I put my gear in my bag, and looked for Neecie. Saw Neecie's head, all shiny yellow in the sun. She was walking the opposite direction, by herself. And even though Eddie was talking to me, I said, "Hang on, I forgot something," and doubled back to the bleachers.

I grabbed her by the shoulder and she turned around, startled, and then she smiled.

"Sean . . . ?"

I just kind of shuttled her body toward me. She wasn't expecting it; neither was I, really. She dropped her bag with a big clunk and made a little noise, like "Oh!" in this tiny high voice, something like a bunny rabbit would make, if bunny rabbits could talk, and she smelled like her nice cake smell, and her mouth was partway open, in a perfect lipstick commercial pucker. So then obviously I kissed her. No tongue, though. And no tongue from her, either, until a minute later, when she opened her mouth more and her tongue was soft against mine and I wanted to laugh, it was so great, but then my water bottle hanging in the net of my bag squirted everywhere and we almost fell over and to steady us, my hand went on her ass. Which was perfect. Her ass, I mean. But then I realized what I'd done, that I'd grabbed her like a total animal, all without saying one word.

I pulled back from her. *She can see my mouth*, I thought. *She can tell what I'm saying. So say something. Even if it's just Sorry.*

She didn't give me much time to think; she just smiled again, like she was thinking of something funny, and she kissed me again, her hand slipping around my sweaty neck. I probably reeked, but I didn't care. I shrugged off my track bag, too, the water bottle now spilling everywhere, but I just kept at it. Smashed her against me, kind of rougher than I meant to, her hair all over the place and getting stuck between our mouths, making her laugh and sweep it away and it was insane and good and why hadn't we done this before?

Someone honked and yelled something, and Neecie pulled back from me. She'd been standing on her tiptoes the whole time. She looked down, her long hair covering her face, and I watched the cars in the distance, recognizing them as guys from the team, feeling weird about it. But proud. But happy.

"What are you doing now?" she asked. Completely calm.

"Going home, I guess," I said.

"Is anyone at your house?"

"I don't think so."

"I'll come with you," she said. In that same calm way, like nothing had just happened. Like now we were going to do something casual and normal where all our clothes stayed on.

Twenty minutes later, I was out of my track gear but had skipped the shower and now was in half-wet clothes because of the water bottle spilling everywhere and I was driving home with Neecie in my rearview mirror, her Blazer sounding loud as hell, and my knees felt all jittery and weird and I didn't know what I'd gone and done with Neecie except I wanted to go and do it again.

Once in my house, we were all cool and casual again. Neecie looked at Krista's latest wedding junk on the table, a big pile of pictures of her and Brad when they were little, and I set my relay ribbon down on the kitchen counter and swigged a bunch of orange juice from the fridge. Then I didn't know what to do.

"You should take a shower," she said.

"Yeah," I said. Not getting what the point of that was. Was it sexual? Or was she dismissing me? Did I smell *that* bad?

But I just dumped my junk in my room and got into the shower. Washed up everything good besides The Horn. Which wouldn't completely deflate, the dumbass. Even when I wrapped my idiot Pokémon towel around myself. So, I brushed my teeth, took care of a zit on my chin, waited a few more minutes. Thought about guns. Thought about carnations. Thought about being in Brad's wedding. Then it was mostly gone.

In my room, Neecie was sitting on my bed, her little pink skirt poofing around her thighs. I could hear the little drips of water from my hair on the carpet. I wondered if she could hear them, too.

"Nice towel," she said.

"Thanks."

We stared at each other for a long, uncomfortable time.

Finally she stood up and said, "Are you sure you want to do this?"

I was next to her in less than a second. "Yes."

She hadn't even touched me, and The Horn, it popped up like toast. Fuck.

Then we kissed again. Her hands were shy on my chest, but mine went straight under her tank top, started shoving it up and when she lifted up her arms over her head, like she perfectly understood what I wanted without having to talk, no rules or routines, it was so goddamn great that I felt like I kind of wanted to marry her.

Her bra was pink and shiny, so smooth, and her boobs were just little tiny things, but they were perfect for her, for her body and its size. I couldn't imagine anything else on her. I couldn't think of a way to tell her this that wouldn't make her feel shitty, though, so I just tried to show her, once I got her bra off, how I couldn't get enough of them, and that led to just wanting, of course, more nakedness in general, and I shoved down her skirt and she easily stepped out of her flip-flops and stood there in her panties, which weren't panties, but a pink thong, the same material as her bra. Hallie never wore thongs; she said they were sleazy. I thought they were sleazy too. Sleazy . . . and *excellent.*

"Jesus," I said, my hands everywhere. I was like a goddamn animal. "You're so . . . god! *Fuck.*"

She laughed. "Eloquent," she said.

I tipped her over on the bed, then, because I couldn't help it and she unwrapped my towel and The Horn was between us for real now, mashing against her thong, and then we kissed again for a long time and everything felt really, really good. So good.

My hand hovered up around her belly like I couldn't decide what do. I kept kissing her, and then she pushed my hand lower, until it was all the way down there.

"Is that all right?" I said.

"It's fine," she said. In that same bunny rabbit tone. It was perfect. She was perfect.

After a while of touching like that, I felt like I might come all over her damn leg so I rolled off her and we just stared at the ceiling for a while. Her hair tickled my face. One hand tucked right into the hollow of my chest, as if it was meant to do that, like that was the point of the cave-in, for Neecie Albertson's hand to hang out there. Her other hand was on my stomach, all casual and relaxed, just above my dick hair, and it took a lot of concentration to chill the hell out about that particular fact.

"You always wear thongs?" I asked. Blurting.

"It depends," she said, "on what other clothes I wear. Sometimes you won't want things to see through, like red under a white skirt or something. Or if your jeans are low-rise or really tight or whatever."

"So why would you wear a thong under a skirt?"

"Because it's hot out and there's no air-conditioning in our crappy school."

"Jesus," I said. Because this changed how I'd look at girls in skirts forever. "Does every girl do that?"

"I don't know," she said. "Ivy sometimes doesn't wear underwear at all."

"Jesus."

"Well, not if she wears a skirt or anything. But with low-rise jeans, you practically have to wax . . . " she explained, then stopped. "Wait. Why do you care about this?"

"It's my continuing mission to understand people better," I said.

She rolled to her side. "By people, you mean girls?"

"Why? Is this a big secret girl conspiracy? You can't tell any guys?"

"No. But it's funny you're curious. I guess I thought this was all common knowledge."

"I don't have any sisters," I said. "What do you expect me to do? Ask my mom?"

She laughed. "Why are we talking about undies?"

"You call them 'undies'?"

"What do *you* call them?"

"Thongs," I said. "Panties."

"Panties, eww," she said. "Don't say 'panties.' You sound like my grandmother. When does your mom come home?"

"Thursdays are her late day," I said. "Usually after seven or so."

She rolled onto her back, then. "Do you really want to have sex, Sean?" she asked.

I pushed up on one elbow, so she could see my face. The clock on my nightstand said 6:38. When I looked back at her, she was looking direct at me, waiting for an answer.

"Yeah, I really do," I said, running my hand over her belly and her boobs. Her nipples twitched in a way that was both a giant turn-on and cute that same bunny rabbit way too. My hand kept roaming everywhere, and her skin was all reddish and rashy, from neck to belly, and she had goose bumps all over but her eyes were shut and she didn't say anything.

After a million billion years, she opened her eyes and said, "You seem worried. Is that why you stopped?"

"I just didn't want to come on your leg," I admitted, dipping my head into her neck so I didn't have to face her.

"That was thoughtful," she said. I could hear the smile in her voice. So we started kissing again, and her hand reached for my dick and it was awesome, how soft and slow she was, touching me, touching it like it was this amazing thing she couldn't get enough of.

And then I had to do it, just had to. Slid down from her mouth to her neck and her boobs and down her belly until I was there. Right there. And just when you'd expect everything to speed up, me being me and The Horn and all, now everything slowed down. Like the opposite of running the relay.

I held her ass in both hands, like something breakable, precious, and slid her thong down her thighs and calves and flung it behind me like a slingshot into outer space. Pressed open her knees, ducked my head down between them.

And instead of freaking out and telling me to stop like Hallie always did, Neecie just let me.

And it was fucking awesome. I thought, *Nothing else is like this. Nothing else in the world.*

But when she was super still, I got worried. Like she'd be like Hallie that first time we'd done it, all tense and strange. But then her thighs started trembling and it was so great, even though I hadn't been sure if I was working it right. Because, actually? I didn't even care. I loved it too much. Every part of it. Listening to her breathing. Feeling the way her stomach was clutching up. Hearing her make a few sounds, the little bunny rabbit kind, then louder, and after a while she was saying words, exactly what I couldn't make out, because I was too busy and what did they matter as long as they weren't *stop* or *no*?

Finally, it seemed like she was trying to twist up and away from me, but I held on until she said my name—*Sean!*, in this kind of whisper, and the thrill of that, of her knees locking and my name like an emergency, *that* was what mattered, *that* was the point of everything in the whole world just then and possibly ever.

When she finally opened her eyes at me, she laughed, all out of breath, but she looked so happy anyway and she said, "I think we're ready, Sean."

And so I got up and got out a condom from my sock drawer

and started ripping into it, standing by the bed as she sat up next to me, and I felt a little embarrassed of how much of me she could see in full daylight. But then Neecie was all involved, and she kept saying things:

"Hold still!" and "You're being a dork!" and "Your bed smells like chlorine. Bleach. I'm getting all rashy. Look, it's all over my shoulders. Is it on my back?"

Her voice was lazy, sexy, even, but she was just her normal Neecie-self. Even if she was holding my dick and looking at it straight, like it didn't bother her. Just kept talking, kept her eyes on it, like it was all a big huge turn-on and not upsetting in any way. I thought I might die, I couldn't wait. We'd rolled the thing on me and then she grabbed my ass ("Come here! You have such a bony ass!") pushed me toward her, so I was above her, stretched over her and she kissed me, right on my chest, not the caved-in hollow, but around my collarbone.

"This is weird," she said. "But I think it'll be good. Don't you?" She smiled, and before I could answer her, I heard the kitchen door open and slam and my mom's keys clanked on the counter and she called out not just my name, but Neecie's too.

We didn't move. My eyes were on the door like it might open any second. Neecie pulled the sheet around herself and we stared at each other, listening to my mom moving around in the kitchen: the cupboards opening and closing, the dishwasher door banging down where it was missing a hinge, the radio news station she liked buzzing away.

Then my mom called down: "You and Neecie want some dinner, honey?"

Neecie shook her head. Looked panicked. "No, Sean. Don't say anything!"

But I just yelled back, "Sure, Mom. We'll be up in a little bit."

"Sean!"

"She knows we're here," I said. "But she doesn't think anything. And if she did, she's not gonna care. I stayed out all night that one time and I told her I was with you and she didn't even care about that."

She nodded. Then she looked at the wall. And I just laid on my back now, looked at the ceiling. My hand was on her thigh and The Horn was totally gone.

Leaving. Never coming back.

Neecie sat up, her hands over her boobs.

"Sean, I need to go home."

I nodded. Stared at her body. She was so pretty, Neecie. All of her. I touched her shoulder where it was sort of red and blotchy and she twitched a little.

"Sean. I mean, I'm sorry, but this is totally weird."

"Yeah," I said. She slipped over me, and we both got out of bed to get dressed. When her back was turned I took off the condom, which was kind of terrible, if you've ever done that, taking off a condom when you haven't even gotten off. Kind of like ripping a Band-Aid off your dick.

"Ouch!" I said, louder than I could help. Neecie smirked at me, put on her shoes. Then she kissed my cheek and ran upstairs. I put on clean boxers and then sat down on the bed. Listened to her talk to my mom. My mom laughing at something she said. They talked some more, about the track meet—"Sean's pretty tired, he won the relay"—and then I heard the door open and shut and her car start and my mom's kitchen noises started back up.

I was exhausted. I laid back on the bed, half awake, half asleep.

I thought about it, for the first time, what it would be like, being Neecie's boyfriend. We could get an apartment or something. Live together. Somehow she'd go to college and do her thing, be smart and nerdy, and I'd go to the grocery store and buy her cases of her weird iced tea and special order that laundry soap she had to use for her skin thing, which her mother said they made in this place in Vermont, and it was genetic, so maybe our kids would get all red in the face, too, and we'd have kids so I'd need a job, something good, not the Thrift Bin, but something. Maybe work with Brad, trimming trees? Though I'd never trimmed trees and I hated working with Brad. Or maybe Grandpa Chuck could hook me up with something—he had lots of friends who owned businesses and shit. And we'd bring Otis to live with us, too, because kids need a dog for when they are lonely or sad or scared, they need a dog for company, for when they come in the door and to sleep on the end of their beds, even if they did hog all the room, the bigger you got. Otis would for sure live with us. I couldn't leave Otis.

Which made me think: I hadn't seen Otis all day. Hadn't heard him when Mom came in.

I threw on some pants and my shoes and pounded upstairs. Mom wasn't in the kitchen. I called for Otis.

Nothing.

I opened the back door, to the deck. Hollered again and flipped on the outside light. There was Otis, standing all weird, looking cringey and shaky in front of the back deck steps, like he wasn't sure how to climb steps or something.

"Sean?" Mom was behind me. "What . . . ?" Then she saw Otis and stopped talking.

259

"He's hurt, maybe," I said. Bent low, slapped my knees to call him. "Otis, come here, boy."

He just stood there, looking like he might tip over. Whining a little, too, a sound he hadn't made since he'd been a little puppy.

"Sean, I think something's wrong."

"He'll be okay," I said, stepping out to him. His tail wagged a little. "Good boy, Otis. That's a good boy. Come here, boy."

My mom started crying. "Sean. *Sean.* We have to take him to the vet, honey."

But I wouldn't listen to her and even when Otis licked my hand, I could see she was right, but I wouldn't believe her and then he sort of sat down weird on the ground, like he wanted to sit or lay down but couldn't figure it out so I went to pet him and saw he was covered in burrs and something wet, too. Piss, his own piss. Which he'd been pissing out everywhere, on my backpack and on the kitchen floor and on a pile of Krista's wedding craft crap, ruining the ribbons for something they needed to decorate the reception with and then I lifted him up and carried him into the house and my mom said that I needed to listen to her, because Otis was hurting and something was wrong and he needed the vet but I wouldn't listen. I wouldn't, because that couldn't be what happened next. It couldn't.

I brought him down to my room and I laid on the carpet with him, just listening to him breathe, his chest rising and falling. I pulled out the burrs softly and gently and wiped him with my Pokémon towel so he wasn't all piss-wet and I just stayed there, all night, telling him I was sorry and it was going to be all right, and it was, as long as I was listening to him breathing and feeling for his heartbeat.

In the morning, when my mom came into my room, I handed her his collar, the little charm still jingling, even though he was gone, and I told her, both of us crying, how in the middle of licking my hand, the sun not quite up, Otis' chest stopped and stiffened and there wasn't anything after that. No more breathing. No more Otis.

# Chapter Nineteen

The day of graduation, my mom and I went to pick up Otis from the vet. My mom didn't want to do it, saying we could wait another day, but I refused to let it go. I wanted him back and I wanted to bury him and I didn't care about graduation or the stupid Senior Lock-In that night either.

"Sean, honey," she said, a million times, until I told her I'd go without her if she wouldn't come already.

But when we got to the vet, I didn't want to go in. I wanted to cry.

"Come on, honey," my mom said, and we went in, and there in the vet's office were all these other pet owners, holding their cats in their laps or hanging onto their dopey-looking little puppies on leashes and all along the back wall were the bags of expensive pet food, which I felt guilty we couldn't afford because maybe if we could have, Otis still would be alive and not dead from kidney failure or whatever the vet said he thought it was.

My mom stood at the counter and got out her credit card, like she was buying something normal, not her dead dog's ashes in a little marble container, and I stood beside her, wondering if we'd have to talk to the vet or something formal, but it was just the receptionist lady having my mom sign a receipt and then handing us a heavy box that was now Otis. My dog, now a box I could hold with one hand. My dog, now a thing that could fit under the seat of my car.

When we got back home, Krista and Brad and Grandpa Chuck were there, all dressed up for graduation, Krista in an orange dress, Brad and my grandpa in collar shirts. It was hot, and I was still wearing what I'd dug the hole in the backyard in and I smelled and I was dirty and my jeans had a big tarry stain on the knee, and but Krista still hugged me and said she was so sorry and she smelled like Juicy Fruit gum, and Brad even looked a little like he might actually feel bad.

Grandpa Chuck helped me put Otis's little box into the hole. And then we all stood there and looked at the box in the black dirt and I didn't know what to say. Though it seemed like we should say something. Like a normal funeral.

"He was a good dog," my mom said. "Gentle. So loving."

I nodded. Krista started sniffling.

"The best," I said.

Then Brad took a picture, with his phone. And I whirled around and screamed, "What the fuck are you doing?"

"For dad," he said. "Dad loved Otis too."

"You asshole," I said. "You are such an asshole."

"What the fuck is your problem, Sean?" Brad said. "You

263

act like you're the only one in the world."

Grandpa Chuck stood between us. Yelled, "Enough. Enough. Brad, I mean it. Sean, go get ready. You need to be at commencement soon."

Krista was crying now, openly, ruining all her makeup. My mom took my hand and led me into the house and said, "Your shirt's ironed and on your bed, honey."

I showered and put on the dumb collar shirt she'd laid out for me and some dorky pants, just like Brad's and Grandpa Chuck's, and slapped on deodorant since it was hot as fuck. When I came out again, Krista's makeup was fixed and Otis's box was covered up by dirt and my mom was finishing planting flowers all over the top of it. Yellow and orange ones and something green with no petals yet and she told me the names—yarrow and poppy and Shasta daisies, "all things that are perennials, so they'll always come back every year" and I wanted to say, *But will we always be here? We don't even own this shithole. Will you? Because I won't.* But I couldn't talk, and then we got into the car and drove to celebrate my graduating from high school.

●

About the actual graduation, well, it was stupid. Because I was trying not to think about Otis and I was sitting by people I didn't want to talk to, even though I'd had my locker by them for years (Charlotte Norton and Asher Nyander) and I wore sunglasses, which was douchey—Tristan Reichmeier wore sunglasses too— but I had an actual reason, because I didn't want anyone to know I'd been crying. Some minister led us in prayer, which seemed like bullshit, because, separation of church and state, right?

264

But no one said anything and then a teacher I'd never had did a funny speech that everyone laughed at and then the genius kid of our grade, this guy named Brandon Houseman, did the speech and because he had gotten into Princeton, we all were supposed to worship him or something. All the fucking possibilities. When it was over, my mom and Grandpa and Brad and Krista took pictures, me with Eddie and everyone, even some kids from the track team, and Neecie and even Ivy Heller, which was a stretch, but everyone had all this goodwill now that high school was over. Tristan Reichmeier and the hockey players posing with the football team and all their dumb girl equivalents from the dance team and it was all so phony but also sincere, with some of the girls crying, which seemed unreasonable, as if this was some accomplishment, surviving high school. And then Sergeant Kendall was there, and he hugged me and said well done, and I introduced him to my family and I thought for a minute that my mom would get mad at him, but then she was nice to him, though distant, while he listed off all my wonderful qualities, which Brad smiled at, as if he knew better. Then Steven-Not-Steve was there for some reason, and it turned out that Brandon Houseman was his godson or something so I got my picture taken with both of them, too. And just when I wanted to leave and go home and lie in bed and never come back out, my mom handed me a duffel bag and said she'd packed some other clothes for the lock-in and my toothbrush and stuff, and I told her I didn't want to go, that I didn't have to, and then Neecie slipped beside me and said, "Come on, Sean. It'll get your mind off things," and I couldn't argue because Neecie knew Otis was dead and my alternative was staying home and doing last-minute wedding crap with Krista and my mom.

"I really don't want to do this," I said to Neecie as we were herded through a line back into the school, the hellhole we'd supposedly officially escaped, but she just pushed me forward to the assembly line, where we all stripped out of our caps and gowns and signed forms and checked in all our stuff and learned all about our diplomas being mailed and whatever.

"You have to go in for a little while, Sean. Just try. Just an hour, try it."

"Then can I leave?"

"If you leave, you can't come back."

"Sounds fine to me."

•

But I stayed, for more than an hour. All the guys went down to the locker room, where people's dads were, supervising that we weren't fucking off or smuggling in booze or anything, just changing out of our dorky fancy clothes and into our normal stuff, and it was loud in the school, all the fans running because there was no air-conditioning. Then Eddie and me spent a while eating all the free food, pizza and sub sandwiches and chips and tacos and Mountain Dew, and after that we ripped open pull tabs for all these prizes, like bicycles and dorm fridges and gift certificates and even a car, and I won a dorm fridge, which I had no use for, so I gave it to Neecie to claim and she hugged me and smelled like cake, and I wanted to get her alone, because, The Horn, of course. I was hypnotized by her long hair and The Horn and how sad I didn't want to feel, because she was smiling that I was still there, staying, like she thought I'd listened to her and taken her advice. She and Ivy went off to the library, which was now a beauty salon where everyone got their nails and hair done and henna tattoos, and it all smelled like chemicals that gave me a headache, so I went to play basketball in the gym with Eddie, and I ended up on Brandon Houseman's team, and he said his uncle was a Marine Corps master gunner sergeant and had been to Iraq three times, and it was badass and congratulations, and then I went to get some water and found Neecie and said, "Now. Now can we leave?"

And she turned, from where she was getting her fingernails painted next to that one Hannah chick, the one who was with (or had been with) Tristan Reichmeier, and said, no, she wasn't leaving, she didn't want to go.

And I might have yelled or gotten pissed, but I couldn't do that, because I wasn't a baby or her boyfriend. I don't know what I was, but I was someone who she tossed the keys of her car to and said that once they unlocked the doors at six a.m., everyone was going down to the trestle to party, and while that sounded horrible, I could go down there and meet her later, pick her up.

"Sure," I said. And then I walked out past someone's dad who told me if I left I couldn't come back again and I said fine.

It wasn't even nine o'clock, so I drove home, and surprised the fuck out of my mom and Steven-Not-Steve, who looked like they'd been fooling around on the couch instead of folding programs for the wedding. Steven-Not-Steve was kind of red in the face and my mom was all giggly and weird, but I didn't say anything to them. I mean, they were grown adults, right?

Then Krista came over with a bunch of snacks, and so I sat and folded programs and watched some TV with everyone and then a dog food commercial came on and I started crying and

Krista said, "Oh, honey" and my mom rubbed my back and said I couldn't keep making wedding stuff or I'd get all my sadness into everything, like in that one movie set in Mexico where the sister cries into the soup and everyone who eats it feels sad.

Then she laughed a little and kept patting my back, and I felt like she was my mom again, like she loved me after all, and I wasn't just tiring her out. She took my hand and led me down to my bedroom and I took off my shoes and got in bed and she pulled the covers over me and sat there while I cried and tried to be cool about it, which is stupid to try to do in front of your mom, who used to give you baths and change your diapers and knew every horrible thing about you anyway.

But my mom didn't say anything. No lectures, no telling me it would be okay. Just scooped a bunch of hair away from my ear—hair that would be gone soon enough—just like she did when I was a little boy and was sick or couldn't sleep, her fingers soft around my temple until I fell asleep.

•

I woke up at five and couldn't get back to sleep. Almost called Otis. Then remembered. A sock to the gut. How many times would I do that before I figured out he was really gone?

Not many. You'll be gone in two weeks.

I pissed. Showered. Dressed. It was raining and grey. I went out back and looked at Otis's grave. The flowers all wet and hanging over at weird angles. A big streak of lightning cracked over the freeway then, and I went inside and drank a ton of orange juice. Then went into my mom's room.

"Sean? Are you okay?"

"Fine. Gonna go grab some breakfast with everyone. The lock-in's done soon."

"Okay."

"See you later."

"Sean?"

"Yeah?"

"I'm really going to miss you. You know that? I really am."

I nodded.

"I'm worried about you, though."

"I know."

"I'm trying not to be," she said. "Steven has been talking me off the wall about it. He's been good at reminding me of my locus of control."

I nodded again. Like I knew what a locus of control was.

"Steven's my boyfriend," she said. "I mean, I don't think you're surprised," she added, sitting up now, her purple-flowers comforter going around her. She tucked her knees up under her nightshirt and ducked her head.

"Thought I might have walked into something there," I said.

"Sorry," she said, looking more embarrassed. "We just didn't hear you because . . ."

"Because Otis didn't bark."

"Right," she said, and she looked like she might cry. I couldn't handle it. And I couldn't cry anymore. I'd cried way too much already.

"Do you like him? Steven? I mean, do you have a good time together?"

She tipped her head to the side. "You know, I do like him. I mean, I wouldn't say he's like a roller-coaster ride kind of boyfriend—having a good time isn't exactly the same for me as it might be for you—but yeah. We enjoy being around each other. It's nice. Very nice."

I was glad about that, though I wasn't in any rush to see her kiss him for real. Not just because it was Steven-Not-Steve, but also because I couldn't remember the last time I'd seen her kiss my actual own father. How depressing that was, to get old and know that you didn't even get to do stuff like that anymore! Like you just had to work and pay bills and deal with your house crap and never have any fun. Never have anyone be nice to you.

"Well . . . good," I said. "You deserve that stuff. To, you know. Make out with someone nice for a change."

"Sean!" She laughed.

"I just . . . I'll make more noise, try to knock, from now on."

"For the next fourteen days, you mean."

"Yeah. After that, you can go crazy."

"Wait till I tell Steven you said so!"

"Do *not* tell him I said that, Mom."

"Oh, I'm just kidding," she said, smiling a little. "He's kind of private about that stuff."

"Well, who isn't?" I said.

"Is Neecie . . . is she your girlfriend or something, honey?"

I sighed. "Well, no. Not really."

"Oh. Did you have a fight or something?"

I shook my head. "I just didn't want to stay at the lock-in thing."

She kept looking at me, though. "Go have your breakfast, honey. I'll see you later. Krista's having us over to the apartment to do the seating plan, okay? Plan to be there around six, okay?"

"Okay."

"I love you, Sean."

"Thanks, Mom." I said. "I love you too."

●

Outside the front of the school, there were Neecie and Eddie and Ivy, and Neecie saw her own car, because I drove her Blazer back, or maybe she just heard it, being as loud as a fucking 747 like it was, and all three of them looked kind of blown-out and hung-over, which was funny, given that the point of the Senior Lock-In was keep everyone sober and not have any tragedy strike on our Very Special Day.

They all got in, Neecie in front, Ivy and Eddie in the back, and when I asked where to go, none of them said to the trestle, because nobody gave a shit about trying to drink after staying up all night. So we went to IHOP and ate a bunch of pancakes and bacon and shit, and Ivy was laughing about how she grabbed this one girl's ass when they were standing in line for popcorn in the movie area, and the girl thought Tristan Reichmeier did it, and then she cried and Tristan got bitched at by somebody's mom, and it was so funny but goddamn was Ivy glad neither of her parents ever did shit like volunteer for things like that, because she would have been so embarrassed, so thank fucking god her mom was never around anyway, because she hated her mom, since she was a fucking selfish drunk bitch.

And I kind of stared at Ivy for the rest of breakfast because I didn't think I'd ever have one thing in common with her, ever, and I kind of wished I could just say things like that, just balls out, about my dad being a drunk and hating him.

Eddie paid for the whole breakfast. I think he was trying to impress Ivy, mostly, but it was really nice of him, and I thanked him a whole bunch while the girls were in the bathroom.

"I'm sorry I hit you," I said.

"What?"

"That day in the library. That was shitty. I shouldn't have."

"Why are you saying this, man? That was like a million years ago."

"Because. Because I should have said it before. It was pussy not to. And I'm leaving soon, and who knows when I'll be back."

"You're not gonna get killed in basic training, dumbass," Eddie said. "It's not gonna be like *Full Metal Jacket* or anything."

"Has everyone seen that movie besides me?"

"You haven't seen it yet? Dude, you have to see it. It's fucking hilarious. Well, not all of it. But a lot of it."

"You and Ivy? You guys should come to Brad's wedding."

Eddie laughed. "Just so you won't die of boredom?"

"No," I said. "Well, kinda. I'm gonna have Neecie come."

"Don't I need an official invitation, though?"

"What? No."

"Dude, you better ask. When my sister got married, my mom was super tight about the invites. Like, I was shocked she let me invite you."

"I came with my *family*, idiot," I said. "Your family probably got an invite, right?"

"How should I know?"

"I'll figure it out," I said. "But it'll be fun, if you guys come. It's out at that camp on Prairie Lake, and we've rented all the camper cabins and stuff, if you want to stay all night. And we can probably drink and everything, too, if we're not too obvious about it. I know Brad wouldn't get married without getting a keg, you know?"

"Cool," Eddie said. "We'll definitely go, then." He slid his arm around Ivy's neck as she came up from the bathroom and kissed her cheek and Ivy said, "Go where? I'm so tired. I just want to go home and shower and sleep for five hundred years."

Neecie stood by me; we didn't touch, just looked at our touchy friends, and I had a feeling like I was not in my body, like I was apart from myself. Like I was dribbling slowly out of my skin into something else. My hands were shaking, and I shoved them in my pockets.

"I'm going to miss you guys so much," Neecie said. "Seriously. I am."

# Chapter Twenty

The day of Brad and Krista's wedding, I had a million fucking things to do. Pick up my tux. Pick up my last check at the Thrift Bin. Pick up a bunch of tables and junk from Grandpa Chuck's. Take a set of Krista's bridesmaids to the camp at the lake and help them move around chairs and crap for the reception. Take another set of bridesmaids back to the restaurant where we'd had the groom's dinner the night before, because one of them had forgotten her cell phone in the ladies' room.

All of that shit took a million years, so the Thrift Bin trip got put off until the end.

Wendy was in the office when I came in.

"Oh, hi, Sean," she said, looking all sad, instantly. "I'm so sad you're going. This is going to suck."

"Did Kerry hire anyone new yet?"

"No, he's in denial, I think. He wants to think you're going to come back and he won't need to bother."

"I think he better get over that quick."

"I know," she said. "Or he'll be up to his ass in baling."

She handed me my check, and I had to sign some crap, and then she hugged me and said to come over to the break room.

Where Kerry was standing, in front of the table. With an ice cream cake and all the cashiers. One of them handed me a card.

"Congratulations, man," Kerry said. I was completely surprised. Kerry, giving me a cake?

"Neecie's on her way," Wendy said. "We didn't know when you'd show up."

Wendy cut up the cake, and I ate it while talking to the cashier girls I never really talked to, and they were giggly and acting dumb but still, it was nice. And Kerry wasn't being a dick, either, which was a shock.

When Neecie showed up, she hugged me and gave me a card that had phone minutes on it and a little good luck key chain that had a dog that looked like Otis on it, and I didn't want to say I wouldn't need a key chain in boot camp since it was the thought that counted.

"Ivy and me are going to get ready for the wedding," Neecie said. "We're staying over all night. Eddie's coming, too. Are you sure that's okay?"

"Yeah."

"Cool," she said and then kissed me on the cheek and dashed off and then it was me and Wendy and Kerry standing over the melting ice cream cake.

"Sean, I'm just so excited for you. I think this is so great," Wendy said. In this voice that was trying-to-sound-happy.

"Yeah, man," Kerry said, in the same kind of voice. "You're gonna do great."

"And if you ever need a job or a reference, don't hesitate, okay?" Wendy said. "I'm serious. You're always welcome back here."

"You won't need to come back, though," Kerry said. "Knowing you, you'll find some other perfectly reasonable person to drive crazy and you won't miss me at all."

●

The wedding itself was kind of a disaster. Brad had gotten super drunk at his bachelor party, which was after the groom's dinner, and Krista was mad at him for being useless and sick on their special day. Once I was in my tux and out at the lake, you'd think I could just have fun, but Krista's bridesmaids made me their bitch. I went back and forth to Walgreens and a million other places whenever they needed bobby pins or cigarettes. The bridesmaid who was my partner down the aisle busted her shoe strap and I had to fix it up with a zip-tie and some glue so she'd shut up already. She was making Krista insane along with everyone else.

Finally, the wedding itself went down. Neecie and Ivy showed up, driven by Mrs. Albertson and Gary, who stopped and chatted with my mother, confirming that all was on the up-and-up about staying out late at the lake. Gary would come and bring her home, Mrs. Albertson told Neecie, over and over. Then Mrs. Albertson hugged me and said good luck and that she was so proud and it was so wonderful and all that crap.

To Neecie she said, for the millionth time, "Make wise choices, honey."

"God, Mom," Neecie said, but she kissed her good-bye all the same.

Then my dad showed up. My chest got kind of tight, seeing him stroll across the lawn in his tux, and for a minute I wished he was gone. Or that I'd already left. But he came over and went through a bunch of hugging and hand-shaking with Brad and Krista and other people and finally got to me, and I was just one more hug, so it wasn't a big deal, really. Though I could only see him that night in the bathroom, still. Half dead and wet.

I had kind of got myself ready to deal with him, but then this woman came next to him, and he put her hand on his shoulder. She was holding a baby in one of those carriers you strap on your body and everyone had to be introduced to her, and the baby. I hung back as my mom approached them, and said hello to the woman and looked at the baby and I wondered what in the holy fuck was going on.

Finally, he came over to me, and the woman with the baby was with him. He introduced them and didn't say who she was, so I guessed he was fucking her. The baby didn't seem to belong to him, though; he didn't seem a part of that. I'd have to talk to my mom if I wanted to know the whole deal. I felt a little numb seeing him, though. Numb from even looking at how different he was now, how pink his skin was, how large he was, just like Brad.

"I understand you're leaving tomorrow," he said.

"Yeah."

"We'll have breakfast together. Tonight will be a bit crazy, I think."

"Okay."

Then we had to get in our places, and the lady with the

baby whisked the baby away because the photographer needed to take ten thousand photos, which was dumb, because nobody was actually married yet, so it seemed like a kind of fake-out to be doing it ahead of time. The ceremony itself was outside, around this decorated trellis thingy between the trees, everything for the wedding having tons of pink ribbons and crap dangling all over it. The actual ceremony was pretty short, too, which was good, because standing there in my stupid tight tux shoes was driving me nuts, and the shirt was tugging at my wrists because it had been fitted wrong.

During the ceremony, Krista cried, my mom cried, my dad cried, the lady he was with cried, and so did her baby. Even Brad cried a little, while saying his vows. Only I, of my family, did not cry. The romance of the day had pretty much been spoiled by bitching bridesmaids. I should have been focusing on my brother, all beefy and handsome in his tux, but mostly I just kept looking for Neecie in the crush of people. She had on this pink dress with no shoulders, a brighter pink than Krista's official wedding colors, tight around the chest, her long hair flying everywhere. She was wearing a pair of flip-flops, too, and when the ceremony and receiving line ended and it was time to line up for dinner, she opened up her bag and handed me a matching pair, black just like hers, but a million sizes bigger.

"Those tux shoes are terrible," she said. "Gary was telling me about it."

"Thanks," I said, sitting down to strip out of the horrible shoes and my socks. "You're saving my life here."

"They're from Walgreens, don't get too excited."

Neecie and Ivy and Eddie and I all hung out together until I had to go eat with the wedding party. The bridesmaid I had to go down the aisle with was having some of kind of fight with her boyfriend, and she was distracted and bitchier than ever. Then everyone clinked their glasses and the toasts started. The best man, Brad's best friend from high school, cracked everyone up with funny Brad stories that made him sound like a loveable idiot and Krista like a smart chick he was lucky to have. The maid of honor did a similar toast, but hers wasn't funny, just sappy, about how she loved Krista like a sister and how she knew she and Brad were perfect for each other and everything was going to be so wonderful in their marriage, blah. So many possibilities.

When it was my turn, I stood up and said it was great to have Krista in our family and I was very happy for them, and then I shut up, because I couldn't stand everyone staring at me all hushed and quiet, and the microphone was spitting static at me. When I sat back down, I caught Neecie's eye and she nodded at me, like I'd done good. Then Brad stood up and said he wanted to say something, even though that's not the rule.

He talked about Krista being so great and thanked everyone for coming and the parents and his new in-laws and whatever. Then he said, "This day is special for our side of the family, too. My little brother Sean is leaving tomorrow for the Marines. He's going to boot camp in California. And we're just so proud of him and want to wish him best of luck. If you'll join me in toasting him . . ."

Everyone sort of oohed, and he said, "To Sean. Thank you for being a good brother and for your service to our country." Then everyone made a little polite cheer and drank. I looked down at my dinner napkin in my lap, then up at my mom, who was crying. My dad was crying too. Krista was crying.

Everyone but me and Neecie was crying, it seemed, when I scanned the crowd. Then the toasts part ended, and I swear, I had about a bucket of sweat pouring down my back. I had never felt so embarrassed about anything; not because it was bad, but how everyone just assumed this grave, special thing about me, and it seemed like two minutes ago since seeing Sergeant Kendall that day at the career fair. I was happy when I could disentangle from everyone, pass through the crowd of people shaking my hand and beaming at me for something I hadn't even done yet.

When the dancing began, Eddie and Ivy and Neecie and I stood around, watching the First Dance and then the parents' dancing and the little flower girl with the ring bearer and everyone was taking a million pictures. Then Neecie wanted to dance. So I danced with her, and Ivy and Eddie and my mother, and Krista, and even the bitchy bridesmaid. During the break after they cut the cake, I took Neecie's hand and led her away from everything, down to the lake, where the dock had a little covered swing thing on the end of the L-shape.

"Pretty crazy, huh?" I said. "I can't believe Brad said all that shit."

"You didn't think he would say anything? I would have been surprised if he hadn't."

"I bet Krista made him. Jesus, I hate weddings," I said. "This fucking shirt is driving me crazy. Thank god you brought the flip-flops, though. And this tie is the worst."

"Take it off, then," she said, helping me untangle it. "Are you nervous about tomorrow?" she asked.

"A little," I said.

"I would be too."

Eddie and Ivy came over, and Eddie asked if we wanted to get high.

"I can't," I said. "They piss test me first thing."

"Bummer," Ivy said.

"You don't want to be around me when I'm high," Neecie said. "I say the dumbest stuff."

"Since when do you smoke weed?" Ivy asked, all outraged.

"Sean got me high once," she said. "Just once."

"She was pretty funny," I said. "But she'll probably go headfirst into the wedding cake if she smokes."

"Neecie, you never tell me anything, I swear!" Ivy said. She turned to me and Eddie. "Did you know that fucker Tristan Reichmeier made her go into the porn store and buy him this special lube that costs like fifteen bucks for a tiny little bottle? Because he wasn't eighteen. And she did it! She went in there and did it!"

Eddie laughed.

"That's what he made you buy?" I asked. "Stupid lube? You can buy that shit at Walgreens."

"Not the kind he wanted," Neecie said sadly, swinging her flip-flops over the dock. "He gave me money for it, at least."

"At least?" Ivy yelled. "After that shit made you all rashy and itchy for a week? He should have paid you more."

"It gave you a rash?" Eddie asked.

"I have weird sensitive skin, I can't help it," Neecie said.

"Even . . . down there?" I asked. Blurting.

"Shut up, Sean!"

Eddie and Ivy went to their camper cabin to get high, and Neecie and I went back to the party. My mom and Steven-Not-Steve were dancing to a slow song. I saw my dad sitting at a table with the lady with the baby. The lady was feeding the baby something from a little Tupperware thing, and my dad seemed really into that, for some reason.

Neecie said, "You should introduce me to your dad."

"He'll just think you're my girlfriend, then."

"So?" she said, dragging me by my hand and going over to him. Introducing herself to him and the lady and the baby in that same happy way she'd introduced herself to my mom. And he stood up and smiled and looked at her, and then we all sat there, talking, and I remembered that my dad used to do that. Be in Athletic Boosters and go to block parties and grill-outs and all sorts of crap, before. He'd been a salesman; he liked being social, talking to new people, that kind of thing.

"Can you believe this one?" my dad said, nudging the lady with the baby, pointing at me. "My littlest guy, a Marine? Been trying to get used to it. You never do, I guess. You think they'll stay little forever, I guess."

The lady with the baby smiled a whole bunch. As if she knew anything about me.

"I'll miss him a lot," Neecie said. "We only became friends this year, you know."

"I didn't know that," my dad said, nodding. "He had that older gal for a while, what was her name . . . ?"

"Dad . . ." I said.

"Hallie," Neecie supplied.

"Right," he said. As if he'd ever known her. "What happened to her, Sean?"

"She went to college," Neecie said. "In Wisconsin. But then she dropped out and came home."

"She's going somewhere in St. Paul this fall, I guess," I said. Just so it didn't sound as bad.

Then someone came around with plates of wedding cake and we ate a bunch of that, the lady with the baby feeding a little to the baby, too, and my dad taking pictures of that, and then Neecie asked my fucking dad to dance, and he was so pleased, you'd think she wasn't doing a whole pity job on him, which I knew she was because I'd told her the whole sad suicide story. But later, when I was dancing with her again, she said it wasn't pity, because she wanted to be nice, and be in my life and know my family, just like I knew hers, and what was the big problem with that?

"He lives in Arizona now," I said. "And don't ask me who that lady is."

"She's his sponsor," she said. "He just told me."

"Oh."

"He won't live in Arizona forever, maybe," she said. "And besides. What do you lose by being nice to someone?"

●

For being such a pain in the ass for most of the year, the wedding party was fun. Especially after midnight, when we all said a big good-bye to Brad and Krista as they got in his truck to drive to their hotel suite. That was also when Steven-Not-Steve and my mom and dad and the sponsor-lady-with-a-baby and a lot of the other adults left and things got really loose. A lot of dancing. A lot of beer getting spilled. A lot of people going into the lake, either in their fancy clothes or stripped down. Eddie and Ivy were running around with cans of whipped cream they'd got from somewhere, spraying them down each other's faces or at people passing by. Neecie was drinking champagne straight from the bottle. Some of the groomsmen started a limbo contest that got really dirty, girls pulling up their dresses and guys stripping down to their T-shirts. I was stripped down to my shirt too, sweating like crazy, and yeah, having a few beers, since my dad was gone and I didn't have to feel weird about that, because what the hell, I could be hungover, I could sleep on the plane. But I didn't feel exactly drunk—maybe because I was dancing and laughing—it was like the beer fizzled through me and I sweated it out or something.

Finally, at three a.m. or so, Eddie and Ivy long disappeared, I took Neecie to my camper cabin. I'd brought sleeping bags and flashlights, and she carried two big bottles of water and she was laughing and telling me to slow down because her dress was falling down, and when we got in the cabin, she was freaked because there was no electricity.

"It's a camper cabin," I said. "You're lucky the windows have screens."

"Jesus. Every camp I've gone to involved dorms."

"Princess."

I laid out the sleeping bags and stuff, apologized for forgetting pillows.

"They probably don't let you have pillows in the Marines," Neecie said, sitting on the bunk and handing me one of the giant water bottles. "Drink some of this. You don't want to be hung-over tomorrow."

"I'm fine."

"Just drink it. I'm going to brush my teeth."

"Jesus, why?"

"Because I believe in dental hygiene, idiot. Didn't you bring a toothbrush?"

"No."

"Gross. You're gross."

So we brushed our teeth, first her, then me using her brush and both of us spitting into the bushes. I remembered Hallie and our first morning together and felt a little weird for a minute.

"You let other people use your toothbrush?"

"No, god," she said. "That's totally gross. I'm throwing that fucking thing away." She chucked it into the bushes.

"Litterer."

She pushed me inside. "Move it, the mosquitoes are all over me."

She was quick about stripping down, out of her dress, the flashlight on the wooden floor in a circle. Folding her dress and slipping into a T-shirt and little shorts and everything, so I did the same, except I didn't have anything to slip into so I just stood there in my boxers for a while.

"Get in, will you?" she said. "I think there's a mosquito in here."

"Just one?" I teased her, but got into the bunk. Which smelled like mothballs and old bug spray. And Neecie's cake smell.

God, The Horn. But I didn't touch her. Even though there wasn't much room for both of us to lie there like that. It felt really good to lie down, though. The breeze from the lake had come up and it was cold, and being under the sleeping bag felt perfect. My head swam, thinking about how still and calm it was compared to the rest of the day.

"That was so fun, Sean," she said. Her hand on my chest, then. Right in the hollow. Right where I wanted it.

I inhaled. Didn't exhale for a while.

"I know."

"I wish you didn't have to leave."

"Me neither."

"Are you feeling weird? With me touching you?"

"No."

"Good."

"But we can't have sex or anything," I said. Blurting.

Neecie laughed. "Why not?"

"I didn't bring any condoms."

"You're not very good at planning, Sean."

"Well, did you bring any?"

"No."

"Well, don't give me shit about planning, then."

"I'm a better planner than you, though."

"Well, no shit. That hardly helps the current situation."

She stretched beside me, her body finally touching mine. She kissed my neck. She smelled like cake. And sweat. And booze.

She said, "The current situation is what you'd call extraordinary. Extraordinary circumstances."

"What does that mean?"

"Just what it means. It's unique."

"Because I'm leaving."

"Yes. But also because of who we are."

"You're not my girlfriend."

"And you're not my boyfriend."

"So, it's just . . . what? Sexual?"

"Not tonight, obviously."

"So what do you call it, then?" I was thinking a bunch of shitty things. Like, sad. Like, desperate. Like, friends with very few benefits

"No, we're something else. Some other thing. I don't know what you'd call it. Maybe there's a word, though. Maybe I'll think of it tomorrow, when it won't matter and you'll be . . ."

"Stop talking," I said. And rolled over on her and kissed her. And we did a bunch of things for a long while, not sex, but still good things, for most of the rest of the night, we did all those things and we didn't talk anymore, just touched each other, on and on, and I wasn't even tired; when I woke up, I didn't even remember falling asleep.

# Chapter Twenty-One

It was weird, how busy and people-choked I'd been twenty-four hours earlier, with all the hugs and handshakes and well-wishes and stuff, everyone helping clean up the day after the wedding, my mother and Steven-Not-Steve and my dad, and Mrs. Albertson and Gary coming to get Neecie and meeting everyone while we all broke down chairs and tables and crap, everyone bossing and fussing and laughing and talking, and then I was all alone, going to my hotel room, my last day before boot camp, just a couple of things in my backpack.

And I was late; my mom had gotten turned around dropping me off at Sergeant Kendall's and then she had to cry and kiss me good-bye and say she was sorry my dad hadn't come with, but I didn't think I could have handled that. I didn't even want to be doing this in front of Sergeant Kendall. Even if it was with my mom.

Then Sergeant Kendall took me out to eat, with the vouchers I'd get for meals, anyway; he said there were other recruits flying out but they'd gone earlier and now it was late, almost nine, and we sat in his car for a minute before I went inside.

"Good luck, Sean," Sergeant Kendall said.

We shook hands.

"You're going to do fine," he said. "I know it."

"Thanks."

"You have my e-mail and phone, right? Stay in touch."

"I thought we couldn't, though? Don't they take everything away?"

"Right, yeah," he said. "No, I mean, for when they give you privileges. And afterwards too. Okay?"

"Sure," I said. Then I got out of the car and heaved my backpack onto my shoulders and went into the hotel lobby.

It was quiet and empty, kind of dark, with the weird mood lighting that hotels thought made them so swanky, though this place was just kind of regular, as far as I could see. I handed the lady at the counter my stuff that Sergeant Kendall had given me. Vouchers and crap, all paid for by the Marines.

She nodded at me and then started typing junk into the computer.

I stood there, my hands in my pockets.

"Sorry," the lady at the counter said. "My computer is being so slow tonight."

"That's okay," I said. I pulled out my phone; there was a new text from Neecie. She was at work, telling me how hungover and tired she still was. And about all sorts of dumb things people were doing, Kerry was bugging her, the usual.

put yr thing up on the shelf.

how does it look.

sad. it missed you.

sorry. tell it to toughen up.

I'd given her, finally, the morning after the wedding, the thing I'd found by the dead turtle aquarium that one day I was pissy at her. It was one of those fucking giant tea cans but instead of pitching it out the window or recycling it, someone had sliced out one side and built a little fucking dollhouse scene inside. Like you could see the people at the kitchen table and sitting on the couch, little metal stick people, curled up and bent into place. Because those iced tea cans were so colorful, so was everything about the little house, and it reminded me of the Albertsons' house a lot. I guess it was weird; it wasn't exactly perfect, except for the iced tea can, which wasn't really that romantic, I guess, but like Neecie had said, we weren't that way. Not something to recycle or trash. Not something shitty to say good-bye to and forget. Something else altogether.

"Here you are, Mr. Norwhalt," the lady at the counter said, handing me my ID back.

Then she looked at me. Smiled.

"Basic training, huh?" she said.

"Yes, ma'am," I said, trying to sound the part. What a dork.

She smiled bigger, looked down at her computer. Then looked behind her, like she was going to say something naughty.

"I'm going do something for you," she said. Typing more junk into the computer.

Fuck. Then I was nervous. She was a cute chick, no doubt. But fucking hell. I didn't want to deal with this kind of weirdness. Neecie was still in my head, tumbling around in there, naked and otherwise, and I didn't need another girl. And this wasn't a girl; she was like a lady. Older. I still didn't have any condoms.

Then she handed me a printout.

"Executive Suite," she said. "Your room number's on this card." She handed me a keycard in a little envelope. "I figure, you might as well enjoy a good night's rest, right?"

"Wait, do I have to pay extra or . . . ?"

"No, it's all good," she said. "Late check-in. Complimentary. I've comped you dinner, too; just dial this number if you want something to eat and they'll bring it up. And the Direct TV too. On us. Watch any movie you like."

"Oh," I said. I hefted my backpack over my shoulder, grabbed the keycard. "Okay. Thanks."

"You're very welcome," she said, smiling down at her computer again. "Enjoy your stay. And thank you for your service."

I nodded. I hadn't done any service; she'd done the service around here, but I didn't want to say that. She looked all pleased with herself, and I didn't want to ruin it.

•

The Executive Suite wasn't messing around.

A king-size bed. A shower with like eight different nozzles aiming in all directions. A TV in the bathroom and one in the bedroom. A giant sofa. A little refrigerator full of stuff to drink, and it wasn't even a mini-bar but all free.

Everything smelled fresh and clean and kind of rich, really. Expensive. I set my backpack on the sofa. Looked at the printout. Looked at the menu on the coffee table. Laid on the sofa, laid on the bed. Took off my shoes. I was tired, but couldn't imagine sleeping yet. My flight took off at 8:38, so I had to be up early, but not that early. I was within spitting distance of the airport.

I ordered a hamburger, fries, and some nachos and a giant Coke. A little while later, a dude brought it up and I ate the shit out of it while watching *SportsCenter* on the flatscreen above the giant bed. Then I felt all greasy and weird, so I took a long-ass shower. Put *SportsCenter* on in the bathroom, too, while I soaped my shit off. Thought about jerking it, but that felt weird because of the dudes talking about baseball and whatever just a few feet away.

Then I got in bed. Naked, because I only brought the one other pair of clean boxer shorts. I watched more TV, then I texted Neecie, asked what she was doing. Eddie sent me a photo of two tanks, one looking like it was humping the other one, like it had accidentally driven up the back of it.

"Good luck," Eddie texted.

I flipped through channels. Watched part of a movie I'd liked a million years ago, when aliens attack the White House. Then I felt sleepy so I turned all that shit off; the TV and the lights all went off with the same remote.

I held my phone for a minute. Looked for new texts. Nothing. Then I had to charge my phone, so I put it up on the little nightstand thing. And laid there. Piled the pillows under my head all luxurious. Kicked my feet through the sheets so they hung out and weren't completely strangled under the blankets.

I liked my feet to hang out while I slept; I'd slept like that for years, since I had to sleep diagonal in most beds once I grew in ninth grade. This bed was the biggest one I'd ever slept in, and I could stretch out in any direction and fit.

A stoplight blinked through the windows, red, yellow, green, red, yellow, green. I waited a long time before I fell asleep.

# Acknowledgments

The following people helped me immeasurably on issues regarding the Marine Corps:

Dennis Durand, Lance Corporal USMC, 1958–1962
Andrew Harris, Sergeant USMC, 1985–1991
Sean Green, Corporal USMC, 1997–2002

Thank you for your insight and service.

Early readers whose insight and attention I also appreciated include Erin Downing, Heather Weiss Zenzen, Trish Doller, Kristin Mesrobian, Ash Parsons, Meagan Macvie, and Betty-Jeanne Klobertanz.

Thank you to the Anderson Center in Red Wing, Minnesota, where I wrote early drafts of this story.

I can't imagine a day without the love of my Secret Friend Cabal: Melanie Cannon, Maria Alisa Blum, Rachel Seres, Megan VanSchaick, Michelle Najarian, and Elizabeth Hutchin-Bellur.

Thank you to Andrew Smith and Christa Desir, for being so unfailingly honest with and kind to me.

Michael Bourret, I just like you so much! It's so great having you in my corner, what with all your Knowing Of The Things, in particular, Things I Don't Know Anything About. Your presence has given me such peace of mind; you don't even know!

Andrew Karre, how did I get so lucky to have you as my editor? What gods did I inadvertently please to earn such rewards? In addition to you doing nice things like preventing me from literally tipping over on my face and buying me lunches at swanky places, you also watch Norman Reedus movies I recommend, visit my Loft classes looking extremely dapper while extemporaneously tossing off brilliant remarks to the youth of our fair state, and—perhaps more than anyone else—take my Tumblr posts extremely seriously. And then we get to discuss via e-mail the semiotics of oral sex! This relationship is like none I've ever had, and I'm grateful for everything you've taught me and continue to teach me.

# About the Author

Carrie Mesrobian is an instructor at the Loft Literary Center in Minneapolis. Her debut novel, *Sex & Violence*, was called one of the best books of 2013 by *Kirkus Reviews* and *Publishers Weekly* and was a finalist for the American Library Association's William C. Morris Award for best debut young adult novel. She was also *Publishers Weekly's* "Flying Start" for 2013. Visit Carrie online at www.carriemesrobian.com.